A Voice from . . . Where?

The service was almost over. When the speaker finished, he grasped a handful of earth from the mound near the excavation and let it spill into the opening. He looked to Joni and nodded piously, until she began to walk to the mound. Then, not knowing how she got there, she was standing in the center of the gathering. The dirt felt cool and moist. She filled her hand and faced the opening.

It came in a faraway lullaby, as though sung by a creature from the surrounding woods, a low incantation carried on the wind. With her hand still outstretched to make the offering, Joni craned her neck to trace the sound and heard it rise to a higher pitch. At once it was familiar: the sound of crying, human crying. Impossibly, when she turned again to locate its source, she was staring at the coffin.

She felt her body tremble but could not move her legs. Her hand had begun to shake and was involuntarily releasing bits of earth, which fell onto the coffin. The instant the soil landed, the cry grew louder.

It was Stephen, unmistakable, her Stephen!

CRIB

HAROLD LEE FRIEDMAN

PUBLISHED BY POCKET BOOKS NEW YORK

Distributed in Canada by PaperJacks Ltd., a Licensee
of the trademarks of Simon & Schuster, a division of
Gulf+Western Corporation.

This novel is a work of fiction. Names, characters, places and incidents are either the product of the author's imagination or are used fictitiously. Any resemblance to actual events or locales or persons, living or dead, is entirely coincidental.

Another *Original* publication of POCKET BOOKS

POCKET BOOKS, a Simon & Schuster division of
GULF & WESTERN CORPORATION
1230 Avenue of the Americas, New York, N.Y. 10020
In Canada distributed by PaperJacks Ltd.,
330 Steelcase Road, Markham, Ontario.

ISBN: 0-671-43115-3

First Pocket Books printing August, 1982

10 9 8 7 6 5 4 3 2 1

POCKET and colophon are trademarks of Simon & Schuster.

Printed in Canada

To Sophia,
with love and gratitude

CRIB

Introduction

The infant slept without dreaming; its tiny chest rose and fell, rose and fell. Temperature had returned to normal, but the frail body was weakened from a long bout with virus. Weight was down, and ever since the beginning there had not been enough sugar in the blood or oxygen in the lungs. Now there was no sound or movement except for an occasional fluttering of eyes beneath tightly clenched lids.

Then from the vicinity of the immature voice box a sudden spasm shook the chest and nudged the upper airways closed. Muscles at the back of the baby's throat seized, locking the air passage shut. Instantly the central control mechanism that expanded the chest cavity ceased operation, and the lungs could no longer ventilate. The baby opened its eyes wide in wordless alarm.

The chest fell and did not rise.

Precious seconds fled and still the infant could not breathe. Its heart was arrhythmic. The nerve reflex center labored in a superhuman effort to reopen the air passages. The dehydrated body began producing salt as the skin turned from gray to blue. The infant struggled to cry out but could not.

Deep within the brain, normally watchful sentinels tried again to trigger the resumption of breathing. When they failed, deadly levels of carbon dioxide began to invade. As the blood was deprived of the oxygen it needed, more of the gas was produced and there was a narcotic effect on the brain—like rapture of the deep. The infant began to undergo hypoxia, suffocation from within. Brain damage was imminent.

Then, for unknown reasons, the throat opened.

As quickly as they had closed, the upper airways relaxed, and in an instant the lungs again filled with oxygen.

The blood, once more enriched, began to evaporate the deadly gas that had invaded the brain.

The skin turned gray, then pale pink.

The brain threw off its lethargy.

The tiny chest rose. And fell. And rose.

The infant slipped back into a deep sleep without waking, without uttering a sound.

Book 1

Chapter 1

It was one of those mornings when she could have stayed under the hot water forever, but Joni Krueger Lawrence now stood naked before the steamy, full-length mirror, watching.

Slowly, as the haze began to evaporate, she studied her reflection, looking for the face and form which the world had once chosen as a standard of beauty. The idea still made her giddy.

The inspection began at the top. Her longish auburn hair looked chocolate brown from the soaking. It was pulled back so that her slightly round face took on a more aristocratic appearance, and her sea-green eyes looked larger than they actually were. The once prominent angles of her cheekbones had softened only a bit, but the freshly scrubbed skin glowed rosy under translucent beads of water.

Joni examined the planes of her face for a hint of the Faye Dunaway others had always seen in it, and found

5

it an interesting if somewhat remote notion. She knew
if she looked more closely she'd see the little lines near
the corners of her mouth and eyes, so she didn't.

The bathroom mirror always made her feel shorter
than her five-foot-five inches, but this morning it was
kind enough to confirm that more of the extra weight
had melted away. Another seven or eight pounds
would do it, she decided, down to a trim one fifteen.

Cautiously, she moved her eyes to her bosom, which
was still fuller than before, but she noted with disap-
proval that there had been no change in the new creases
that had etched the top of her breasts, the *desecration*,
as Doug had once joked hurtfully.

There were matching marks on both sides of her
hips, where the skin had expanded steadily for nine
months and one week. They weren't going away, she'd
finally been forced to admit, no matter how much
weight she lost.

She drew a deep breath and let it out slowly.

Joni pivoted to a side view. Her legs had suffered the
least from the changes and were still nicely tapered and
well-defined, longer than they should have been for her
height. She always felt her legs were her best feature,
an opinion with which her agent and the photographers
had disagreed. They favored the profile.

She faced forward again, put her feet together and
searched for the three diamonds, the empty spaces
formed by meeting points of thighs, calves, and ankles.
Having three diamonds was the test of perfect legs, the
more worldly models had told her.

"Well, two out of three ain't bad," she said aloud
with a wink at the mirror.

Joni responded to a sudden chill and felt snug again
once she'd wrapped herself in an oversized bath towel.

She was a mother now.

It was the beginning of summer.

And, all things considered, she was a happy woman. What the hell!

As she was dressing, Joni was alerted by soft cries of protest from the nursery, but a few seconds later she heard the comforting brogue of Lottie, the nursemaid, in his room and decided Stephen was in good hands. His fever still worried her. It had gone back over 101° for the first time in several mornings. Joni's thoughts strayed back, as they often did, to the night Stephen was born. She'd been both deliriously happy and scared to death at the same time. It wasn't the prospect of a painful labor that frightened her, although that's what she admitted to. She knew that she'd be able to handle the pain.

Instead, it was the possibility that something might go wrong in the delivery room—with her baby—that terrified her. It had proved an important distinction, because when she realized the source of her fear, she knew how much the baby had come to mean to her.

It was still all so vivid. She was back in delivery near the end of a long labor, and an incredible thing was happening. A small part of her body had stretched until it took a shape beyond all reasonable proportion, and she felt certain she'd burst apart at the seams. The reason was to make way for a miniature human being, in part of a copy of herself, who had lived inside her stomach for almost thirty-seven weeks, able to breathe, feed and move about on its own. And right at that moment, a time of its own choosing, it had *decided* to leave its growing place and join her in the world outside. And as if that weren't enough, while this perfect little person had miraculously taken shape, he'd also learned the *capability of independent thought*.

His existence still seemed extraordinary even though she'd lived the moment in her mind over and over again. But in the end there was Stephen, an absurdly comic little character, red-faced, lumpy-headed and soaking wet, with too much hair and tiny little fingers and toes. He looked as if he just knew that he belonged with her.

The immediate bond between them. That was the feeling she remembered the most, but when she'd tried to express it, the thought came out as the silliest question the delivery team probably ever heard:

"This is *my* baby?"

The blissful reverie abruptly changed to a memory of what had happened when she was in her hospital room with Doug and they brought Stephen in. Her body was like a single muscle that had relaxed after hours of painful spasm. Doug was attentive, though he'd been unwilling to be with her during the actual delivery. All at once, as she was clutching her newborn infant to her breast, she found herself yearning to be held, too. Suddenly she needed Doug to make it complete, to love her and their baby. The two needs magnified each other and became the same. Finally, Doug came forward and gently held her in his arms, but she'd found it strangely unreassuring.

She convinced herself she was imagining it at first. She knew her emotional state was undependable, her hormone levels so abnormal it was bound to affect her judgment. But part of her knew something *was* wrong. Could his hesitation, his slight withdrawal just be the normal uneasiness of a new father? In the end, though he'd used all the right words and performed all the tender rituals of concern at bedside, she'd remained uncertain.

Doug had only looked at Stephen once, and not

never touched him.

The rude thought put her squarely back in the present with a sudden urge to go to her son, even though his crying had stopped.

Even though she'd only put on one sneaker.

8:45 A.M.

Joni neared the mile-long path into the park that she'd chosen for the first run in a year and a half. She could feel her anxiety growing. It had been with her as soon as she left the house, a premonition that something was going to happen to Stephen because she wasn't home to take care of him. A ridiculous idea, she told herself; what could possibly happen, in her own house, with Lottie there?

Joni forced the thought from her mind and arbitrarily picked a starting point on the path, but a few minutes into the run the feeling came back stronger. By the time she passed the old stone fence that marked the half-mile point, her fear for Stephen had mounted dramatically.

The feeling was heightened by the interior of the park itself. Now she was in a section that had an eerie, brooding quality. It was misty with a number of deep pockets of ground fog the late spring sun still hadn't burned off.

Determined, she tried to shift her attention back to the running. The strain was already more than she imagined it would be, showing the changes her body had undergone hadn't all been on the outside.

In a few minutes the steepest part of the hill came into view, and Joni set herself mentally for it. She could feel her perspiration soaking her baggy sweatshirt.

Nearing the start of the rise, she began to feel an aching weakness in her calves and tendons that momentarily broke her confidence, stabbing needles of pain in her thighs. Her heart was pounding, and the hill swam in her eyes until she was able to blink it clear. She focused on the pain and tried to examine it as though it were a slide under a microscope.

She raised her head to locate the top of the hill still more than a hundred yards away, then lowered it quickly. She'd seen a turn to the right where there were bits of loose tar and some treacherous potholes. Better not to think about all of the hill at once, just the next step and the next. Like her marriage.

Nearing the end of her endurance, Joni directed her thoughts to Stephen, her refuge, her solace. She could envision him in his crib in slumber, his deep blue eyes hidden by filmy lids that fluttered slightly even in sleep. Those soft, searching mirrors to the soul that spoke volumes about his fascinations, his peace, or inner turmoil. More and more as his personality emerged, she found herself communicating with him through his eyes. In the absence of real language they talked to each other in an intimate, spiritual way. She felt it from the beginning and the feeling had grown with the months: theirs was a special connection.

Joni moved ahead torturously, each breath of air searing her shocked lungs. She climbed, turning with the path as it moved right. All of a sudden the thick trees that had obscured the view fell below her line of vision, and in the distance she could make out the tall outline of the new colonial house she and Doug had fallen in love with. The image bounced each time her feet landed on the narrow path, but she was able to trace the roof-line to where it angled back and down toward the rear porch. In front, like colored patches on a giant white quilt, two brown shutters flanked the nursery window where there were delicate lace curtains she had made.

Joni looked front again, just in time to avoid a deep rut which could have meant a sprained ankle. Only a few more steps now, if her wind held out. She was excited.

She was just turning back to finish the last section of the course when she saw something out of the corner of her eye. Quickly she again looked back toward the house, almost breaking stride. At first it appeared to be one of the many tall shadows from the trees or giant hedges that flanked the house, but she could have sworn the dark area moved slightly from a moment before. She fought her way past the pounding in her temples and tried to hold focus. The dread feeling was back, stronger than before, fighting for possession of her mind. Her head was racked by a sudden pain. Migraine! She was running nearly out of control as her imagination became her enemy and filled her vision with terror.

Stop it, you idiot!

The fear would not abate. It closed her throat a bit more until breathing was nearly impossible, and she fought for breath and mind control at the same time.

Again she turned her head sideways and strained to see movement near the house, anywhere. Steps from the summit she saw it again, this time more clearly, in silhouette on their front lawn. The tree closest to the house. Something about the angle was wrong. The distance to the foundation had closed. It looked alive!

The moment she knew, the last air escaped from her lungs in a gasp, her legs faltered, and she lurched to one side. The tree had become a long, narrow finger that moved forward and pointed up to the nursery. But

there was no tree on that part of the lawn! It was a man,
and he was going to the nursery.

Stephen!

Without warning, her right foot dug into a section of
the eroded tar surface. The toe of her sneaker caught in
the hole and pulled her down. It was another second or
two before she felt the stinging pain and lay defeated a
half-dozen yards from the finish.

1:30 P.M.

The most tender spot was around her elbow, and when
Joni probed it the pain closed her eyes. She pictured
herself sprawled out on the pavement like some soggy
bag of laundry with legs. When would she ever learn to
do things gradually?

The silly clock-on-a-dish showed it was a half hour
later than the arranged meeting time with Jeremy. The
timepiece was one of a number of knickknacks that had
begun to clutter their home: macrame planters, em-
broidered pillows, little glass animals. But were they
evidence of the new family forming—their *nest*, as
Doug used to call it—or only bits of camouflage against
the growing discord?

When the doorbell chimed, Joni was holding a pot of
steaming coffee, and found herself comforted by the
thought that it was Jeremy and not Doug. Doug would
still be able to see the residue of alarm that lingered.
He'd never understand how a swaying branch could
look like the movements of an intruder. He'd be telling
her again that she was obsessed with Stephen.

She caught the coffee pot as the liquid began to
spill.

*   *   *

It was at times like this Jeremy Goodwyn knew he should have retired at sixty-five. Somehow he'd managed to find every pothole between New York and New Jersey and gotten lost in a maze of signs that greeted him after the George Washington Bridge. People who thought of him as a kindly old patriarch would have been shocked at the things he said aloud in his rented Ford LTD, especially when he missed his turnoff and couldn't get off the express lane to turn back.

Jeremy had been lost in thoughts about his favorite topic, the celebrated Femme Model Agency, of which he was the founder. He thought about how it would fail without his continued leadership. "Flounder without the founder," was his motto. At work they were sick of it.

He had also been thinking about how much it would mean to Femme if he could entice Joni Lawrence back to work by a week from Thursday, the deadline set by his biggest client. And that it was time to find out.

Jeremy had played a waiting game with Joni ever since the day of her surprising marriage to Doug Lawrence, a newcomer to the music scene. When Stephen was born less than a year later, he'd nearly panicked. Six months was what he'd finally decided to give it, and June 7th was only a week short of six months. By now she'd have had a good dose of motherhood, enough to really miss the excitement that he could still offer. Even if she wouldn't admit it, the business was in her blood. It had to be. Few models had done better than she.

The main problem was that Joni Lawrence would be hard to convince. She made such a big speech about having found "real values" and such when she quit. He'd have to pick a good moment and be at his best as a salesman. In his bag of tricks he had a plum of a job, his inestimable charm and, of course, the knowledge that Joni could almost never resist him.

Why then, he continued to ask himself, did he have the feeling he was going to fail?

Aside from the obvious reason, her baby, other answers came readily to mind. Joni had always displayed the disturbing characteristic of thinking independently. He'd seen it right away, during their first meeting in the ad agency where she was working as a copywriter. When she'd balked at his suggestion that he arrange a screen test. Instead of being awed by the opportunity, she was suspicious and put him on the defensive. Although she'd never thought about modeling for herself she had strong opinions about it. Clearly she thought modeling was removed only by a degree from a life of prostitution. She also believed that sort of success had to change a person for the worst, that it would inevitably lead to a false sense of self-worth and would force her into unwanted relationships in order to succeed.

What really made her different from all the others, though, was her shocking closing argument. She said she wasn't pretty enough.

In the end Jeremy had prevailed, and Joni's modeling career was launched. In truth, her belligerent attitude had actually endeared her to him, but the strength and complexity of her personality had always kept him off stride.

Restlessness was one of the things he sensed in her. Evidently she'd been searching for *something* but didn't seem to know what it was. Then, when she suddenly announced she'd found *it* in Doug, he hadn't believed her.

There'd always been an impatient quality about her, too, as though she heard a clock ticking and wanted to get on with it, whatever *it* was. She was surprisingly unsocial with men in a city where sociability was the rule and, in all the time he knew her she'd only made one close woman friend, a photographer named Josh. On the other hand, she was exceedingly loyal to those she cared about. He remembered how Joni once cancelled a badly needed vacation to stay with a distraught, evicted Josh when she could have simply offered her apartment like most people would have done.

Joni had given him his share of fits, too. A sunny afternoon was all it took for her to cancel a booking and head for a park or beach. Also, she had a pressure-cooker temper that could burst loose violently, and she was sometimes foolishly brave, like the night she kicked a would-be mugger on Lexington Avenue. It was an admirable but reckless thing to do, but at least she'd known where to place the blow. The attacker had run off howling.

Then there was her drinking problem, the problem being that she almost never drank, and when she did she invariably went too far. Luckily, the result of her inebriation was a tendency toward incessant, high-pitched giggling.

All things considered, Joni's faults couldn't compare with her good points, Jeremy concluded as he finally drove up to her house and squinted at the brass numbers on the door to confirm the address. Then, with a groan, he swung his overheated, corpulent body out of the LTD, lamenting his half-smoked Cuban cigar, which he knew enough to leave in the ashtray.

A moment later he stood poised to ring the bell. This was one gutsy lady, he was telling himself again with a renewed sense of imminent failure. He thought of the day she'd slapped an important client for an off-color remark, actually slapped him like in the movies! It

could have cost them a good fifty thousand, but the
businessman called back to apologize and Joni accepted
it—after he agreed to double all fees. The client said
her behavior convinced him she was the woman they
were looking for. And she was.

Jeremy swallowed hard, adjusted his tie, and pushed
the button. He was trying not to recall the below-
freezing day she'd worked fifteen hours straight out-
doors. Jesus, he thought, if she'd been a man, she'd
have been Joe Louis. A lovely lady Joe.

1:55 P.M.

Overweight and overworked, the tired cleaning woman
checked the wall clock one last time and locked the
door to the wash closet. She'd made her decision. The
work wasn't complete, but her patience was at an end.
She'd been trying to get into the messy meeting room
for over an hour. The old man was still in there.

It was downright spooky for Mr. Aaron Schecter to
linger there like he was, in the dark, in the middle of
the afternoon. Just sitting without doing anything. The
thought that he might have passed away had occurred
to her, and she'd hurriedly crossed herself. Folks said
he was over eighty, and in her nine years cleaning the
council chambers, his one o'clock departure was something you could set your watch by.

On her way down the hall, the cleaning woman
peered through the glass doors one more time, but she
could not bring herself to call his name. There was
something about the way the old man looked . . .
something. She scratched her head. *Pitiful*, yes, that
was the word.

*   *   *

Aaron Schecter did not hear the maid until she closed the metal front door. It sounded like the sealing of a tomb. He continued to sit at his desk, the shades drawn shut, the lights out. He was rocking gently, his completely bald head clenched tightly between two alabaster hands that seemed to glow in the dark. His head was propped up by elbows planted solidly on his desk and his hands were shaking so badly he shook like he was in a vibrating vise. Ever since the afternoon mail, his heart had been racing at a perilous rate and he found it difficult to breathe.

But the old man was oblivious to everything except the brief news story from the Sparton Oakes–Northmont *Reporter* that rested in front of him on the desk.

The fact was, at eighty-four Aaron Schecter was in perfect health.

He was shaking from fear.

MYSTERY SICKNESS CLAIMS INFANT OF PHARMACY OWNER

June 6—The eight-month-old son of Ellen and Irving Kalish, proprietors of the Paris Pharmacy in Northmont, died suddenly Tuesday evening of unknown causes. The infant boy, Kenneth, was pronounced dead by the County Medical Examiner at Concordia Hospital.

Shortly after the baby's death, Dr. Jerome L. Gleason, the child's pediatrician, issued a brief statement on behalf of the bereaved family.

According to Dr. Gleason, the infant had been in perfect health with no

> prior history of special illness. Asked to
> speculate on possible causes, Dr. Glea-
> son said only that such things were
> "more in the hands of God than in
> man's."
>
> Burial of the Kalish infant will be
> tomorrow. Funeral arrangements will
> be through . . .

Aaron Schecter lifted his leaden head and tried to
stand. For a long time he had held back his terrible
suspicion from the rest of the council, and now he'd
have to tell them. He could no longer dismiss his fear as
paranoia.

With a mighty effort, Aaron Schecter worked himself
to his feet with a groan more appropriate to a wounded
animal than to a man. For the first time since 1942, he
was beginning to feel sorry he'd ever been born.

2:15 P.M.

For a few moments Joni loomed up in his mind as the
slightly younger woman he used to know, brash and
unwilling to accept a compliment until she knew what
was expected of her in return. She had been thinner
then, leaner, but not that far from her present appearance. Most importantly, her face was unchanged. She
still had that certain something, the *angle* as they used
to call it. Seen from the right perspective and with
proper lighting, Joni Lawrence could go head to head
with the best of them, this despite the fact that she
wasn't really an archetypal model. She'd been the first
to point it out. She was shorter by several inches than

the usual requirement. Her eyes were a bit too small for the planes of her face. Too guileless and innocent, too, he had added to her self-critique. Then there were her arms, a shade too solid near the shoulders. The cameras would make them look even heavier. Not to mention that in the beginning she didn't know how to wear makeup or walk, nor did she care to learn.

On the plus side of the ledger, Joni did have marvelously full auburn hair, a smile that could melt ice, gleaming white teeth (including a Huttonesque space at the bottom), and a remarkable ability to look statuesque for someone so short. Somehow Jeremy always attributed that to her determination more than anything physical. Once Joni set her mind to something, nothing on earth could get in her way. So if she wanted to look tall, by God, she found the clothes or the attitude to bring it off.

What had transfixed him, however, was her spectacular profile. No matter what else might have been lacking or imperfect, the *angle* held pure magic. Now, two years later, it was still the reason he'd come to talk to her. But not yet, something told him.

"Stephen is fine," she said, forcing a new direction to the conversation. "Almost six months, you know."

"The very next thing I was about to ask. That dear little boy, tell me, he's healthy? He looks more like his momma than he did at the hospital?"

"I'll do better than tell you. If you'd like you can see him, and that's not an offer I make to everyone."

"I was hoping you'd suggest it before I had to."

Halfway up the staircase that led to the nursery, Joni suddenly checked her eagerness and turned to Jeremy with a serious look.

"I have to ask you not to get too close to him, Jer. He's had a bad cold for almost a month, and I'm trying to be careful."

Jeremy shrugged. "Not to worry. After all these years I've built up an immunity to almost everything."

"Not what *you* might catch, Jer—" she started, then saw him beaming. "Oh, you!"

He could see her cheeks go flush with embarrassment. With all her acquired sophistication, she still had a gullible streak a mile wide.

The world she ushered him into was as alien as the inside of a spaceship. Half-moons were suspended in a heaven of outsized stars, a blue sky with puffy clouds rained little lambs on soldiers with mushrooms for umbrellas. Footballs, candy apples, and neon tortoises were in abundance. The floor had been carpeted one layer upon another until it became difficult to walk.

The crib itself commanded the room. It was made of delicate brass and could have been something out of the Victorian Age. The headpiece was a brilliant yellow and had been hand-painted with a floral motif. In one corner there was an antique treasure-chest-turned-toy-box, which refused to close to an overflow of fuzzy ostriches, stuffed bears, Slinkies and countless games from well-wishers who'd obviously overestimated Stephen's level of accomplishment by several years.

Jeremy kept beaming and shaking his head as Joni introduced them and went on with stories about her son, but then, she stopped abruptly.

"What you're thinking, you old stinker, is that Stephen is just like every other baby you've ever seen."

"No, not at—"

"Lumpy, Toothless, Gummy and Dopey. The Seven Dwarfs rolled into one, right?"

Jeremy laughed and tried unconvincingly to protest.

Actually, his mind wasn't on Stephen at all. He'd noticed it first when she talked about the baby's illness, the way she'd share his symptoms right down to the fever that knitted her own brow in remembered heat. For a time it was as though she and the baby were alone in the room. This was a side of Joni he'd never seen, doting and completely unselfconscious, so removed from her past it made him even more uneasy.

When they were downstairs again, Joni was still buzzing about the baby, but when Jeremy became quiet she asked him what he was thinking about.

"The other Joni Lawrence," he said with nostalgia. "In a way I miss her, that beautiful young woman with a big adventure ahead of her. A little frightened, but also very excited."

"Scared stiff, if you want to know. I used to lose my breath in the auditions. It was absolutely amazing that you got me to those first jobs."

"It was in you, otherwise I could have done nothing. You had guts, pure and simple."

"Nope," she insisted, "the fact is you pulled off a miracle of perseverance. All I did was let you persevere."

Jeremy turned his head sideways and lowered it. It was time.

"Well," he sighed, "I suppose if one were serious about it, it might be possible to . . . persevere again, if you know what I mean."

The surface look that greeted Jeremy depressed him. It was genuine amusement, but he could also detect that inside she was undergoing a mixture of feelings. His suggestion had conjured up old memories and, after the nostalgia passed, there was visible excitement in her eyes. Then, just as quickly as it had appeared, it vanished.

"As if anyone would care about an ordinary house-wife from the sticks," she answered. "You once said it yourself, 'I'm living out here in the land time forgot.' How about the *model* time forgot? Thirty-two isn't exactly a model's prime of life, you know."

"There are exceptions," he said with great uncon-cern. She wasn't taking him seriously, and his eyes probed hers for a weakness. But he did it for too long.

"You son of a gun, you came to get me to work again, didn't you?" she exclaimed. "I don't believe it!" She threw back her head and gave into a comfortable laugh.

"It was only an afterthought," he hastened to say. "I came with no such intention."

"No such expectation, you mean."

"Actually, I don't care whether you take the job or not," he paused, "no matter how wonderful it might be."

She raised an eyebrow.

"No matter how perfectly I've set it up," he added.

"You are an incurable rascal. And a liar, to boot."

"I never lie for business. For love, maybe," he allowed with a crinkly smile that was intended to be adorable.

"Well, I'm listening because I know you'll tell me anyway."

It had to make her feel good, he thought. He put on his most serious face and leaned across the kitchen table toward her. "It's so beautiful, Joni dear, and so right for your new . . . situation." His hand went into his jacket and produced a cluster of papers, which he waved in the air. "It's all here. Sixty thousand against first-year bookings. And listen to this. It's the whole line of Camille baby products: diapers, detergents, the whole *megillah*. Think of it, 'The glorious model-

turned-mother shares her tips on bringing up baby.'"
He slapped his cheek. "What an idea! What an idea!"

She said it simply. "No, Jeremy. Just no."

"But you haven't heard the best part yet. You make
your own schedule. You need time for the child?" He
snapped his fingers. "You want to make some money?"
Snap, snap. "What do you think, that I didn't consider
the reason you left? The wonderful values that you
pointed out? It's a dream job, sweetheart, with everything taken into account. The best deal I ever negoti-
ated."

She looked him squarely in the eye. "Not a chance,
but thanks."

He stood excitedly, trying not to hear what was
already apparent. "A guaranteed education for Stephen. I'll put it in the contract." He lit up further. "My
God, what an idea. More proof to the public of how
much you care for your baby."

She started to protest, but he caught her with a finger
over her lips. "Don't say anything now. Think it over.
It could be good for you." He waited before the next
part. "You have till next Thursday."

For a few seconds she seemed to let herself marry the
twin concepts of mother and model, but soon she was
shaking her head again.

"No, Jeremy, it just doesn't fit any more. It's like
finding an old prom dress in the attic. It might still
make me nostalgic, but I couldn't wear it any more."

Jeremy slumped back into the chair, his worst fears
realized. Nothing had worked, not even the college
education bit. He tried to start again, fishing for a new
angle, but her hand came out to stop him.

"I know I can't expect you to really understand," she
said softly, "but please try to listen to me. When I had
Stephen it was the best thing that ever happened to me.

It was like an awakening, Jeremy, a change that I could feel inside. And I needed it. Nothing I ever did gave me what he does, not the modeling, not the glamour, not the money. It's not just that Stephen is more important than anything else, he *is* everything. He and Doug," she added. "If you can't understand it, at least accept it. I won't do anything that takes me away from him."

Jeremy was listening intently. When she finished, he shifted his weight uneasily.

"All right," he said, "I give up, but only if you listen to one last idea."

She shook her head.

"I respect your choice. I know that nothing I can say will change your mind. For now." He took her hand and began to stroke it. "And that's why when I talked to the client I included a delay clause in the starting date. If you change your mind, say up to a year from now, you can still have the best of both worlds."

"Dammit, Jeremy. You haven't been listening."

"Not that I expect you to feel any differently a year from now. It's just in case you—" He stopped in the middle of a thought. "What are you doing?"

Joni hadn't waited for him to finish. She had come to her feet and was staring at him intently, while her fingers were busy on her blouse. For some incredible reason, she was starting to unbutton it.

"I'm sorry to resort to this, but you won't listen any other way."

The second button gave way and the silk designer blouse fell limply forward, exposing part of a breast that was still larger than normal since her pregnancy.

Jeremy suddenly felt the tightness of his own collar. He was mesmerized by the spectacle unfolding inches away, and made stuttering sounds of protest that Joni ignored.

The third button squeezed through the narrow opening and the garment fell away. When the fourth button was undone, Joni took hold of the blouse from each side to reveal the top of her breasts.

Instantly, Jeremy understood. Although he had never seen Joni without clothing, it was apparent that her breasts had undergone a change. There were a series of deep creases; it was as though a vandal had been there and defaced a work of art. Jeremy stared at her, unable to look away.

"This was part of the decision I had to make, Jeremy," she was saying. "Having Stephen has changed my body, and I made that choice happily, even though I knew it would mean the end of Joni Lawrence the Model."

"For heaven's sake, cover yourself," he finally stammered.

She closed her blouse. "I only did it to show you the changes, the obvious ones. Breast-feeding made me look this way, not exactly a pinup, huh?" She'd said it without apology, a matter of fact.

"There have been other changes, too. In my thighs, my skin, my weight distribution. And I want you to know I haven't had the slightest regret. Really."

"Now," she said, folding her hands delicately in her lap, "does that tell you how strongly I feel about it?"

Later, when she had stuffed the contract firmly back into his jacket pocket and walked him to the car, Jeremy was still in shock. Soon he was planted inside the LTD and the electric window hummed open.

"No big deal," he said dejectedly, "they don't want you for your body, you know."

Joni's look held a mixture of exasperation and affection. "You're something, you know?"

"You'll think about it?"

"You stink," she answered with a scowl.

"Good. There's another contract in the mailbox. I left it there, just in case." He winked.

Shaking her head, Joni leaned into the front of the car to kiss him on the forehead.

Before the oversized automobile disappeared from view, Joni stiffened and spun around to face the house. Upstairs in the nursery, Stephen was crying loudly.

10:30 P.M.

Lottie O'Hare felt a cold hand on her, woke, and thought about putting on the light. Instead she clenched her hands and began to pray.

"Blessed Virgin, Mother of God, Protector of the Innocent, watch over this house and all therein. Make us safe from the evil which surrounds us."

It was the prayer she had intoned earlier that evening and which now passed her lips again with more urgency.

She felt it in her bones all day: something horrible and evil lurking close by; something without a name.

It would do no good to warn the mistress, she knew. When she told her the last time, her warning had met with ridicule. The mistress called herself a believer but wasn't, not according to the true meaning. And her husband was worse, an outright atheist. He would think her superstitious, a foolish old lady.

But the feeling was stronger this time, and the feeling

was never wrong. She knew about such things from experience. She had seen the face of the demon and knew its torments. It was time to place one's trust in the Lord.

Lottie O'Hare crossed herself three times and lay awake in the darkness with her eyes wide open.

Chapter 2

Tuesday, June 8
1:00 A.M.

When Joni rearranged Stephen's cotton coverlet he woke to her touch, his huge blue eyes struggling to focus. She thought his expression looked troubled, and she leaned forward to nuzzle his neck and feel his warmth.

He was hot, but not alarmingly so. He'd been perspiring in his sleep. Though he still hadn't shaken off the virus, Dr. Geffs said he seemed healthy overall. Why then, she wondered, was he so listless, so bored? Could the doctor be wrong?

Be healthy, my darling. Please be healthy.

The urge to seek an emotional haven with Stephen was stronger than ever. The tension she'd felt in the bedroom clearly signaled another storm. When she said she was leaving to check on Stephen, she'd felt Doug's angry, unspoken thoughts, but she'd gone anyway. What else could she do? She was Stephen's mother, she couldn't ignore ignore her responsibilities just because of Doug's craziness.

28

It was sad to realize how far she and Doug had drifted from each other in the two years since their marriage, how increasingly irreconcilable their differences had become. Joni sighed deeply with memories. She'd met Doug during one of his studio sessions in New York. Jeremy had insisted that she meet a new client, but she'd also been curious to to learn more about the music business. At first, Doug hardly seemed to notice her, but it was impossible not to be aware of him, such was the fury with which he threw himself into his work. Doug was one of those human dynamos who seemed to inhabit the special world of creativity. He couldn't sit still, working first as the music producer, then as an engineer on the unfathomably complex music console, then dashing into the recording booth to rewrite a line of music or sing a difficult harmony part for a singer.

After three solid hours of activity, the client finally prevailed on Doug to take a break, and that's when they were introduced. Within a few minutes of conversation, they found an easiness with each other it should have taken months to feel.

Her first impressions of him physically were of his hands and eyes. His fists were large for his frame, big and hard like she remembered her father's. He was not a strikingly attractive man, but that had never really mattered to her. His face was rather boyish, with oversized hazel eyes and a little nose that had a snobbish bob to it. His skin was etched with the strain of uncountable late hours in studios, and he was so pale that his close-cropped reddish beard appeared to have been affixed to his face as an afterthought. At forty he'd already lost a good deal of hair, but though he was thin for his six-foot height he looked wiry strong and commanded the stuio like a feudal baron.

Within a few weeks, they were spending almost all

their free time together and Joni soon found in Doug many of the heretical beliefs that she shared, which were irrelevancies in the society of models and agents in which she traveled: a yearning for an old-fashioned marriage, kids and kittens and homemade pies—the whole package. He wanted a home away from the artifice of the city and a backyard where they could see the seasons change firsthand; fidelity, loyalty, and "me and you against the world." Doug was a clear voice speaking the truths for which her heart had secretly yearned. It was too good to be true, but he was too adamant not to be believed.

Doug had been married once before to a temperamental artist who had competed with him, he said, and taken her lack of success out on their marriage, but though none of his love affairs had become permanent, he hadn't burned out emotionally as had many of the middle-aged men Joni met in the city. In fact, he was as romantic as she, maybe more so. He was the sort of man who would surprise her with a thousand-piece jigsaw puzzle that turned out to be a picture of them, who planned celebrations for anniversaries measured in days, and who wrote a very special love song just for her. In a burst of typical romantic frenzy, he'd written the lyric and melody and played every instrument in the band, one at a time, as he put the music tracks together.

Being with him in those days was like living in a valentine. He was an amateur pilot and flew her over her Manhattan apartment house and gave her the controls when she jokingly asked him to. He loved to cook for her (he was the worst cook she'd ever known) and he quoted Emerson and Keats, her favorite poets.

They'd gotten to bed on their third date, right after she told him not to get his hopes up. Their lovemaking was neither kinky nor athletic, but tender and considerate with nothing to prove. She'd never known how complete a physical union could be until it was consummated within a context of deepening love.

But Doug had his problems, too. From the beginning he'd always been overly aggressive with a need for praise. His competitiveness made her wonder about his first marriage and just who competed with whom. Also his moods would swing wildly. He could come home absolutely elated over a new job he'd landed, only to become morose a few hours later over his ability to handle it. In those early days, though, the problems didn't seem too grave.

They were obviously compatible, but the actual breakthrough to intimacy proved painful. The years of disappointment with other would-be loves had cultivated well-developed distancing patterns in both of them. Trusting was the hardest thing. Luckily, whenever there was a crisis one of them could usually identify what was happening. It was Doug who first pointed out that her migraines struck when she felt herself getting "too close." After thinking about it, she realized it was a pattern of hers for many years. "Excess baggage," his psychologist, Dr. Baum, had called it, and like everyone else, they both had their share.

Then, after one memorable night of fear and trembling over some hobgoblin from the past, when it could have all ended but didn't, they took their stand against a lifetime of fears and woke the next morning to a whole new set of possibilities with another human being.

The way he'd proposed on a cool October night epitomized his creativity and romance. He'd marched her to Broadway, told her to close her eyes, and repositioned her. When he said it was time, she looked up at a dazzling display of moving electric lights over Times Square. Doug had rented the giant display to

deliver a message all the world could see. The sign
read: *I love you, Joni. Marry me.*

But it had been a long time since their sides had split
with laughter, since they'd kept a diary of their mile-
stones with each other, since they'd ridden on the
carousel. And without question, Doug's change had
begun with her pregnancy.

She'd known about some men's difficulty with wives
who had suddenly become mothers, but she'd never
realized how fast things could change, or that for some
men it was a chronic affliction. On the news of her
pregnancy, Doug went into a series of depressions that
he tried to hide but couldn't and that never really lifted.
He had used all the right words to reassure her of his
happiness, but there was little genuine feeling behind
them. Often he'd steer conversations about the baby in
another direction. He was more subtle in the beginning. He'd spend hours helping plan the nursery, but
soon the room seemed more important than the baby.

By the time Joni was nearly full-term, Doug required
almost daily proof of her love for him, insisting that she
become more of a homemaker, that she help him more
with business by joining him at client dinners, which he
himself hated. Bed was where it showed up the most.
His lovemaking became rough and selfish and, strangely, experimental at a time when even normal sex was
difficult.

It became worse when Stephen was born. Suddenly
she had two children, one who needed her for life itself
and one who acted that way and competed with his own
powerless son. Soon he began to complain about their
new expenses, even though their mailbox was constantly filled with royalty checks from his music business.
He'd hired Lottie, it was clear now, not to help her but
to regain some of the attention he'd lost.

This was another Doug, out of control and unaware
of his duality. His was the same clever mind, but it was
now at work to service the needs of a hurt little boy.
She resented having to deal with his neurosis when
most of her attention had to go to Stephen. Nor could
she tell him that part of her increasing concern for
Stephen stemmed from the fear that he might soon be
all she had.

Stephen was clutching her thumb in his soft palm and
trying to put it into his mouth. He looked contentedly
amused again, his color better than in the past days.
Joni turned him on his stomach and tucked him in
snugly, feeling warmth flow between their bodies.
When she retreated to the door and shut the light, she
paused. He was making soft nasal sounds. A shadow
cast from the streetlamp played across his face, darkening a part of a nose, an ear, half a chin. She felt a
momentary wave of cold air from somewhere and made
a mental note to check the window in the hall. Watching him, she thought of his tender body stretching into
manhood and wondered whose qualities he'd take with
him. Silently she prayed he was too young to pick up
the tension that held their home in unhappy times.

With apprehension, she turned to the bedroom
where Doug was waiting.

1:20 A.M.

He could see her in the dressing-room mirror, watching
him. He lay on his back in bed, his hands clenched over
his belly, his chest bared to where the summer blanket
met the beginnings of a paunch. He noticed her hair
needed a layering and that she looked tired. Also that

she was wearing a nightgown he didn't like, even
though he'd told her about it. The fact that she'd
chosen to put it on again was a signal, the code that
meant *stay away*.

They lay next to each other in the dimly lit room for a
long time without exchange. She'd closed her eyes in an
effort to negate the talk they needed to have. Finally
the silence was starting to make its own statement and
he couldn't allow that.

"Stephen all right?" he tried.

"His temperature is down, but I don't like the way
he's acting," she answered without opening her eyes.

"Acting? I thought he'd been sleeping."

"I mean in general." She turned to face him. "Listen, Doug, if you want to know how he is I'm glad, but
please don't bait me and then disagree with me. I don't
want to fight tonight." She turned away to stare at the
ceiling.

She was acting as though he'd attacked her, Doug
thought. He could hear air escape from her nostrils in a
short burst. Language. It would probably he better to
wait for breakfast, but his gut was burning.

"Did you ever think it would get to this?" he said
finally.

"You sure you want to start?"

"If we can keep it sane this time."

She seemed to relax. "All I know is that we were
pretty idyllic at one time, before Stephen came. That's
when it seemed to come unglued between us."

She was right about that. It had been the issue all
along, but she'd never come right out and said it.

"Stephen changed things," she continued, "our privacy, our mobility—"

"—and some other things," Doug interrupted.

"What?"

He propped himself up to confront her. "Listen, I admit I haven't been especially terrific at adjusting, but at least I tried. It wasn't easy for me, but dammit, at least my reactions were normal for a man. With you, though, you're so obsessed with him there's no time for anything else. You make me feel like a fucking guest in my own house."

"Stephen needs me now is the only reason, Doug. Can't you understand that simple fact and accept that it has nothing to do with my feelings for you?"

Doug shook his head. "Don't you remember how it used to be? How there were never enough hours in the day for us? Hell, I know Stephen demands a lot of your time, but what about us?"

"He doesn't demand my time, it's something I want to give him. Besides, just because we have less time to spend with each other doesn't mean the quality has to change."

"You've changed," he snapped. "You're different now, like a recluse. You're afraid to leave the house."

"Oh, Jesus, Doug, do you really believe that?"

"If we're not talking about *him,* you don't seem to have anything to tell me."

"Well, I'm sorry. I don't have a fascinating job like you do any more. If you remember, I gave all that up to have our son."

"You couldn't wait to, and you want to know something? Forget about me, you don't even care about yourself any more. Look at you. You're overweight and out of shape; sometimes I think you're trying to make yourself look unattractive." The outpouring of pent-up frustration felt good. It was a relief to have finally said it. "Whether you're aware of it or not, you're out of control with this Stephen thing," he added more calmly.

Joni was seething, but there didn't seem to be any battle in her.

"One of us is out of control, that's for sure."

"It's a matter of degree, that's all, considering us for once and not just the baby."

"But I'm part of that *us*, Doug, and I think you're talking about your needs, not ours."

"Well, now that you mention it, I do have some basic human needs, but ever since Stephen came along you seem to have said the hell with them, too."

She recoiled. "If you're talking about sex, you brought that on yourself. You never even let me get back to normal before you put the pressure on. Besides, you act like we haven't made love in years. We're not doing that bad."

"That's your opinion," he snapped. "Let's just say I'm not doing so good with your new schedule."

"You would think that. You'd have to."

Doug thought about the possible ways to reach her, a more forceful approach. Suddenly his concentration was broken by whimpering from across the hall. Stephen was up.

"Guess who," he said sarcastically.

Joni made a point of ignoring it. "You know," she said, "sometimes I think we simply got out of step and couldn't pick up the beat again."

Stephen's crying became louder.

"What are you going to do, run to the nursery? We finally get to something here and you take off?"

She was about to move. "For heaven's sake, it'll only take a minute. I just want to make sure he's all right."

"It's what it represents. That's *exactly* what I'm talking about."

He watched her head drop back down into the pillow. The chance for conversation seemed to have ended. He searched for words, for a bridge. The only sound in the room was the crying from across the hall. Then it suddenly rose and Joni was off the bed and throwing on her robe.

"If I don't go to him, we'll be up all night."

Nothing he said had made a difference. His arms stiffened and he bolted out of bed. He stood poised to go after her.

"Don't make a big thing of it, huh, Doug?"

"Uh, uh. Not this time. As of now Stephen isn't going to come between us any more."

She froze, looking him in the eye. *"He* isn't," she shouted back. *"You* are."

He could feel it burning deep in his belly, something separate from the anger. The look on her face, it was like some crazy, taunting teenager testing him. If she was determined to turn it into a test of power, he was ready.

"What's the matter with you, Doug?" she shouted.

He caught her arm as soon as she started to turn away, but with surprising strength she shook off his grip and planted herself firmly, half facing him in fierce defiance.

The instant he felt it come over him, they both knew. From behind him the dressing table lamp threw illumination onto the visible part of her face, highlighting her features. Her profile was a determined silhouette against the dark wall. That profile! A layer of perspiration blossomed on her upper lip and brow. Her hair had fallen with the activity, framing one side of her face. Doug felt like he could hardly breathe.

She was no longer Joni but an abstraction looming out of the night, with one gleaming eye that transfixed him. She was all women, animal. She stayed motionless, except for rhythmic breathing that exercised a vein on her milky-smooth neck. Her eye tried to dissect his sense of control, and her taut mouth teased in a primal challenge.

Unable to hold back any longer, he moved forward. He could see the muscles in her jaw go rigid. Her eyes were still riveted on him as she groped for the door somewhere behind her. He knew what she was thinking. He was going to hit her.

But she was wrong.

Chapter 3

Even in slumber the infant was aware of the danger. The Presence was not always the same. Uninvited, it sometimes entered its host slowly, meek and insidious, struggling for a foothold, probing for weakness. Then, abruptly, its power would wane and it would seem to be gone entirely, only to return more virulent and fighting for total possession. That was the most threatening time, when it could hold the baby's very existence within its grip, taunting with its own sense of supremacy. It was impossible to know its source or whether in the end it would win.

It had not always been this way. Within memory were recollections of a better time of comfort and security, easy rhythmic breathing and fascinating dreams. The infant remembered the many warming contacts with the gentler of the two beings in the next room, blissful touchings which came even when there was something unpleasant that could be felt in the space between them. Once existence was smooth and relatively untroubled.

Now it was filled with uncertainty and sinister apprehensions.

Reality and fantasy were hopelessly confused. Her baby needed her, but his father wouldn't let her go to him. Her husband had become a mad, frightening stranger.

The idea was ridiculous. Any second his crazed expression would change and it would turn out to be a bluff. Then he dragged her toward the bed, wrenching her arm too painfully for it to be anything but real.

Violent hands lifted her off the ground and flung her down hard at the mattress. She landed flat with one arm trapped beneath her. Before she could recover, he was on top of her, tearing at the thin robe that had come unfastened. On one level she understood what he wanted all too clearly, but because he was still her husband the disbelief continued.

"Get away from me," she shouted, but he wouldn't obey.

She struggled free for a second and drew a long scratch across the side of his face.

"You've brought it to this," he snapped, "don't forget, it was because of you."

He caught her arm in midair and pinned it behind her. Joni struggled furiously, bucking underneath him.

Most often it came during sleep, when the vulnerability was greatest, or after a sickness, when the infant was weakened. During these times the Presence could sense its advantage and used it many times in a single night. Now, as the infant slept through more and more of the night, the Presence came more and more often.

The outside world had become more complex, too. The senses were feeding in tens of messages a moment,

*which further confused what was happening from with-
in. It was getting impossible to distinguish between
internal danger and external experience, so the infant
cried out in confusion.*

Stephen's chilling scream sent a wave of cold panic
through her. She fought with renewed strength to
overpower Doug and get to her baby. His full length
was on top of her. She jerked her body one way, then
another, trying to dislodge him. For an instant one of
her arms came free and she pounded his back. As she
fought, everything went unaccountably into slow motion, and then she was somehow outside the struggle,
experiencing a series of ghostly impressions. There was
a vivid memory of her mother and a childhood warning
that boys would hurt you if you trusted too much. The
images passed quickly, until she got to the most frightening one. She was six again, lost in the woods a long
way from home. They were calling her, but she didn't
care because her father had died and gone to a place
they called Heaven. It was dark when the laughing man
came, in filthy clothes that smelled of urine, into the
woods. There was something wrong with his eyes; she
saw it when he spotted her huddled against the fallen
tree. That's when she knew he wasn't one of those sent
to find her.

There were some that would try to hurt you.

It felt bad when he touched her, like it did now in the
bedroom. He touched her all over, the man in the
woods—the man in the bedroom—Douglas, her husband, the rapist.

*A chill gust of air spread across the exposed parts of
the infant's flesh. At that instant, infinitesimal sensors in
the brain signaled a warning to the limbs and the baby
stirred. It was the coming of the Presence, the brain*

*thought, the most logical explanation it could find in its
limited experience. The sinister intruder had never announced itself in exactly this way before, but then the
Presence had shown itself to have many forms, no two
of which were the same. This time the feeling of dread
that came with the warning was stronger, different. The
Presence seemed to be lurking in the darkest corners of
consciousness, creeping, stealthy. This time it was both
inside and outside its vulnerable body, which waited to
be terrorized in unimaginable new ways. This time it had
come to stay. Again the infant cried. Soon, it knew, the
ability to make any sound would be gone.*

Lottie O'Hare bolted upright in bed. Stephen was
having another horrid dream.

"Poor thing," she said aloud in her small but comfortable room. Then she thought about the premonition and felt a drop of perspiration fall from her armpit.

Her instincts urged her to go to the nursery, but
certainly the cry had alerted them, too. She calmed
herself and waited. Even now the mistress would
probably be on her way to the baby.

Lottie rolled over and reached for her pocketwatch
and tilted it to the dim light from the streetlamp.
Almost two in the morning, five hours more before first
feeding. She debated between sleep and a visit to the
child. It would be a blessing to spend time with him
alone, and it would alleviate her sense of danger. She
had been dreaming something the cries had interrupted. Something dark and slippery.

As the crying continued, it frightened her to think of
the little soul lying there unprotected. Where was his
mother? The mistress had been clear in saying she
would go to him at night if he became disturbed, but
why was the crying going on so long?

Lottie O'Hare lay in her bed, arguing the merits of

two courses of action, unable for the moment to decide between them.

Stephen's cries filled the bedroom and echoed in the house. He needed her desperately. His calls were different this time, pleading. She had to get to him. A bolt of fear shot through her and she felt herself panic. She was helpless, beyond strength. It was useless to beg for her release for Stephen's sake, but she did anyway. It enraged him further. Joni tried to convince herself that it wasn't happening, that her son wasn't calling for help, that her husband wasn't part of his danger.

She tensed her muscles and tried to shut out all feeling, but Stephen's strident scream broke the night apart.

Stephen!

In the pitch dark of the nursery, it was impossible to discern one blackness against another, so when the infant struggled to open its eyes it could not be certain whether it had or not. In fact, its eyes were wide and searching. The imagination began painting images on the brain, yielding line and shadow where there was none to be seen. As shapes became grotesque, the baby grew more afraid. It felt trapped by the thin cover and kicked feebly to free itself from the constraint. The struggle failed. The baby's legs became hopelessly snarled in the layers of fabric until it could not move them at all, until it could not move any of its body, nor cry out for help.

She refused to accept it, but without her consent, against all will and reason, she had to acknowledge the faint but pungent scent of her own moisture.

The despicable pleasure rippled through her in sensations that became more and more intense. It was an

irreversible passion with its own essence and a duration
now beyond her control, a denial of her greater need to
be with Stephen. His fingers moved on her forcefully
and her legs thrashed under the insistent tickling. She
felt her resistance ebb and heard him sound his satisfaction, a malediction. She could feel the surge building,
rage and lust fusing into one as the body allowed what
the mind sought to reject. Once set in motion, it was an
undeniable course which she despised herself for needing.

*Without warning there was a stabbing pain to mingle
with the fear. The Presence was all-encompassing, a
suffocating force that spread throughout the body and
claimed the baby for itself. The power was of inestimable magnitude and held the infant against its waning
ability to resist. Instinctively the small being tried to turn
toward the next room, where there were two others with
whom its existence was somehow tied, but it couldn't.*

The pleasure ignited her body in sensations which
became kinetic. It was at the same time ice cold and
searingly hot, a vulgar ecstasy that veiled all other
thought. The will to withhold it was gone, and it grew
to envelop her spirit, her whole being. It rose within as
a seething river, which drowned all protest. It was not a
single explosion but an infinite series that fed on each
other in a chain reaction. Before long, the gates opened
and she felt the flood wash over her in a crashing
torrent.

*It began as a thought, not a feeling, and it spread like a
gentle river down its left arm and into its belly, where it
caressed the center of fear. The waters went forth
through the legs and up into the chest and neck.
Wherever the river touched went still, as though a great*

*storm had passed and left the shoreline in ruin. As the
river passed over the upper portion, it numbed the
enfeebled muscles made to exercise the chest. Rising
further, it narrowed the passages to the lungs and closed
off the inadequate openings in the nostrils. With a virtual
end to the air supply, the heart slowed, then nearly
stopped. The river moved higher and burst into the brain
with the force of a torrent. There was stillness everywhere.*

*Its bout with the terrible Presence at an end, the gentle
face went slack and found exquisite peace.*

The tiny chest did not rise.

At the moment of its crescendo, their chorus was
joined by a third voice, distant but pervasive. As theirs
began to diminish, the new one increased until it took
on a recognizable shape that froze them in the after-
math.

In the nursery, Lottie was screaming hysterically.

2:05 A.M.

When the cry pierced the night there was no thought of
Doug and what he had done to her. It had come from
the nursery. Instantly, she'd put on her robe and was in
motion toward the hall. Her mouth opened, and nothing came out.

Doug yelled from the bed, but it didn't register.

The blood surged in Joni's brain. *Stephen? Something's happened to Stephen. Please, God, let it be
Lottie, not him!* Even as she made the denial, her body
was gripped in a tight vise of fear, which sent her
hurtling into the nursery.

The first thing she saw was absurd: Lottie, trying to

lift the crib off the floor while Stephen was in it, sleeping.

"What is it, Lottie? For God's sake?" she screamed. Then she realized the nursemaid was beyond speech. She had slumped to the carpet and was holding the crib for support, making sounds like she was getting sick.

For just a second Joni hesitated at the light switch with the thought that everything would be all right so long as the room remained dark. She shot her hand to the switch anyway, and the room jumped into bright clarity.

Doug was right behind her, insisting on knowing what was happening, but she fled to the crib.

"Stephen?"

He wasn't moving. The light should have awakened him. Or the noise.

"Get back. Let me see him," Doug ordered, trying to push her to one side.

Again the unthinkable forced itself on her and she swallowed the hateful thought.

My baby has stopped breathing!

Her body was vibrating. She willed herself toward him, her hands outstretched. *Could he be asleep? Yes, that's it. The fever came back, that's all.*

She forced herself to think it over and over, but the idea didn't work. Lottie was on the floor beneath her. There was something terribly wrong. She could feel it.

She picked him up and felt it and saw it. The coldness, the blue, bored expression. *Maybe it was the light?*

Doug grabbed her from behind, saying something angry.

"Get away," she shouted, feeling the scream just beneath the surface. He was trying to keep her from him again, but there was no force on earth that could do that now.

Wake up! Wake up, Stephen! You're so cold and mommy will give you her heat. Wake up! Please wake up!

She pushed her baby's face to her own, skin on skin, pressing him tightly against her, thinking warmth into his frigid little body. There was no reaction.

It was a dream. Some terrible nightmare. *Let it be a dream!*

Was there a clue? Something out of place in the room that proved it wasn't real? She shot a glance around the nursery. *No, I'm not asleep.*

God in Heaven, I think he's dead!

Her entire body was bathed in a thick coat of perspiration. Her mouth was on his. How many breaths, three? Then rest? Five? *Pass the breath, let his lungs give it back. Pass. Give. Pass. Give. Give it back, Stephen!* Why wasn't he moving?

Because he's—

—choking? Something caught in his throat?

She went to a sitting position on the floor and held his body upright. It was like rubber. She opened her knees and put him between them, looking at this back.

Hands under the ribcage . . . *just there* . . . the bottom one a fist, the top one over it.

She picked one racing moment and tightened her grip. Hard, hard enough to hurt. His body wheezed. *Breathing?* She jerked him back and forth, but this time there was no hissing air. No sound.

Try to stand, Stephen!

She loosened her hold on him, but he pitched forward until she caught him.

Wake up, Stephen. Please! Mommy's so scared!

She was shaking him. He moved back and forth, his arms flaying at his sides in the same rhythm she imparted.

God, don't take my baby!

She laid him on his back.

Thump it. Wake the heart!

She delivered the blow. Thump. *He's so blue.* Again.

Doug caught one of her hands, but she had another. She pounded with it. Once . . . twice. *I'm sorry to hurt you, Stephen.*

The last thing she heard was the sound of her own scream.

PLEASE CRY!

Chapter 4

Lottie sat opposite the washing machine, staring at her clothes. Like her mind, they were spinning round and round. It had been nine hours since Stephen and she hadn't slept.

During the bedlam that followed the final pronouncement at the hospital, Lottie tried to reconstruct the story for the doctors. Her account was marked by bitter self-recrimination and a number of references to evil and premonitions. Also, she couldn't understand why no one had gone to Stephen before she arrived.

Unable to sleep, she'd crept into the hall and listened from outside the nursery. It was after two in the morning and the crying had stopped for five minutes before her intuition drove her to the room. When she got there, the door was ajar as always. Once inside she found her way in the dimness until she touched the crib.

The first thing she noticed was that Stephen was lying on his back, though he never slept that way. Except for where his legs had become entangled in the blanket, his body was uncovered and marred by a strange pattern of light and dark made by shadows from the window.

Cautiously, she reached over the railing and tried to work his legs free of the cover, and by the time the coldness registered she'd already separated his body from the material. In alarm, she reached for his forehead with her palm. It was shockingly chilled. All of him was.

When she tried to lower the railing, it had jammed and she had to lift him out of the crib. Holding her breath, she moved her ear past his face and pressed it to his chest. The silence was something she could feel. Quickly, she put him down again.

She was shaking uncontrollably as she turned toward the door like an automaton. Her legs felt wooden. She took another step and froze, knowing she'd fall if she tried to move again. It was then that she convulsed in the blood-chilling scream that summoned her mistress to the nursery.

The drug had let Joni sleep through most of the next morning. It had been nine hours since she'd been pulled, screaming, off her baby, and the migraine that ensued had not let up. But it wasn't the headache she woke thinking about.

Please let it be only a nightmare!

The bedroom took shape through a haze of tiny dots. Doug was sitting near the foot of the bed with his head in his hands. He hadn't shaved and it appeared that he probably hadn't slept either. He looked like a dog awaiting a beating.

"Doctor Geffs?" he called when he saw her wake. He rose and approached her carefully, but moved back when he heard the moan.

A few seconds later Geffs was at the bed.

"You're all right now, Mrs. Lawrence, just try to

calm yourself." Instead of his normal bedside manner, his face was grimly set.

Joni was having trouble feeling. Her limbs were numb and hardly responded when she tried to move them. The thin summer cover felt like a straitjacket. The main feeling was weakness, allover weakness.

"Stephen?" she said limply. "It happened? He's—"

"There was nothing else we could do," Doug answered directly. "Nothing."

The events of the night before returned and she fought to maintain control over the knot of fear gathering in her belly. Dr. Geffs was leaning close to her and saying it over and over, "Try not to think about it. Don't let yourself think about it."

Her mind conjured an image of a world without Stephen and then denied it. He couldn't be dead, he was only a baby. She imagined he was still there. It was time for his lunch. She wanted desperately to hold him, felt her arms ache for his touch. She needed to press him to her breast and show them he was still alive. Not think about him? Were they stupid? He was her life, and they couldn't exist one without the other.

When Doug rose and came toward her, the rest of her memory returned and there was heat with the pain. What she remembered was too disgusting to believe, but the confirmation was there in his eyes. She'd made love while her baby was dying. He'd forced her.

"Let me talk to her alone," Doug said to the doctor, who nodded but kept looking at Joni, studying her.

"No, please stay," Joni managed. The sedation still had a hold on her, and words came out with other sounds she didn't intend to make. Then, all at once, the idea was exploding in her mind.

"I did it, didn't I?" she cried. "I made a mistake that took him."

As she had the night before, Joni frantically searched

her memory for something she'd done wrong. She struggled to remember hundreds of incidents during the months of pregnancy, a doctor's appointment she skipped, a fall she might have taken or medicine she forgot to give him. She'd been so careful, but there might have been something. Closer to the present, she tried to make a list of all the foods she'd cooked for him, especially on the last day—*the last day!* Yesterday. There was the clothing she'd bought for him, the soap she washed him with. Some deadly chemical in the cloth of his new diapers? The cold that wouldn't go away? Something. Anything. *Dear God, why didn't I see the sign?*

Geffs was trying to calm her. "Not you, not anyone," he was saying. "It had nothing to do with anything you did, not with any of us."

Any of us? Is that what he'd said? Was he feeling the same way, sharing in the blame?

The doctor took her hand and cupped it between his. "Don't even let yourself think about it."

His words were futile. Her baby gone for no reason? Dear, sweet little Stephen dead with no one to blame? No. It must have been something she overlooked, her fault. She was his mother. The frustration rose in her throat and came out in beads of stinging water from her eyes.

"Tell me what to do. Tell me what to think." Her body was racked by a spasm that cut off her wind until she wept deeply and without relief.

Geffs waited patiently. Doug was staring at the floor, bereft.

"My baby died last night, my six-month-old little boy," she sobbed. "One minute he was alive, the next . . . Why?"

The doctor took a long breath and spoke in a monotone. "For whatever it's worth, it was as peaceful a passing as we know of. In Sudden Infant Death the baby, well, just goes to sleep. There is no awareness, no suffering. We don't know much about the syndrome, but we do believe babies like Stephen don't suffer."

The weak promise came wrapped in a cloak right out of the Dark Ages.

"There must have been something I could have done," she insisted.

"All you have to do is rest. We can talk about it later."

"No, tell me why I couldn't have saved him. I have to know."

The beleaguered family doctor looked older than his sixty-one years.

"Don't," Geffs cautioned. "It's hard, I know, but don't blame yourself. It's nobody's fault. We just don't know why."

She took a deep, long breath. He was looking at her, perplexed, trying to be of help and not knowing how.

"My baby died last night, my six-month-old baby," she began. "You're a doctor," she said, riveting Geffs. "You're supposed to know. You've saved hundreds of babies from every sickness. Why couldn't you save Stephen?"

He took the accusation stoically.

"How do you live with your helplessness?"

After a long pause, he answered. "Not much better than you do, I'm afraid."

"Oh yes, you can. You're only the doctor. I'm his mother."

"I don't blame you for being angry. It's normal after a time like this. It will leave you."

She was not pacified. The hollowness of his assurance had left her empty. The idea of a doctor not being able to say why a human being had died was absurd. Something out of the Dark Ages.

"If it were your baby, would that be enough for you?"

"No, I guess not."

"Is there anything you *do* know about it?"

"SIDS is a highly organic area of medical research, by which I mean it's an active field of investigation. I'd guess there are more than a hundred specialists at work in this country alone trying to find its cause or causes and, hopefully, its cure."

Geffs rose off the chair and paced toward the open window. The air was sultry. The new leaves outside hung like hundreds of limp hands. The breeze had died, too. "Like everything else in medicine these days, infant death is a specialty area, and the people who are most knowledgeable are not practitioners—but researchers. They are at the front of their science, well ahead of doctors in practice. It may be discomforting to hear, but the best a family can hope for is a doctor that is well-informed about the topics most likely to come up in his day-to-day experience."

"And crib death isn't likely?"

"Not very."

"You're saying . . . you weren't ready because it's so rare? Is that it? You just weren't expecting it?"

"There are only eight to ten thousand Stephens a year."

"Only?" She bolted at the idea. *"Only?"*

"There are millions of babies born each year," he said quickly.

She thought bitterly about what society would have done by then if ten thousand . . . soldiers died a year, ten thousand third graders, ten thousand doctors!

Before she could respond the door flew open and Lottie came running into the room, collapsing in a flood of tears at the bedside. She clasped Joni's hand in a frantic grip. "It's the Lord's way, Mrs. Lawrence," she blurted out. "Don't blame yourself. There was nothing you could have done." She looked down, full of grief. "Forgive me. He was gone before I got there."

Joni pitied the woman as she was pitying herself. Lottie loved Stephen, too. The younger woman pushed herself into a sitting position and stroked the nurse-maid's head. "There, Lottie, I know how much you cared for him, I know. It . . . it couldn't be helped." Now she was giving the same reassurance given her even though she didn't believe it.

The doctor went to pry the wretched woman from the bed. "Come, Lottie," he implored. "I think we should let Mrs. Lawrence rest."

Lottie looked up in bewilderment and allowed her-self to be lifted from the floor. As she was escorted away she stopped and turned, and there was an evange-listic fervor in her words.

"You can't question, you know. When it's His will, Thy will be done. Trust in Him, Mrs. Lawrence, and know that Stephen is with Him. It's the only true comfort."

Trust in Him, Joni repeated to herself as Lottie went to her own quarters and a job that had ceased to exist. *Trust in Him? He* who had taken her little baby in the night?

Then another thought, perhaps more terrible, re-placed it and she pictured Stephen's face one last time. "I never even kissed him good-bye," she remembered.

Doug had prevailed in the end and they were alone. He was sitting close to her on the bed, his eyes red. He looked pitiful and sounded worse.

"I'll help you, Joni," he was saying. "I'll do anything I can to help you get through this thing, I promise."

Somewhere in the recesses of her mind she wanted to hear that they'd help each other, but it didn't make much difference.

He moved closer. "Please don't judge me for what happened to Stephen, for what I did last night. It was only a coincidence . . ." His voice trailed off.

She wasn't able to talk for a long time, but when she could she felt pity more keenly than anger. She said it without emotion, and without looking at him.

"I feel close and far away from you at the same time. I know Stephen is your loss, too, but I can't forget about last night. And even now the first thing you chose to tell me is about your needs, that his death isn't as important as your need to be forgiven."

"But there's nothing I can do or say that will bring him back, don't you see? I know what you're feeling. What I did was stupid, and I didn't have the right, but please don't make a connection. You can't, or else we can't go on together."

He couldn't even understand what had really happened, she thought.

"It's not just the violence or what you did to me. I could probably get over that." Her head came off the pillow to confront him. "But my instincts said Stephen needed me, and I might have been able to help him if you hadn't stopped me. That's what you did wrong last night, damn you! Because you held me back I'll never know for sure if I could have saved him."

Doug was groping for an answer he didn't have.

"They told me at the hospital . . . Stephen must have always been at high risk and we didn't know it, that if it hadn't happened now it probably would have later. It was only a coincidence that it happened last night."

It was meaningless information. All Joni wanted was to be alone. To think.

"We need each other now," Doug pleaded. "Don't you want my comfort?"

It was the wrong time. He should have felt it. Joni turned to him, but this time even the pity was gone.

"What you've done has made it impossible for me to come to you. That's the biggest hurt of all. I can feel sorry for you, like I do for myself, but I can't forgive you. At least not now."

"But you've got to, you must see that. I don't know why this thing has happened, either, but I do know we had something good together long before Stephen came along. Maybe we just weren't meant to have children."

She felt a flash of heat. "Don't say that to me, Doug, not now."

"Think about it, though. We can be like we were before, maybe better now that the pressure . . . well, you know what I mean."

She couldn't believe what she was hearing.

"Without the pressure of a baby that I loved as much as my own life? Is that what you're trying to tell me?"

"Look, I'm not in such great shape myself, so don't judge me for using the wrong word. What I'm saying is, as much as we loved Stephen, when he was here there was an imbalance, like a wedge driven between us. Whether that was because of you or me isn't important any more. Now what matters is that we don't let his death ruin what's left, that we use it to heal ourselves. I want to heal, Joni, don't you?"

His logic was twisted to suit his own purpose. He'd dismissed Stephen so lightly!

"It's easier for you than me," she shouted, "I can see that now. I wanted Stephen and you didn't, right from the beginning. And now that he's gone you've gotten your wish, so don't you dare talk to me about healing."

He moved closer, oppressively close. "We could have another baby, then."

"Leave me alone. I don't want another baby, I want Stephen."

Again she asked him to leave, but he was intent on making his case. Slowly, Joni pulled herself out of the bed and started for the door. It didn't matter where she went, just not in the bedroom with Doug. The migraine had become brutal.

Her legs could barely carry her, but she went forward despite Doug's rising protests until she was in the hallway. At least he hadn't tried to stop her.

Once out of the room, she stopped in indecision. The weight of the night before pressed down on her shoulders. It bent her over and she began to feel nauseous. For the first time in her life, she knew she was unable to deal with the world and she felt herself sinking under wave after wave of dashed hopes. She was dizzy and struggled to focus on her surroundings.

Finally she stepped forward again, turning in the direction of the nursery. Suddenly it had become crucially important for her to be there. It was the last place she'd been with him. She needed to feel his presence, or find some meaning she could draw from the room.

Doug followed her into the hall, loudly calling her name, but she didn't stop. A few feet from the entrance, the strength in her legs was used up and the right one buckled. She pitched forward, her hands outstretched to cushion the impact, and slammed into the closed nursery door. The door flew open and she fell to the floor. Shakily, she tried to gather herself and came to a kneeling position. She raised her head, then began blinking her eyes repeatedly.

It was impossible, she thought. It was supposed to be Stephen's room. Her eyes raced from one wall to another. There was nothing. The furniture had vanished. The linen chest was there, but open and empty. There were a row of cardboard cartons along one wall, and her eyes went over them one by one. Each was filled to overflowing with the missing pieces of the room. She came to the last one and saw a gleaming yellow board that protruded awkwardly and, when she saw the hand-painted flowers, she screamed out in anguish. It was the headboard of his crib.

Doug was over her, towering, gesturing wildly. She forced herself to concentrate, but there were only fragments of what he was saying: ". . . for your sake . . . rid of the reminders . . . start over . . ."

He was asking her not to look at him that way. She pushed herself around on the floor until she was facing him. The rage was uncontrollable.

"You bastard," she screamed. "You never wanted him, never. Isn't it enough for you that he's been taken away from me? Did you have to steal his memory, too!" She broke down, sobbing.

"For you," he said one last time, but now she could hear that even he didn't believe it.

"I'll never forgive you. Get out! I'll never love you."

There was nothing more. Slowly her head came to rest on the carpet. She was on her side. Her knees moved toward each other until they were touching, and together they began to creep toward her chest. Her arms bent inward at the elbows and went to her waist. Her back became an arc that fit itself around her rising limbs. She lay there, embryonic. It was over. Everything. All over.

Chapter 5

Wednesday, June 9

The morning of the funeral dawned cruelly beautiful. To Joni, the speed with which Doug planned the service appeared to be only further evidence of his obsession to put Stephen completely out of their lives. When she requested they wait longer than the day and a half since Stephen's death, Doug was adamant. Once again, he cited their need to put their son behind them. In the end she'd been too weak to fight.

In the midst of the painful preparations, Joni contacted her mother in Florida. It had been months since they'd spoken and years since they'd harbored any illusions about their relationship. As a child, Joni remembered her mother as a morally upright woman, but though she achieved many good works in the community they were seldom performed at home or for her only daughter's benefit. Emma Krueger was a strict, elegant woman, impeccably tailored but not accustomed to expressing her emotions. So when she heard the news about Stephen, the outpouring of sympathy that followed was surprising.

It was difficult to talk to her, though. Her mother was a reminder of the other painful loss Joni had suffered in her life—her father's death. Seeing her mother vividly brought back the night when her parents had returned from a party to find their house in flames and Joni trapped in the upstairs bedroom. Ignoring her mother's pleading and the restraints of firemen, her father had raced into the thick smoke and brought her out to safety. But he'd been badly burned and later that night he suffered a fatal heart attack. Joni had always been convinced that her mother blamed her for his death.

But now her mother was her only living relative and in a way she never felt before, she needed her, wanted to see her.

Looking very much in control, Emma Krueger arrived at the house after an arduous early morning flight from Miami. When they faced each other for the first time since the wedding, there was a long, awkward moment, but soon their mutual tears softened the stiffness. Suddenly they were holding each other in a rare expression of closeness it had taken the death of a little boy to bring about.

Emma Kreuger sat across from Doug and Joni in the hearse, still unaware of the other reason for the silence. For Joni, the silence was better than their brief but icy exchange on the way to the funeral home earlier. Doug had announced he'd arranged for a van to move some of his belongings, but that he'd only be taking enough to get by for a "brief time." At that moment, the subject of his leaving was a matter of indifference, and she hardly heard him.

"But I can't believe you'll feel this way once it's over," he'd added strongly.

"It's better this way," was all she could manage. It

was the first and last thing she said to him, though, in truth, part of her ached for him, even then.

The few bereaved who managed to attend the service on such short notice stood next to each other in grim silence. Aside from Joni's mother, Doug's brother, Eric, was the only other member of the immediate family. Joni had liked him when they'd first met, but hadn't seen him since leaving New York. Doug's father had been confined to a nursing home for a number of years. Except for Josh Kokai, her closest friend from the city, the rest of the people assembled were the few friends they'd made in Edgewood.

Arriving ahead of the procession of cars, a haggard-looking Jeremy Goodwyn stepped out of the crowd and met Joni getting out of the limousine.

"I share your sorrow, Joni dear," he whispered weakly as she entered his consoling embrace. He also cast a sympathetic glance at Doug, but saw that the man's expression didn't change.

"Thank you for being here, Jeremy. Will you escort me, please?"

Jeremy looked surprised at the exceptional request, but after another futile glance at Doug he kept her arm and walked her to the ground that had been torn open to admit her son. Doug followed ploddingly.

Soon the somber funeral language rang out in the thick summer air and Joni focused on the casket that had been lowered halfway into the grave. She'd never seen an infant casket before; it looked pathetically small. The box was a hateful thing, a cold, impersonal container that separated the living from the dead, mothers from their babies. For a split second, she started to reach for it, but instantly drew back, remembering what had happened a few hours before.

She'd come to the chapel by herself, well before the

service was to start, and she arrived with a cruel fantasy. Despite what she knew to be true rationally, something inside still believed Stephen to be with her. In the midst of her loneliness she'd reached out to him with yearning and actually felt Stephen touch her. Then, she'd gone to the closed casket, praying against all reason that when she raised the cover there would be life in the vessel. Kneeling in the silent chamber, she struggled with the heavy lid until it opened suddenly.

She couldn't bring herself to look at first. Her eyes clenched tightly shut, she held her breath and fought off a flood of horrifying images that defiled her mind. She imagined his face and wondered if she could endure it, if he showed signs of suffering. She knew she must be nearly crazy to even be there, but something had driven her: the need for proof it hadn't been her fault, to be forgiven by the only one who could.

Finally her eyes opened and she looked down to see the body covered by a shroud, a custom of which she'd been unaware. She felt like she was in a state of suspended animation. Slowly, her shaking hand moved to the material and tugged at it until it came loose. Not yet able to look at his face, she drew it over his feet, then his legs, his waist. She felt sick to her stomach. When she unveiled his hands she stopped. They were intertwined and had been folded across his stomach, clenched against the fate some unjust power had chosen for him. For a second she wondered how he'd learned such a grown-up posture, until she thought of the mortician and went weak.

It was an endless time before she dared to place her hand on him and the second she felt the cold putty of his arm she withdrew it. Torturously she removed the rest of the cloth until she was staring directly into his face, and she gasped aloud at the lifelessness etched upon it. His skin was a grayish color, inhuman. The rash was gone, his eyes closed as if in normal sleep. She waited for the lids to tremble as they always did, but gave it up. There was no expression, not anger or pain or accusation. Just nothing.

She drew back for a moment to study the statue of her baby. He looked like a soft rubber-doll replica of life. There was the faint smell of talcum, and she was vaguely aware of a steady but light hissing sound in the room. At first she thought it came from under the coffin somewhere, before realizing it must have been the air conditioners.

Before she closed the coffin and raced out of the room, she leaned down and put her lips to his cold ear.

"I'm sorry, my baby, so sorry," she cried, her tears leaking onto his small cheek. "Forgive me."

But she never found a way to say good-bye.

The service was almost over. When the speaker finished, he grasped a handful of earth from the mound near the excavation and let it spill into the opening. He looked to Joni, nodding piously, until she began to walk to the mound. Then, not knowing how she got there, she was standing in the center of the gathering. The dirt felt cool and moist. She filled her hand and faced the opening.

It came in a faraway lullaby, as though sung by a creature from the surrounding woods, a low incantation carried on the wind. With her hand still outstretched to make the offering, Joni craned her neck to trace the sound and heard it rise to a higher pitch. At once it was familiar: the sound of crying, human crying. Impossibly, when she turned again to locate its source, she was staring at the coffin.

She felt her body tremble but could not move her legs. Her hand had begun to shake and was involuntarily releasing bits of earth, which fell onto the coffin. The instant the soil impacted, the cry grew louder.

It was Stephen, unmistakable, her *Stephen!*

She spun around to Doug for confirmation, but there was no awareness in his expression, only impatience for the ceremony to end.

Frantically she scanned the other faces and saw their frozen looks of curiosity, but they were for her and not the sound.

She turned back to the coffin and watched as it began to shake. The crying had become steady, a baby bawling for its mother. She shook her head to clear the sound that couldn't be there but wouldn't end.

A-waa! A-waa!

Too late, Doug realized her confusion and put an arm out toward her.

"Make it stop! Please make it stop!" she cried.

She whirled around in panic and screamed again, but saw only pity on the faces that stared back at her.

The crying was deafening, an assault on her sanity.

A-waaaaa!

Half mad, she held her hands over her ears and took a step toward the coffin, imploring it to stop. The movement of her foot loosened the mound of soil and some of it spilled over the edge into the void. When it hit the coffin, the crying grew louder.

Against the power of Doug's arm, she moved to the brink of the opening. The wailing was so strident she couldn't hear the voice that commanded her to come away. She was going to Stephen. To be with him. To get inside.

I'm coming, Stephen!

Before she could take the last step forward, the hands on her shoulders became stronger and held her back with a purpose mightier than her own. Steadily they forced her away from the grave, back past the mound of earth and the faces with open mouths. Supporting her firmly, they urged her to a faraway place where the grass was cool on her skin and the crying became distant, then ended. Near sleep, she turned to Doug with a distant sense of gratitude, but when she focused on his face she found instead the gentle features of Jeremy Goodwyn.

Chapter 6

Friday, June 11

The man in the doorway reminded her of someone from another age. He was Captain of Detectives William Thompson, a rough-hewn man in his late thirties, a bit shorter than Doug but more solidly built. He scanned the twenty-foot square that formed the master bedroom and saw it was in as much of a shambles as the rest of the residence. Three days after the baby's death, it still looked as though some giant hand had gripped the house and let things fall where they may.

The officer from the Edgewood P.D. tried to look pleasant and came into the room.

"This will only take a minute, ma'am," he said softly, turning his attention from Joni to her doctor, who insisted on being there for the interrogation. "Sorry to bother you at a time like this."

Geffs nodded and Thompson turned back to Joni, who lay in bed.

"Your maid, Lottie O'Hare, was kind enough to spend a few minutes with me, but she seemed anxious to leave."

"That's because she's not needed here any more," Joni said, hearing the self-pity in her own voice.

"Yes, I understand, but I wonder if you would corroborate a few of her facts?"

"You wonder, or you demand?" Joni checked herself. "I'm sorry, what is it you'd like to know?"

"According to Mrs. O'Hare, your child passed away about two in the morning. Mrs. O'Hare actually made the discovery, at which point you and your husband went to the nursery. Can you confirm the time?"

She wondered why he needed her side of the story when he seemed to have all the facts she could supply.

"I wasn't . . . thinking about what time it was."

"One of you called the ambulance?"

"My husband."

"But before it got here you decided to drive to the hospital yourself?"

The picture he was painting was all too familiar.

Geffs came to his feet for attention. "Really, captain. Mrs. Lawrence is still on medication for—I can't see how she can be expected to—"

"Well, I don't mean this to be unkind, but we've found that the best time can be the earliest."

"For your purposes, maybe," Geffs retorted.

"I'll tell him anything he wants . . . to get it over with," Joni said. The last thing she needed was another fight.

"The ambulance? You didn't wait for it?"

"My husband called as soon as I saw Stephen wasn't . . . breathing. I tried to revive him the best I could, but I was alone and unsure. The rescue squad . . . it seemed too far away to wait for."

"Excuse me, but you just said you were alone, yet a moment ago you also said your husband was with you."

"For heaven's sake," Geffs interrupted, "she only

meant she was without any medical help. Alone in that sense."

"Wouldn't it be normal for her to call you in that situation, doctor?"

Geffs was caught offguard. "Why, yes, but—"

"And *did* she call you that night?"

He shook his head.

"It was already too late for Dr. Geffs," Joni said loudly. "We needed faster help." Why was he torturing her? He was making it sound as if—

"Of course, but there *was* a nurse on the scene, was there not?"

"Lottie, yes."

"Did she give the child medical attention? Isn't she trained for this type of situation?"

"She wasn't in any . . . condition. It was already too late."

Thompson wrote something in a small notebook.

"What did they tell you when you got to the hospital?"

She forced only enough of the scene to mind to answer the question.

"I was begging them to keep trying. They were telling me my baby was dead, but I made them keep trying." She recalled how one of the nurses had looked at her. She had seen it clearly in her eyes, but only remembered it now. Suspicion. "Why do you want to know all these things? What good will it do?"

"The law requires us to investigate this category of death, Mrs. Lawrence. The normal procedure. I'm sorry."

Geffs was impatient for the interview to end, but Thompson noted it and faced him down until he looked away.

"Can you think of anyone who might have been with

your baby recently that you didn't know very well? A stranger or new friend? Perhaps someone new in the neighborhood, who took an unusual interest in him?"

"No, nothing like that. I never let anyone near him I didn't know. Never."

"Yes, of course." He paused. "By the way, can you tell me when your husband might be home? I'll need to talk with him also."

"My husband doesn't . . . stay here any more." She didn't like having to tell him something so private, but there was no choice. "Not for the time being. He's with a friend in New York. I can give you the number there."

The officer's puzzled look was understandable. It must have seemed terribly strange for a husband to move out at the same time his baby died. It still seemed that way for her, too.

"It has nothing to do with what's happened," she added quickly.

Thompson put down his pad. "Would you mind telling me why he would choose this time to leave?"

"Yes, I would mind very much."

Geffs took a few steps forward and placed himself between Thompson and his patient.

"I think you have what you need, officer. Frankly, I'm beginning to find your line of questioning a bit overzealous, given the circumstances."

Thompson was considering the doctor's criticism. For some reason, Joni's mind had fastened on a comparison between the officer's reaction and her mother's when she'd been told about their separation. All the compassion she'd shown Joni regarding Stephen had suddenly turned into an empty, moralistic speech about the sanctity of marriage and the shame of divorce. It was something she would have expected more from Lottie and, when they'd said good-bye, she knew the gulf between them had widened. Now, although she resented the motive behind the officer's intrusion into her personal life, at least he'd asked why.

"All right, Mrs. Lawrence, I guess that's enough," Thompson said, stepping away from the bed and the confrontation with Dr. Geffs, "and I'm sure when I talk with your husband there won't be any further need for questions."

He asked for the address in New York and Joni found the folded-up piece of paper in the night table.

"Again, I'm sorry I had to bother you. I hope things go better for you now."

"Thank you," she said curtly.

She'd expected him to leave right away. Instead, the officer seemed to be debating with himself.

Geffs became impatient at the delay and cleared his throat.

"Thank you, officer . . . and good afternoon."

Thompson continued to stare at the night table after Joni went to it for Doug's number. He was studying a picture of her and Doug that she'd been unable to put away. When Thompson heard the doctor asking him to leave, he addressed Joni.

"I'd just like you to know," he said, with a gentleness that hadn't been apparent up until then, "I didn't find it easy coming here today. I have some idea what you must be going through, and I know the last thing you need is the police butting in. But I do want you to know that if there's anything I can do for you, please feel easy about calling me."

His unexpected offer disconcerted her, but before she could respond he'd nodded his good-bye and turned away. After he'd gone she felt confused about the interrogation. There was something about the officer she found comforting, but he also made her feel curiously paranoid. The way he focused on her separa-

tion and looked at their picture. In addition to her
original doubts, she now felt as though she'd been
accused of something and had failed to satisfy her
accuser.

Later, after Geffs had gone on to his next house call,
she closed her eyes and wished she'd told the cop about
the tree that moved.

Chapter 7

Monday, June 14

The Visitor was extremely tall, middle-aged, and spidery thin. He could have been a neighbor from down the block. His well-groomed Afghan pulled against him on a firmly held leash, threatening to take him away from the imposing Tudor he had come to investigate.

But he ignored the dog, which was no challenge to his own strength and kept walking until he could verify the number over the door. It was correct. He scrutinized the residence with intense attention, not blinking once. As he watched, a girl of about six crossed the street and came toward him, clutching a bag of groceries she could barely handle. For a moment their eyes met, and after she'd gone by, the Visitor turned to watch her from behind, thinking how easy it would be, if she were the one he'd come for.

The Visitor continued past the house, then stopped to look up and down the secluded street. When he was satisfied it was deserted, he reversed direction. The area was new to him. It was a rich neighborhood of large houses and swimming pools and parents who let their children run loose without any thought of their protection. It made him feel good to know what he was about to do would also be a blow against the rich. He despised their arrogance. The Visitor laughed. It wasn't his kind of neighborhood, that was for sure. It wasn't even his dog.

The front edge of the ample lawn was shut off from the street by dense brushwood hedges and backed by overgrown blue spruce. The thick foliage ran along both sides of the house to where it disappeared in the backyard and blocked the view from either side. Satisfied that no one was watching, the Visitor let go of the long-haired animal and instantly reappeared on the other side of the thick bushes. The dog immediately bounded in the opposite direction, free again to search for the man it knew as its owner.

The Visitor surveyed the distance to the house, then traveled the relatively long space within a few seconds. When he was abreast of the building, he flattened himself against it. An hour earlier, the area would not have been in a protective shadow. Everything else had been planned down to the smallest detail, but the shadow was just good fortune.

Pausing in the calm that followed his first movements, the Visitor felt reassured. The homes he visited were always so defenseless, and his victims so unsuspecting, waiting for him and their destiny.

There was only one window on his side of the house, and the Visitor inched toward it until he could look into the empty room. His eyes scanned the interior, but there was no one inside. He crept forward to the end of the house and the sheltered backyard—where the mother might be. Alone, or maybe with the small being.

The Visitor quickly looked around the corner of the house. The woman was there, lying on her stomach by the pool. The part of her face he could see showed her to *be pretty, young and ripe in a bathing suit that barely stretched across the two plump spheres of her buttocks. She was sunning herself, the straps of her bikini undone at the top. He studied the lines of her almost nude body and thought about what he could do to them if he wanted to, the rich bitch!*

As he watched, his face pressed tightly against the siding, the woman stirred. Heedless of her bikini top, she pushed off the ground with one hand and turned onto her back. Now her large, white breasts were completely exposed to the sun. Slowly, she took a bottle of lotion and worked the creamy liquid into them.

For the first time, the Visitor felt himself losing control. His breathing became irregular, and it was a while before he could restore enough self-discipline to take the mental picture. Once he did, he compared it to the one he'd already filed in his mind. There was no doubt, she was the one the Planner had sent him to find. The other, her infant, would be nearby. The Visitor came alive with confidence. He would retain the image perfectly in his perfect mind.

For an instant he thought about doing it to her and then going to the baby. Incredibly, as he debated, the woman began to squirm as her hands moved to her waist to remove the bikini bottoms. Quickly, before it was too late, he turned away. The discipline. He'd come back later, when it was dark and there was little chance of being seen.

Having made the right decision, the Visitor moved back along the side of the house. On the way to the street, he paused only long enough to step back from the building, look up to the second-story window—the nursery—and take one more picture.

Book II

Chapter 8

Monday, July 19

It had been almost six weeks since the night Stephen died. Doug was already settled in his new Manhattan apartment and Lottie had gone on to another family. The house echoed with emptiness. Even Dr. Geffs had confined his contact to an occasional phone call. But as lonely as it was, the outside world had become a frighteningly alien place that, except for brief trips of necessity, Joni was able to avoid completely.

Though the decision to separate from Doug had been born in a moment of hysteria, the dark cloud had never lifted. In the days that followed she knew that she could never live with him again. Still, it took more strength than she knew she had not to change her mind.

The nights were the hardest, long, empty and dark places with dreams so vivid they'd wake her in fright. Sedatives, books, music—all of the normal tranquilizers—failed to stem the wave of confusion and dreams that night brought. And the most uncertain part was why she should want to go on at all.

It was excruciating to remember how her life had

changed into such a surreal nightmare. Just a few short weeks ago there was a family in the house, a baby, a husband, a hope for a long future of belonging together. Now they'd all been taken away and there was nothing left but the belief that she would always be alone. Doug and Stephen had made her believe, but when they were gone again the belief became just another empty promise, the echo of a lie.

Often Joni stayed awake for more than twenty-four hours, overcome by exhaustion and yet unable to sleep. During that period, the slightest occurrence could upset her tenuous emotional stability. A broken faucet meant an invasion into her cocoon by a stranger that could not be trusted. A knock at the door warned her to retreat into the recesses of the study until the potential threat had passed.

Rain became an ally. It soothed and insulated her island against disruption. What courage remained was used to do watchful battle against the urge to escape through alcohol or drugs. It was a time for extreme isolation.

There were nights then when she lay behind the locked door in her bedroom, trying to understand why there was no one she could turn to for help, not her mother whom she could never reach, not neighbors who hadn't looked her in the eye since that night, not Jeremy who would try but was hopelessly outside of what she was feeling, not even Josh, who would have understood but whom she couldn't face in her present state of deterioration. The truth was, she didn't want to be reached by anyone. She was utterly alone and by choice.

But even in the midst of her suffering there was a part of her that needed to believe something could be saved, a truth or strength that she could take from the experiences, however painful they had been. Even in the depths of despair, she tried to remember that life always held new and unpredictable possibilities. It was the thinnest shred of belief, but for a time it had kept her going.

Then, on a morning when the earth was bathed in sunlight, she awoke to the sound of starlings nesting in the ivy that embraced the brick chimney. She lay in bed, unaware of the difference between that day and the one before until the chorus prodded her interest and she knelt to peer out the window. In the past weeks she had rarely taken notice of the outside world, but on this morning she awakened to an inexplicable peace.

Nearly ripping the curtains away in haste, she opened the shutters and let light flood the room. Out there a hundred shades of vivid color exploded in a bouquet of living things that her mind recorded as though for the first time. The emptiness and fear that only a day earlier had made her an invalid had been miraculously tempered by the most tentative sense of renewal, and she wept in the hope of a possible redemption. Unable to alter the past, something in her had chosen to look forward again.

Chapter 9

Wednesday, July 21

It was as though Providence had decided to become kind all at once. The same afternoon she realized she might be able to put her life together again, Joni impulsively called Jeremy with a single request: a job, any job, as long as it was fast. At first he was shocked but quickly understood her need. After a much-welcomed and very supportive talk, Joni waited for him to call back as promised.

Within hours Jeremy rang her with good news. The same client he'd come to her house to talk about was delighted with her acceptance and could offer her a small print ad that was shooting in two days. Although he was already negotiating with another model for his line of soaps and cosmetics, nothing had been firmed up.

The best part was that the Camille Company was using Josh Kokai, Joni's dearest friend and their photographer for many years. It was the same way they'd met originally, at many similar work sessions in the old days. It was a marvelous turn of events, a new beginning with an old friend. Fate seemed to be smiling on her.

By the time Friday came, Joni had become more and more nervous, and when she arrived at Josh's studio she entered the place with a sense of foreboding.

The room was as high as a two-story house, white, and all windows on the side facing the street. The floor met the far wall in a rush of curved, seamless plaster so the camera could not tell where one began and the other ended.

Josh Kokai was in the middle of a tirade directed at her makeup man. Even in the so-called enlightened age it was rare for a woman photographer to command the respect and earnings Josh did, rarer still because she was also Japanese. She'd made it in a man's domain because she was better than most men, a photographer's photographer, and her use of dramatic extremes to highlight her product's attributes had earned the prized reputation. Joni could still picture the eagle's claw with nail polish on it, the Tiffany necklace hung on the panther's neck.

Josh was small, sharp-tongued and as beautiful as the models she worked with, and when her own beauty became provoking to the models, she used it as another tool. All was grist for the photographic mill.

"You bet your ass you do," she said after they'd exchanged a warm embrace and made their way to Josh's private quarters, not a dressing room as Joni had expected.

"Do what?"

"Look as good as the day you left the business."

"Except on the inside I'm a tired old model trying to make a comeback."

"Except you look better in retirement than most do at their peak."

Joni turned to the mirror and shrugged. "No comment. Besides, if anyone looks good it's you. You're absolutely dewy."

Josh started to smile, but didn't let it happen. She moved closer to Joni. "Hey, listen, I'll cut the bullshit if you do. Tell me about it. Are you okay?"

Joni sighed deeply.

"'Okay' about describes it, Josh, but where I've been, I'll settle for it."

"What about Doug? I couldn't believe that on top of everything else . . ."

Joni reddened. Absently she reached for a bottle of Pink Chiffon nail gloss and unscrewed the cap. "Doug and I are separated for the time being, but there's little hope. It's not news, though, not really. I think it's been ending for a long time."

"But at a time like this?" Josh asked with pain in her face.

"No choice. He's been living in the city for almost six weeks."

The Japanese woman pressed her shoulder gently.

"What can I say, I misjudged him. He's a good person deep down, more sad than anything, but I don't think he knows how to give, how to be part of a family." Joni suddenly stared at her hand. It was shaking so hard she almost spilled the nail polish. She cleared her throat of the discussion. "Listen, I appreciate your concern, really I do, and there aren't many people I could even talk to about it, but I got my eight hours last night and if you get me going it's gonna turn my eyes red."

"Well, I'll say one thing for you," Josh sighed. "You have guts."

"Wrong," Joni replied, "what I have is no choice."

Josh looked uncomfortable. Her normally high energy was absent.

"What's the matter?" Joni asked.

"Well, I don't know how to tell you this, but we're not shooting today."

"What? Why not?"

"There's been a change in the job, Joni. The client killed the one we had scheduled."

Joni noticed the way she turned away. She was hiding something.

"Josh? There's something else, isn't there?"

Josh nodded.

"What I said was only half-true. Yes, they changed the job, but yes, you could still do the new one they substituted."

"So? What's the problem?"

"The new one is for another part of their line, soap, not cosmetics."

"And?"

Josh sighed. "Christ, Joni, the damned ad's got a baby in it."

Joni sat upright at the word. The last thing in the world she wanted to confront on her first time out was such an obvious reminder.

"Why didn't you tell me before? How could Jeremy have let me come? He must have known—"

"The change happened less than two hours ago, phoned into me directly. Jeremy probably doesn't even know. I tried to reach you at home, but you had already left."

Josh came over to her and sat down. There was a warm glow in her almond eyes.

"Listen, why don't we just forget about this one. Like they say, jobs are like men, are like buses. A new one comes around the corner every five minutes."

Josh was undoubtedly right. If she were smart, she'd get the hell out of there. It was a long time before Joni answered.

"Can you still cancel the other model, the backup one you must have called?"

Josh brightened. "Can the Pope make pizza?"

"Then I'll do it."

"Are you sure?"

"Hell, no, I'm no hero, but I know that sooner or later I'm gonna have to face a world with babies in it, so better sooner."

"You could easily wait for something else. Sometimes it's better to play safe."

Joni stood with a sense of purpose. "Why should I start now! Which way?"

Josh jumped to her feet. "I was hoping you'd say that." She rubbed her hands together in anticipation and escorted Joni to the biggest dressing room, where she was seated in a barber chair. Instantly a male stylist came into the room and had his hands in her hair before he stopped walking. He was humming something from *Peter Pan*. Josh leaned over the back of the chair and gave Joni a kiss on the cheek.

"Okay. We go inside, shoot our buns off, and be a hero. Then we'll catch a drink and hang out, okay?"

"Okay."

The professional photographer whirled to the door and instantly was at full energy. "Oh, Maurice," she called back to the stylist, "go easy on the eyeshadow, for chrissake. This isn't an ad for Hooker's Anonymous."

When Josh came back in the room a moment later, she had an artist's rendering.

"By the way, here's the bullshit we're doing."

Joni unfolded the paper the rest of the way and felt a wave of uneasiness. The ad showed a mother carrying an infant. They were surrounded by a circle of washing machines and detergents. The machines were sinister, the mother and child vulnerable, but they were obviously going to find their salvation in the bar of Camille Baby Soap at the bottom.

The headline read: *Camille Baby Soaps—Safe Enough for Your Most Delicate Washable.*

When the lights came on in a blinding flash, the heat on her skin felt like tropical sun and it took a minute before Joni's eyes got used to the glare and she could see the camera. After the stage was set, the stylist brushed back a loose hair from her forehead and Josh called for the infant. There was no telling how coopera- tive the baby would be or how long it would take before the hot lights would affect him. That's why bringing on the baby was always the last step. It was also why there was a backup infant waiting in the wings. To Josh's credit, Joni never heard or saw either of them until they were almost ready to shoot.

"You got him?" the young mother asked as she placed her child in Joni's arms.

"Yes . . . there." It was the oddest sensation, like feeling a flow of current between herself and the child, a bonding of skin to skin as though it would be difficult to pry them loose. "I have him," she said as evenly as she could.

The baby's mother was staring at her. "You sure you're all right?"

"Of course. Just that he's a little heavy is all. What's his name?"

"Brando. From the movie, *The Godfather?* It was a nickname at the time, but it stuck."

Joni was trying to smile politely, but as she looked at Brando for an instant she thought she saw something in his eyes, a glowing reflection of . . . something in mini- ature. She could not look away until Josh was calling her name loudly and she forced her head to the front. *Stop it!* she scolded herself, adjusting him until they both were comfortable. *Don't talk yourself into it. You can do it.*

She drew a deep breath and listened for direction.

"All right now," Josh called, her body bowed over the lens. "Relax. You're one of the good guys. Doting. Concerned. You wouldn't use anything on that sucker that was bad for his skin. You're secure in your relationship with him and with Camille. That's it," she purred as Joni took a good read on the character. Joni could feel her breath coming at more regular intervals as some of the insecurity began to melt away. She was becoming comfortable with the camera, "making love to it" as Jeremy had once observed. After all, she was Joni Lawrence, thirty-two and still in her prime. Well, almost.

"No, uh, uh. You lost it." Josh was scolding. "Back to the beginning. Problem, then resolution. That's it, keep it going."

Flash.

"Beautiful."

Flash. Flash. Flash.

The encouragement continued, punctuated by bursts of electrical energy as the shutter opened and closed on a moment in time. The heat was becoming intense, as was the exhilaration. After a while the baby became a bit restless in her arms and began to squirm, but he did not utter a sound. Offstage, his real mother watched proudly. She had buttonholed the bored stylist and was telling him about her son.

"Okay," Josh sang. "Now from full profile. Turn to your right and raise Macho Man about two inches. Two more. Bang!" Her hands were animated, but the rest of her was motionless as she stayed glued to the lens. She clicked off dozens of shots in an amazingly short time.

There was only one break after the first half hour,

mostly to spell the model from the weight of her bundle. Coffee and doughnuts covered with compliments were followed by the second series of pictures. Josh was glowing with dedication to her art. Her aura was an extra light that brightened the room.

"Last one, gang," she shouted to the crew, attentive to her every need. "This time some low-angle stuff." To Joni: "I want you and Edward G. independently looking at camera. You're together but separate, as though you both have legitimacy without the other. So don't look at the baby, Joni, just know he's there."

She nodded slightly, but not enough to change her angle.

"More intensity. Epic."

Carefully she thought herself into the role and challenged the lens with her knowledge. The flashes of light were vindication. Josh didn't shoot until she saw that Joni was perfectly attuned.

When the baby began to become irritable and whimper, Joni's first impulse was to abandon the pose, but any decision to halt the shoot was the photographer's, not hers, so she continued to play to the camera.

There were many more small explosions of light coming faster. Now the baby had begun to cry softly, and Josh's continuing could only mean there was some new inspiration as her mind calculated ways to exploit the new chemistry.

"Howya doin', Joni? Don't move. Just answer by stomping your foot like Trigger."

If she wanted her to laugh she had her way. Counterpoint? Baby crying, mother laughing?

The infant was beginning to make such a clamor it was getting hard to keep her focus, but Josh kept the shoot going way past the point where other sessions would have stopped.

The flashes continued blindingly as the baby's voice became strident. Joni thought of stealing a quick glance at the mother. Why wasn't she concerned about her child's welfare?

When the migraine struck like lightning, the atmosphere in the studio changed. As the wailing continued, she began to hear another texture in it, that of another little boy who used to cry in the same way. It was like having him in her arms and—*STOP IT!* Her imagination was getting out of control; the foolish, self-defeating artist in her mind.

But again it was Stephen she was holding, then Brando. Not even the self-administered lecture could stop it. The baby was screaming; it was a wonder it wasn't losing its voice. Josh was telling her not to move, to smile. She could hardly hear her any more as the din filled the room. The weight of the child was an unbearable burden she had to put down. It seemed she'd been in the pose for hours.

From somewhere outside the noise, Josh was calling her name, ordering her to break. There was a rough pressure yanking on her arms. The real mother was trying to pull her baby away from her, pleading with her, frightened. She could feel her own hands, burning where she touched him, and she knew she couldn't put him down—ever—because they were one.

Finally she forced her head to turn toward the infant and when she saw him her heart nearly stopped in disbelief. Although the screaming continued even louder, the child's face wasn't moving. He was peaceful, completely quiet. He was asleep.

She staggered, and people were struggling to catch her as she pitched toward the floor, still clutching him. The crying filled the room and she was swallowed up in it.

*   *   *

She awoke on a couch in Josh's private rooms. It was still midday, with sun filtering in from a double sky-light. The tumult of the session had been replaced by gentle stroking on her forehead and soft whisperings.

"What some people won't do for a spotlight."

Joni blinked away some fog and forced a dry swallow.

"Want to talk about it? It's okay if you don't."

She pushed herself into a sitting position, the returning color from embarrassment. "I made quite a mess of things out there, didn't I?"

"You mean did we blow the shoot?"

"Yeah."

"Honey, when you came to ol' Josh you came to play hardball. I had this deal wrapped in the first series, the rest was padding."

She shook her head, still unnerved. "It was the crying. Spooky, Josh. I couldn't look at the baby because it would have broken my concentration. I thought you saw it too and were using it. Then, when I finally did look, he . . . he wasn't crying at all. It was all in my mind." She looked away. "Stephen, again. The way it's been happening ever since . . . I don't think I'll ever get over it."

"You heard a baby crying and it wasn't Brando? That what you just said?"

Fighting tears, she nodded.

"Well, I got a news flash for you. That's exactly how it was."

"What do you mean?"

"It's a fact. Brando wasn't crying, but Georgy boy was, and that's what you heard."

"I don't understand."

"Our backup kid, George Tabor Nelson. The one we never used? The goddamn makeup man stuck him with the scissors when he was trimming his hair and the kid started screaming bloody murder in the wings. Thought he'd never stop. I didn't know that's what was bothering you until just now."

Out of the corner of her eye Joni saw one of Josh's assistants following the exchange from the doorway. Being the largest helper, he'd been given the job of carrying her in.

"I was really hearing a baby, not imag—"

"I'd show you the kid, but I sent him home with the professional opinion that he should consider becoming a gas station attendant."

"And I thought—"

"I can see now what you thought, that you were going bonkers. But it was just circumstantial, you fool. The crying you were hearing and the baby you were holding. Just your luck they had to come together first time out. We won't let that happen again. No more baby ads for you for a while."

Joni smiled sheepishly. "You got that right."

Josh clapped her hands and stood up. "You up to some lunch? Personally, I could use some air. What do you say to the Russian Tea Room while we wait for first negs?"

Joni took a deep breath and felt relaxed. "Assuming I can still walk, you've got a deal. And assuming you've got a bathroom."

"First door on the left."

Josh helped her to her feet but wasn't needed further. When Joni was out of the room, the assistant was glowering.

"And just what does that mean?"

"You told her the other baby started crying. How come? It never happened."

She walked up to the young man, who dwarfed her, reached way up to his shoulder, and pointed him out of the room. "I know what happened and what didn't happen, Johnny boy, and also what I think that very brave young woman has to hear right now. And until she can get her act together, I'm not about to send her on her way thinking she's flipped out."

"But don't you think it's—"

"And the only question left to resolve as I see it is just how much *you'd* like to become a gas station attendant."

The assistant blanched. "I'll go tell the makeup man to be more careful next time."

Josh smiled contentedly. "There's a good boy."

Chapter 10

The young couple had tired of the company picnic and retreated with their baby to a remote part of the park. There they were hidden from view by the tallest of the Bear Mountains.

The location not only secluded them, but conjured up warm memories. They'd visited the spot before; it was even possible that it had served as the bed in which their infant had been conceived.

The three family members lay on the blanket in contemplative silence, breathing air thick with moss and fern. Then the husband remembered the rock, and, with a wink, hopped up to find it. Soon after, she heard his shouts of discovery and came to her feet to join him.

For a fleeting second, she debated about leaving the baby. There was no reason to be afraid, she thought. He was in the center of the blanket, sound asleep on his stomach. And there was no one even close to where they were. Still, she hesitated before finally bending down and kissing him on his soft forehead. Then she rose and bounded to the man she'd married in her grandmother's dress.

She found him just beyond a stand of beautiful white birch where he took her in his arms and pointed proudly to the names he'd chiseled in the boulder before they were married. He held her tightly and wouldn't let go until she'd told him how much she loved him, until he'd returned the assurance with an impassioned kiss, until their baby sensed the Presence enter its body and began its futile struggle with the apnea.

Instinctively, the Visitor had crept up to where the baby lay. He could hear the parents' muffled cooing in the distance and, when he estimated the time it would take for them to get back to the spot, he stepped out of the thicket.

The infant awakened to a snapping of twigs and made a low, gurgling sound. In a second, the Visitor took three quick steps and knelt.

The dangerous time was in the beginning, when the small body had to be touched, when the being might cry out, so the first thing he did was cover its mouth. After that, speed was all that was required. And, of course, the Instrument.

The baby's eyes opened in alarm when it felt the cool hand on its skin, but the hand prevented it from making any sound. The Visitor was already reaching for the small glass vial, opening it and looking for the exact spot on the baby.

It was always amazing to watch the speed with which the Instrument did its work. It was so predictable, so quiet. The chosen subject never stirred, not even near the end.

The Visitor was well away from the scene when the first screams of discovery pierced the quiet of the forest.

As he slithered through the trees, feeling safer with each step, some of the other names came back into his perfect mind, as did the series of events that would follow his visit: the parents calling for help; the arrival of the ambulance; the unsuccessful attempts at revival; and then, later, the second visit.

Chapter 11

It was no small task bulling her way into the private offices of the famous Dr. Jonah Amaloff, and once there Joni found staff assistant Angel Dominico cordial, if protective of her superior. The article she then gave Joni to read while she was waiting was a reprint from the *Journal of Medicine* and the difficult narrative was highly technical. It was an extensive summary of Dr. Amaloff's specialized field of medicine and therefore a source of facts about crib death, or Sudden Infant Death syndrome, as the article called it.

But try as she could to untangle the complex jargon, she became hopelessly lost. The author had made no attempt to weight his findings. It was as though all the researchers were working in a hundred different areas at the same time without a clear sense of direction. Amaloff's work was mentioned several times and in one instance his efforts were described as "pioneering."

Nurse Dominico met the middle-aged doctor in the

hallway before he could enter. She wore a things-are-out-of-my-control look that made him pull up short.

"Except for calling the police, there was nothing to do," she said, looking back toward his couch. "When she got past security, she came in here and said she wouldn't move until she spoke to you."

"One of the mothers?" Amaloff asked. As he studied the simply dressed woman more closely, his curiosity rose. There was something extraordinary about the way she looked. She was pretty in a simple but elegant way, and there was something about her profile that was both intriguing and familiar.

"No, just a very pushy lady who got your name from reception." She saw her boss's fascination. "Also *muy bonita*, eh? God knows what she did to get past Waters at the desk."

"What does she want?"

"She wants to talk to an expert on the syndrome."

"Well, I guess that's a compliment, at least. What's her problem?"

"Beats me, you're the doctor," Dominico said cutely.

"Did you tell her we run a busy private facility and don't do individual counseling?"

Aware that she'd become the object of his scrutiny, Joni looked up in time to catch the distinguished-looking man with a faint smile. He was a composite of every television doctor she'd ever seen: forty-five to fifty, slim, salt-and-pepper hair and handsome in an unshowy sort of way. Even from where she was sitting, she could tell he was going to see her.

"Never mind," Amaloff said to his nurse. "I'll tell her myself."

"What makes you think it was a case of sudden infant death?" he asked her later in his private office.

"That's the question *I* came to ask," she said. "In fact, you're the first person to allow for any other possibility."

"Do you know that a number of deaths labeled SIDS are actually not?"

"No, I didn't. I don't know much of anything, except what a few people told me and what I read in a couple of trips to the library. And I think you need a Ph.D. to understand that."

He was unamused and impatient. "Well, I'm sorry, really I am. I know how hard it is to search for understanding when there's none to be had, but I'm not set up to dispense information. Perhaps I could send you a list of articles and we could discuss them at some . . . future time." He stopped cold when he saw her annoyance. "I can tell you're not too pleased with what I just said."

Joni squirmed uncomfortably in the metal chair and placed her hand hard on his desk.

"Look, Dr. Amaloff, I didn't come here to be a pain in the neck or to trade favors. In the last few weeks I've done a lot of soul-searching and heard from a lot of people just how screwed up I am. I've been questioned by the police, silently accused by friends and relatives, and been through a dozen bouts of panic. And today I almost had to let your security guard molest me just to get in here. Meanwhile, a voice inside me won't let me alone until I find out what only someone like you knows. Now, will you help me or won't you?"

The mannerly man was taken aback by her sudden offensive. In his lofty position at the hospital he was unaccustomed to ultimatums. He pushed himself back from his oversized desk covered with piles of neatly stacked papers, took off a wristwatch, and set it face up in front of him.

"All right, Mrs. Lawrence," he said, surrender in his

voice, "I'll give you a half hour, not a minute more. I hope that will satisfy you."

"Will that be enough?" she demanded further.

He weakened even more and leaned forward.

"Let's start with that, okay? We'll see what happens."

Once he became communicative, Amaloff was an encyclopedia of information on his topic. The questions Joni piled, one upon the next, never failed to elicit a learned answer, usually supplied with an appraisal of its reliability. The exchange was relaxed and they became more comfortable with each other. Amaloff opened the door to a strange new world and did not bother to edit insights it had taken a lifetime to originate.

The facts about SIDS were themselves stunning, particularly since so much was known and yet there was so little progress against the dread sickness.

"The incidence of the syndrome is highest among infants between two and four months old," he said. "After six months, only ten percent of all SIDS babies are at risk, and the number falls off to almost zero after one year. It might interest you to know that this single fact forms the basis of my work."

"In what way?"

"It makes more sense to me to devote our resources to the maintenance of life during this relatively brief period than to spend untold years in the pursuit of elusive if not unattainable cures. This is where I differ from my colleagues." He was getting wound up, but abruptly halted the direction. "But this must be rather off the topic for you."

"Not at all."

"In any case, there are between eight and ten thousand cases of SIDS a year, probably a lot more that we don't know about. It ranks as the primary cause of death in infants."

Dr. Geffs had named the same figure, but it didn't lessen the shock.

"Almost ninety-nine percent of all deaths occur during sleep, and almost all are silent. It's a cruel anomaly of nature, you see. Most living things emit screams of warning when in danger, except babies that succumb to the syndrome."

Joni was confused. Hadn't she heard Stephen cry out before he died, or did he stop for a time before, during their *struggle?* It was hard to know exactly when the attack came, and if it was the reason he fell silent.

"I've read a lot about *apnea.* That's a period of time when the baby stops breathing altogether."

"Yes and, if I can anticipate your next question, we're not certain why."

This part of his explanation was more bizarre, like something from science fiction. A sudden cessation of breathing occurred regularly during sleep in almost all babies. Usually the chest stopped its contractions and this set off a closure of the airways in the throat. The amazing thing was that it was so common and not just a SIDS phenomenon. Unbelievably, even normal babies experienced up to twenty bouts of apnea a night, each lasting for up to twenty seconds.

As the doctor spoke, his energy for the topic increased and for a while Joni lost herself in the lecture. But then she was aware that her half hour had elapsed and there was so much more she needed to know.

He'd also checked the time. "One tends to get caught up in it, but now I'm losing my day. Sorry."

She took his hand, shook it warmly. "When we started to talk you asked me if I was sure my baby died of the syndrome."

"You didn't seem certain yourself. Also, you're here, after all this time. It's not usual for the doubt to persist with such intensity."

"If it's possible my son's death had another cause, I have to know."

"You mean you're worried it might have been your fault."

Had she been so obvious, or was the feeling that common? "I don't know why I'm worried or, to be honest, what I believe." She took a deep breath. "Something took my son that no one understands, and ever since it happened I've had strange forebodings, feelings I never had before. They're not easy to talk about. A lot of people tell me I'm going through this because I'm feeling guilty, that most parents do. What do you think, honestly?"

He was about to answer, but suddenly the room started flashing and a buzzer went off somewhere. His alarmed assistant dashed through the door.

"We have an arrest. The Greer baby," she shouted, not waiting for a response before darting out again.

"Right behind you," Amaloff said and turned back to Joni. "Now you'll have to excuse me, but perhaps we could continue this another time when I'm free to—dinner or lunch, perhaps?"

"I'll call your nurse for an appointment. Would that be all right?"

He paused for a moment and finally nodded. "Yes. Do that."

His disappointed smile stayed in her mind as he fled the room.

Chapter 12

Thursday, July 29

The meeting progressed with no certain plan. It was an unstructured time, designed to meet the particular needs of its members, to provide information and serve as a gathering place for people like Joni with a history of familial crib death.

The SIDS parents group that met in neighboring Cedal Hills was typical of the centers around the country. It convened once a month in the evening for couples, once a month in the morning for a mothers' group. It was attended by anywhere from three to fifteen members, depending on the session.

In addition to the monthly meetings, the local chapters could arrange for private counseling with a public health nurse or social worker. It was customary for each chapter to have a twenty-four-hour hotline, run by staff members.

Joni and Doug had been notified about the group right after Stephen's death, while they were still together. Doug had scotched the idea of psychiatry in general, but now, especially with him gone, joining the SIDS group seemed a natural step.

"It's not surprising, these continuing episodes," the counselor was telling them. She was in the home of Claire and Kevin Rheingolde, SIDS parents. Normally a family therapist or lay counselor chaired the meetings, but this night there was to be an infrequent visit by Hilde Lange, a fortyish woman on assignment from the foundation itself. Her job, Joni soon learned, was to visit as many existing group chapters as she could and establish new ones in local communities. Mrs. Lange was well-respected for her knowledge and compassionate works, and the visit was a welcome occasion for the eleven assembled members.

"Typically there is a return of depression after the initial period, usually three or six months later," the slightly overweight, red-haired lady said. She stood in the center of the room, her audience in a semicircle in front of her. "We don't know why for sure, but it might be that these are normal anniversary dates for parents and the missing presence is magnified then."

The others at the session were couples in their twenties and thirties, except for one who appeared to be closer to forty. At first Joni had felt awkward in the setting, like becoming part of the circle of the damned. Also, being there alone, she felt conspicuous, so she had hardly spoken after introductions.

"That makes sense logically," she finally said, interrupting Mrs. Lange, "but in my own case the anxiety is set off by the slightest thing and at times which don't seem to relate to special dates or such."

"It was like that for me, too," said a trim, pale woman who sat holding her husband's hand tightly. "But it did let up with time. It's been eight and a half months since ours," she looked to her husband, who nodded kindly, "and it's taken until the past few weeks to be able to return to anything like a normal life. Of course, we do have another child, another reason."

Lange indicated that she understood, then broke off to go to a woman of about twenty-five. She was the only other one who had come alone, and earlier she too had been apologetic about it when asked if her husband planned to join them.

"It's been harder for Ann," Lange said sympathetically, "even though it's been—four months now?" She put her hands on the young woman's shoulders from behind and Ann raised a polite eyebrow in acknowledgment. "But it's only a matter of time, no matter how hard we try to hang on to the past. Time ushers us all into a new phase of our lives, even if we have to be dragged, kicking and screaming."

The other listeners agreed, with sounds of knowing.

"No one understands that better than me," the oldest woman there concurred. "I was a case and a half, but it does end. Trust me, it ends."

Joni studied the instructor, the broad face and wide-set eyes, small hazel marbles that twinkled brightly. Why did all the evangelists have those sparkling eyes, she wondered.

"Is there a normal amount of time when it can be expected to end?" someone else asked when there was a lull.

"Not really. It varies with each person, each family."

A new speaker took a turn, again the female of the couple. "I'm two years since the ordeal, and I can't say I'm really over it yet."

"Have you been coming here all that time?" Joni asked.

"No, we thought we could work it out by ourselves, but we've just had another baby and we're uneasy about being on our own."

"It was a good idea to come," Lange responded.

"Oh, not just for *our* sake," the new mother continued, "the odds against our second one are higher because we've already lost a child to SIDS."

"But still remote, dear, don't forget."

"One in seventy will never seem remote. We couldn't beat the original odds and they were a lot higher."

The leader nodded, then pivoted to face the newest member again.

"Because it's your first time here you probably have other questions about the way you've been feeling, Mrs. Lawrence."

Attention focused on Joni, who was thoughtful. "I should be honest," she offered after a troublesome decision, "I don't believe I came here with the same motive as most of you."

"Why do you say that?"

"Well, from what I can gather my problem is different. The rest of you are willing to accept your tragedy as an act of fate, and I'm not ready to do that yet." Said aloud, the main point of difference generated a feeling of distance between her and Lange. The counselor looked disappointed with what she'd said. No, *patronizing* was what her expression read.

Lange waved off one of those about to answer.

"You only think you're the first one to have those thoughts, but you're not, Mrs. Lawrence. Acceptance isn't the first step, it's the last."

"Forgive me, but I came here for information, not to learn acceptance."

"What kind of information?"

"Everyone tells me what happened to my child is the same thing that happens to thousands of others across the country every year. I'm supposed to believe that, and in truth I guess I should. The only trouble is, I don't. Something is terribly wrong in my case. I can't tell you what it is and there's a good chance it's just my unwillingness to accept the reality of his death, but I still have doubts about what happened. Somehow I still feel him in my life and the feeling won't go away. If anything, over the past few months it's gotten stronger." She thought of telling them about what happened at the funeral and later at the photographer's studio, but she suspected it would only convince them she had emotional problems. Maybe she did. The memory of the crying still terrified her.

Lange drew a deep breath. "When a baby succombs to the syndrome there are many things we don't understand and a few we do. One is that the parents feel terribly cheated and paranoid, like they've been singled out for punishment."

Joni detected a subtle change in Lange's tone. Some of her cheery veneer had worn thin and there was annoyance and condescension in her manner.

"The reaction to this very natural feeling is anger, and although anger can get in your way—by alienating those who want to help, for instance—it is also a sign of recovery, and as such is to be welcomed. If you look around the room, you'd find that everyone here had the same history of anger, plus another emotion you haven't mentioned."

There was something about Lange that alienated her. The woman wasn't really trying to help her understand, it was as though she was competing with her, as if her credibility was on the line.

"Guilt. I think what I'm hearing from you is guilt, Mrs. Lawrence, and that, too, is unavoidable. Your baby dies with no warning. Your doctor, all the doctors, can't give you a good reason. Neighbors, friends, even family look at you with their own doubts, after all, their babies haven't died in the middle of the night. The same is true of your relatives. If you're like most SIDS parents, the death may even bring on a temporary breakdown in your marital relationship, so for a while your main support system becomes unreliable. Put everything together and you have a situation tailor-made for self-pity and self-blame. Take it from me, the main source of the bad feelings you're experiencing is internal, not external."

All eyes were on her now. It would have been so easy just to shake her head in agreement and let it end, but she knew she couldn't take the easy way out. It wouldn't be fair to Stephen.

"I know about the guilt, Mrs. Lange, and I admit it's part of it, but I also know what I'm feeling is a separate thing. The two are different, and you'll have to take my word. What I don't understand is how after all this time my sense of something being wrong is still so great."

Lange reacted as though she'd been personally challenged.

"I'd like to ask you a rather intimate question, if you don't mind. It may help us all to, well, experience what you're going through."

Joni nodded.

"Did you have sex with your husband on the night your son passed away?"

The question took her and the room by surprise. On the surface it was a total invasion of privacy, an insensitive irrelevance, and Joni felt a flash of anger. Several of the others present fidgeted nervously, too.

"Not . . . really," Joni answered with open hostility, forced to think again about the kind of sex they'd had. "I don't really see how—"

"It may have a lot to do with your inability to stop blaming yourself. Forgive me, but the night your son died—perhaps at that very moment—were you receiving pleasure? It's not that uncommon. Whether or not you made that connection consciously, it's a likely reason you're suffering so much now, feeling so guilt-ridden."

Joni felt an almost irrepressible urge to run from the room. "You are completely wrong in my case. That was a cheap guess and I resent it. Whether or not I had sex had nothing to do with it."

Lange's face went slack. "Come now, Mrs. Lawrence. How can you ignore the possibility? What makes you so certain?"

"I know, that's all."

"You *did* have sex that night? Am I right?"

The urge to bolt from the inquisition was growing. They all seemed to be ganging up on her, waiting for the inevitable confession. But they didn't know what she did, and if they pushed any further—

"Did you or didn't you, Mrs. Lawrence?" Lange repeated. "That's all I want to know."

Rising, Joni looked around at the faces hungering for disclosure. She was beginning to lose her breath and knew her face glowed deep crimson.

"If you must know," she answered with forced assurance, "it wasn't what you have in mind. It's just that—"

"Please don't beat around the bush. Sex is sex, or have I lost my memory?" she chuckled, turning to meet the pleased glances all around.

Lange had chosen to make her light remark at the worst time, and it finally pushed Joni over the edge. She took a step toward her, a tightly wound spring of emotion.

"I think perhaps it's you who've lost your memory, Mrs. Lange," she said icily, "and what you've forgotten is how to counsel someone in a professional manner. I find your line of discussion and your weird fascination with my sex life *and* your clever little joke grossly insensitive. In deference to the good things I've heard about you, I won't say any more, but neither will I sit through an inquisition just so you can impress this group with your ability to bait me and ridicule me for my fears."

Joni gathered her coat, and there wasn't a sound in the room as she stormed to the front door without looking back. She closed it hard behind her. The tears came as soon as she was in her car. Lange had been unbelievably cruel, but not totally wrong. She had to admit some of the guilt did stem from what happened in bed, and there was only so much of it for which Doug could be blamed. It was true, she hadn't made love, she'd been raped, and that's why she couldn't get to Stephen, but when Doug had gotten what he wanted and she could have fled the room, she'd stayed there instead. That's what plagued her now, she'd stayed. Stayed there to finish her orgasm.

Chapter 13

This time the taunting had become too much for the eleven year old. Once again, his relatively small size proved an irresistible instrument of torture for his classmates, the taller, sturdier boys who always got the most attention, at school, on the ballfield, from Cheryl Adams McChesney. It didn't matter that he'd been smart enough to skip a grade. He was short. Period.

This time, though, there were special reasons not to accept their challenge, even though the giant, red-haired pitcher had mocked him loudly when he asked him to take his turn at bat. For one thing, he'd promised his mother not to hang around the school-yard. Once around the block was what he'd promised her, and it wasn't easy for him to lie to his mother. He wasn't like the others. Also, he'd probably do badly if he took a turn. He had the power, all right, but they'd all be thinking he'd miss the ball and that would make it more likely.

But the most important reason to ignore them was because he hadn't come to the schoolyard alone.

111

They were still looking at him, waiting for an answer, when he made the decision. His father had said it: "They'll make fun of you unless you stand up to them." That's what he said, now he'd have to understand.

Making up his mind, he scouted the area. A short distance away there was a small lawn, the waste space between the nearest house and the ball field. It was the perfect spot for the stroller. He'd only be gone a few moments, and nobody would bother his baby brother. He couldn't let them think he was some dopey baby-sitter. A few moments later, he'd parked the stroller on the grass, turned, and trotted to the batter's box.

. When he swung the bat on the first pitch he felt the pleasing, unexpected shock of wood colliding with the baseball. He could see the surprise on all their faces as he rounded first and kept going. He could see the center fielder racing backward, still hopelessly far from the long hit. They were already making fun of the big, red-haired pitcher. And, as he pulled up at third, he could even see Dad thumping him on the back, *and* the adoring face of Cheryl Adams McChesney.

What he couldn't see from where he was, what no one could see, was the stroller with his baby brother in it and the Visitor, who'd waited all day for the chance to be alone with the younger being.

Chapter 14

Wednesday, August 4
3:30 P.M.

Dr. Amaloff was noticeably more at ease than he had been the first time they'd met, with none of the grudging courtesy he'd shown previously. Another surprise was the way he looked: remarkably better groomed. His suit was stylish and brand-new and his hair had been trimmed. The doctor had called her at home personally and, since she hadn't left her number, he had obviously taken the trouble to look it up.

"I thought I owed you an answer to your last question," he said from behind a desk, which had been cleared of paper. "Well, I'll be frank. When the emergency arose last time, it relieved me from having to tell you what I really thought."

"That I was driven to see you because I blamed myself?"

"Yes, I'm afraid that's what I believed."

"Do you still feel that way?"

He sat back without answering. "There's something I

think you should see first as background. You'll at least find it interesting."

He reached into his top drawer and then handed her a cotton mask. Before she'd had a chance to figure out what he was up to, he was on his way through the two large glass doors at the rear of his office that led to his research facility. Joni quickly followed him. On the other side was a world of pure science fantasy. There was one central aisle, about fifty feet long, with a huge computer at the far end. Along the sides, more than two dozen cribs were lined up, hospital-style infant beds, each occupied. The infants ranged in age from a few weeks to just under a year, and their position in the file appeared to be according to age or size. As Joni soon learned, the entire chamber glowed pale green from ceiling fixtures that provided light to people and death to bacteria, and the temperature was kept at a constant 80°. The room was a giant incubator, a hothouse that grew babies. The concept of a clone factory suggested itself to her. Suddenly Joni felt a rush of anxiety.

"I can assure you that these babies have natural mothers and that I am not Dr. Frankenstein," Amaloff said, reading her mind.

"I'm not sure I'm ready to be here—yet."

He gave her his full attention. "Because of your son?"

She released a short burst of nervous laughter. "Sorry, I'll be all right. I know I can't hide from babies the rest of my life. Go on, please."

"Fine, now let me explain what you're looking at." He took her arm firmly and strolled to the first crib. "Say hello to Michael, the newest of our family and the luckiest. He'll get to spend most of his first six months with us, but his sister wasn't that fortunate."

Joni understood and quickly diverted her attention to

an array of gadgets and wires that surrounded the infant.

"Are we still on planet Earth?"

"We are. Most importantly, so are they, for a good long life, thanks to *Baby Watch*. That's what the manufacturer calls this system. It's the most efficient and, I might add, the most expensive baby-sitter in the world."

"What does it do?"

"Think of it as a twenty-four-hour watchman. It's a very sophisticated monitoring device to watch over these infants when people can't be around." His finger traced a wire from where it entered the crib's zone and attached to a rectangular box about the size of a clock radio. "This is the sensor for the system. You'll notice it has two circular grids aimed at the baby's chest. They're sensing devices that send out a signal, a wavelength based on the movement of the infant's chest, which is constantly measured by the computer over there. To put it simply, the unit *expects* a certain number of breaths or chest expansions per minute, and if the baby should stop breathing for twenty seconds or more, an alarm is activated."

"Why twenty seconds?" Then she remembered. "The longest apnea period?"

"Right. When it lasts longer, it usually indicates an arrest that may not be self-correcting. That's when we come running."

She could see each infant was identically wired. About half were awake, accepting their common domicile, a massive live support system. As she watched, her face went slack.

"If my son had been part of your program, would it have saved him? For certain?"

Amaloff looked at her and nodded. There was a change in his usually stern eyes. "With adequate monitoring, I'd have to say yes, there's no question it would have—if it was SIDS that took him."

"So in a way, it is my fault after all, for not—"

"For not knowing what you couldn't know? That your son was at high risk? Nonsense."

"What do you mean?"

"Did you have any reason to believe your child was prone to the syndrome?"

"No, of course not, how would I?"

"There are some symptoms that point to an increased risk. As a matter of fact, after your last visit I compiled a list of them. For now, just remember that you're no different from all the other parents who suffered the same tragedy. There's a mother just like you for every SIDS baby, and you're no more to blame than they are."

She thought about what he said, trying to picture ten thousand mothers that felt like she did, but it didn't matter. All that counted was that somehow she had failed her baby.

"I showed you my facility to give you an idea of how many potential SIDS infants there are. If you think there are a lot of babies here, remember that this represents an infinitesimal fraction of the total, but even so, the odds against you or your doctor finding your way here were prohibitively high. Don't blame yourself, Mrs. Lawrence," he said vehemently, "what you did or didn't do was perfectly normal."

She heard his intent, but was not reassured.

The baby closest to her looked up and widened his mouth to emit a bubble. His cherubic face relaxed, as though ready for slumber, but then, unexpectedly, he opened his eyes and fixed a glassy stare directly at Joni. The effect on her was instant. When she tried to shift her attention elsewhere, she couldn't move. Pins and needles traveled up and down her arms. There was something magnetic in the deep brown eyes that pulsed slightly and seemed to penetrate her thoughts. She felt it at the back of her head, the beginning of vertigo, a shortness of breath. Her head started to ache when Amaloff pulled her from the spot to which she'd become rooted and she finally broke contact with the infant.

She didn't know how long she'd been out of it, but there was nothing unusual in Amaloff's treatment toward her.

"Nature's greatest show," he was saying, "like looking at the ocean." He bent down and chucked the baby under its chin. "I'll tell you a secret," he said, as if afraid of being overheard, "I could watch them all day, too."

She smiled and, mercifully, he ended the tour.

When they were in his quarters again, he took a folder from a drawer and put it on the desk.

"During the time between your visits I had a chance to think about your problem."

"Which is defined as what, just so I know," she said. She felt better once they left the ward.

"Your search for knowledge. I'm not here to pass judgment, just to help you find whatever it is you're looking for."

"Thank you."

He produced a page of legal paper from the folder.

"This is a list of facts I've compiled—the state of the art, so to speak—on the syndrome. The best guesses by the best guessers in the world. I've made it as nontechnical as I could." He pushed the page toward her on the desk. "It's an outline of the symptoms of SIDS that are most often identified. The items are in random order, and I should add that an exhaustive list would run for several more pages. But these are the most important."

Her adrenaline was surging as she focused on the top

of the page. What he'd written might be crucial in determining the truth about Stephen—or about her.

"Just one background fact before we start," Amaloff said. "The odds of any given infant becoming an SIDS casualty are on the order of two or three out of a thousand."

Joni's body tensed. Two out of a thousand was five hundred to one that Stephen would have been normal. Put that way, the numbers seemed so unfair. They were the shocking large odds that Stephen had not been able to beat.

Amaloff pushed the paper in front of her and, after a fearful moment, she began to read.

Sudden, unexplained, unexpected.
Silent.
90%-95% while asleep.

The list brought back the terrible memory, but it was exactly what she needed, something against which to check Stephen's symptoms. So far, two of the three held true. He might have been crying near the end, but she couldn't be certain.

Recurrent, sometimes chronic apnea episodes.

"Most parents wouldn't know if this was a problem unless there had been a history of it in the family. Also, since it's common in all babies, it's one of the weakest identifying symptoms."

Peak periods of occurrence: 2½ to 4 months.
30%-50% have mild infection prior to event.

"Stephen was six months old when he died, but he did have a cold."

Low body weight at birth.
Physically underactive.
Abnormal feedings (exhaustion during feedings).
Unusual temperature regulation and motor tone.

She felt a shiver of foreboding as Amaloff pointed to the first of the new symptoms.

"Babies weighing less than four pounds have ten times the risk of normal-weight babies."

"Stephen was seven pounds eight ounces," she answered indignantly. Her sense of confirmation from the first few items had begun to dissolve as she continued. If anything, Stephen was hyperactive and his eating habits were the envy of most other mothers. True, his temperature showed large swings, but that was true of all babies.

"Well, that one's not too telling," Amaloff reassured her.

Abnormal crying.
Underventilation of lungs (breathlessness).

"How would I know if my son underventilated?"

"You wouldn't, except it would probably show up in underactive behavior."

"He never sat still except to eat, or when he was sick."

Amaloff was perplexed. "Curious."

More common among premature babies.
One parent with abnormal heartbeat.
Occurs in late winter or spring, between
midnight and 9 A.M. on average.

"The abnormal heartbeat referred to is also known as the 'long Q-T' syndrome. It's a condition which predisposes people of all ages to sudden death. Adults have been known to have prolonged apnea and die, although it is not connected to SIDS."

The information had begun to make her nervous. Neither she nor Doug had a history of heart irregularities. Also, her son had been a week late, not premature, though he had died in the spring. The evidence that would make a strong case for crib death was rapidly shrinking.

More victims in blood group B.
Most common among black males (3 to 2 over
   females), the malnourished, and siblings of
   SIDS victims.
Frequent oxygen therapy after birth.
Low scores of tactile stimulation tests.

There was nothing in this group that correlated, and another negation in what came next.

Low or high maternal age of mother at birth.
Mother smoked.

Here were two that could have tied her in directly, but she'd never smoked and thirty-one was not a young or an old mother.

When she finished, Amaloff was waiting for a reaction, but seeing how shaken she was he didn't press her.

"Seven out of twenty-two, maybe only six," she said weakly, allowing only the symptoms she'd been sure of. She pushed the paper toward him and took a deep breath. "What would you say the chances are we're talking about something other than SIDS?"

For a moment he appeared to be confused.

"Are you certain you made an accurate count?

Perhaps we should take them one at a time, to re-check."

"No, there's no need to do that," she said. "Since my son's death I've spent almost every waking hour re-viewing the facts about his life in the minutest detail. I've even gone back to before I was pregnant and thought about what I ate and drank then. I can tell you every medicine he was given, when he was sick and how long it took him to get well; every nuance of his behavior, everything. Do you understand? When we went down the list I was absolutely certain of each item except for the crying." She raised her voice. "Seven out of twenty-two!"

He was thinking hard, being careful. "It's difficult without knowing all the other factors, of course, but if what you say is true—and I believe you—I'd have to say that's a startling percentage indeed. But," he added quickly, "you must remember that any one of these factors could conceivably push the fragile infant chem-istry over the edge. You wouldn't need all or even a lot of them to do it."

"Which of the causes could have been responsible by themselves?" she demanded. For the first time, she found herself half-wishing it *had* been the syndrome. If not, it would surely imply other reasons which she might not be able to face.

He gazed steadily at her, his expression more grave than his words had been.

"Ruling out the causes that are normally present but not in themselves critical," he said, scanning the list, "we are left with . . . underventilation—".

"Which we said wasn't likely, because of his ac-tivity."

"—parents with heart problems and, of course, a deceased sibling who died of the syndrome."

She had become agitated and suddenly wanted to be anywhere but there.

"None of them," she shouted. "None!" Ever since his death, she'd sensed something was wrong, and now there was concrete evidence to go along with the feeling.

Amaloff stared at a point on the wall behind her, then turned in his chair and gazed out the window. He did not speak for a long time, and Joni could almost hear his mind working. Finally he was ready, and when he spoke he seemed to be taking all of her in, as though who *she* was formed as much a part of his judgment as the facts about Stephen.

"I hadn't wanted to upset you any more than you already were, but now that you've demanded an opinion . . . In my years of working on the syndrome, I've developed a feel as well as a science for identifying high-risk infants, and your case bears little relationship to what I've learned. If I had to guess, I'd say that you should have serious reason to suspect something other than the syndrome may have taken your baby."

"How sure are you?" she demanded to know.

He folded his hands and leaned across the desk toward her.

"No one can be sure, but I'd be willing to bet on it."

His final pronouncement was like a sharp, cutting knife that tore at her belly. She'd learned what she'd come to find out and hated the new knowledge.

"And now what, now that you believe me, now that I've finally found someone who believes me—what am I supposed to do?"

Amaloff was pensive. "Maybe I can help you."

"How?"

"You understand that I'll have to check the facts of your son's death, of course?"

She nodded.

"But, assuming that everything is as you said I believe we have quite a strong suspicion with which to go to the authorities."

"The police?"

"Possibly. I'll have to think about whom. There are others, people of position within the medical profession whom I know. I think they might be interested, or at least could direct us to highly placed authorities. Cut through the red tape and all."

As he continued, his conviction became stronger and Joni felt a wave of relief begin to wash over her. At long last, she had a champion and would not have to fight her battle alone. Wherever the new path led, at least she had finally found one.

"Whatever I can do to help you, I will," she said gratefully.

"Just give me some time, that's all. And sit tight until you hear from me."

There was nothing left to say, nothing to do but wait. As she took her leave, Joni wanted to hug him, to let the tears of redemption flow freely, but all she could manage was a simple statement of gratitude.

Walking down the hall that led to the hospital lobby, she knew she had opened a door on a vast dark chamber and, though she felt haunted by what she might find inside, there would be no turning back.

Chapter 15

After the deeply disturbing meeting with Amaloff, Joni
found the normally heavy crosstown traffic a welcome
distraction. Her thoughts were getting crazy again. She
knew that if she told anyone what she'd just learned
they'd only think it a continuation of unending hysteria.

At the beginning of the rush hour one could sense
the common urgency to get out of the city. The drive
led directly across Manhattan into the heart of Central
Park where the mood changed abruptly. It was one of
those rare summer days when the park took on an
amber glow and became a mellow profusion of color,
fragrance, and activity. The last tenacious petals of
forsythia were long obscured by mimosa and magnolia
blossoms that shouldered over the silken ground and
lent a fairy-tale charm. There were daffodil and hya-
cinth planted in flamboyant displays by city fathers. As
she drove through the park, she could see dozens of
separate paths that meandered as if by their own whim
past ball fields and into thickets, which further north

became too primeval to be growing in the heart of a great city. This was New York at its peak vitality, a dogpatch of flowers, joggers, bikers, giant elms, Italian ices, fountains, statues and Hansel and Gretel running around the clock at the Central Park Zoo. Part of her still yearned to be where the beauty and possibilities of life seemed so boundless.

She left the park with regret, then steered past the stately apartment houses on Central Park West. Soon they gave way to the modern facades of Lincoln Center and the Metropolitan Opera House. Here she had drunk in Verdi, Puccini, and Wagner so often in the old days, so often in the standing-room section, before the money came.

Further south, Broadway still staggered the senses, but if Central Park had been the oasis of hope, then Times Square had to be its enclave of despair. Once called the center of the world, it had deteriorated into a shoddy gallery of topless clubs, porno movies, and drugs. The area was teeming with threatening-looking youths, black, white and Spanish, for whom the area seemed to serve as a mecca.

Without realizing it, Joni looked up from inside her car and saw the large electric display for the first time in over two years, the same one Doug had rented to make his proposal. Now, as if in parody of that night so long ago, it was being used to advertise honeymoon vacations in the Poconos. Fighting back a bitter tear, she looked away.

Later, she wouldn't remember whether she'd been aware of it for very long or even if it had happened at all. Her mind was still digesting the day's events as her car was forced to stop in heavy traffic on the approach ramp of the Lincoln Tunnel. Absently, she shifted her gaze to the car just behind her in the lane to the left, a

new Mercedes. From that angle she could just see into
the car through its front windshield to where there was
a young woman behind the wheel, smoking a cigarette
nervously. The prettyish blonde was impatient and
seemed caught out of her element. All the windows
were closed, indicating air conditioning, though the
afternoon wasn't very hot. Obviously annoyed at having to wait, the woman blew a cloud of smoke that
came back at her from the front glass, and it was then
she leaned to her right, in Joni's direction, to investigate something on the front seat next to her.

Joni could just make out part of the object, two
upright posts of an infant seat and the top of a baby's
head. The mother reached down, as if to tighten a
strap. The infant's hair was blonde, just a little lighter
than—

As Joni kept staring at the child, the cars ahead in the
Mercedes' lane inched forward, and when it stopped,
the two cars were exactly abreast of each other. Now it
was possible to see the entire front seat through the
passenger window. The baby was bent over, facing
away. For a few seconds, the child's mother looked
over at Joni staring in rapt attention, but then she went
back to fussing with the infant. Then, abruptly, the
baby straightened up so that Joni could see part of its
face.

At first she remembered thinking the infant bore a
strong resemblance to Stephen and, just to put the
thought to rest, she scrutinized his mouth. Like Stephen's, one corner turned upward.

Quickly she looked for a small indentation at the tip
of the button-nose and found it. She gasped.

But his hair was different, more golden and longer.
Her mind was clearly playing tricks on her. Then,
suddenly, the child jerked around completely, looked

directly at Joni and she saw it: the small dark spot at the
base of the cheek where his smile started. It was the
birthmark, where the cold cream always collected.

Suddenly she was screaming his name, clawing at the
handle of her door until it burst open. In an instant, she
had become obsessed with getting to him. The baby's
mother heard muffled cries from outside and turned
quickly to see a crazed woman with wide, anxious eyes,
approaching the car. Frightened for her child, the
mother lunged for the lock on the baby's door and
slammed it down an instant before Joni pressed on the
handle. The baby looked out at Joni as she yanked on
the locked door, and he beamed with delight at the
show. When the door wouldn't open she began to
smash her fists on the window. She was calling a name,
over and over: *Stephen, Stephen*.

Joni looked beyond the child to its mother and
pleaded to be let in, but then the traffic in both lanes
started moving again and the Mercedes lurched forward. Joni struggled to hang on, but couldn't, and
when her iron grip was broken there was blood across
her palm.

There were horns honking angrily behind her. At
first she started to run after the car, but a few seconds
later, seeing she was being hopelessly outdistanced, she
reversed her direction and flung herself back to her own
car. She got in and her car leaped ahead.

There was a long, empty space ahead in her lane, and
she quickly began to make up the distance between
them, but when she'd gone less than half a mile she
caught up to the cars in front of her and immediately
slowed to a crawl. The other lane was still moving
quickly, and again the Mercedes shrank in the distance.

The stream of cars to her left poured by in an endless
and unbroken line, like links in a never-ending chain.

Turning the wheel sharply, Joni tried to get into the faster-moving lane, but each time she crossed the solid white line their horns shrieked and they wouldn't let her in. She felt as though her body was going to explode as she was forced to sit and wait.

When she was able to move ahead again, she still thought she could overtake them; the need was so intense that she didn't stop to question the incredible hallucination she'd accepted as fact. Then, though it was impossible to believe fate would keep the two cars apart, the Mercedes became smaller and smaller. It was like a fevered nightmare in which survival depended on running, but her legs wouldn't work. She was a hopeless prisoner in the tunnel when the Mercedes disappeared completely.

It was a miracle she'd been able to safely negotiate the rest of the narrow underground road, but when she exited the tunnel and saw the number of possible routes the car could have taken, she knew there was no hope of catching them. Recklessly, she swerved onto the emergency shoulder and hit the brake, feeling as though she was going to pass out. Her head was pounding. It swam with visions of Stephen and a hundred questions that chiseled away at her slim hold on reason. How could she have seen him? Who was the woman he was with? Did he recognize her, too?

Then, resting her head on the cold chrome of the steering wheel, thinking about what she'd been trying to believe, the obvious truth shattered the illusion to pieces. She had wanted to see him so badly she'd invented the vision. The progress she thought she'd made, her recovery, was all an illusion, merely a period of remission within a lingering illness. The realization swept over her and threw her into despair. For a second her mind flashed to a picture of Amaloff saying he would help her and she clung to it. Without him she knew she wouldn't be able to push down another thought she was having, of putting the car in gear, pressing down hard on the accelerator, and closing her eyes.

Chapter 16

Before the council session had broken up in a furor, Aaron Schecter had resigned his post as chairman at least twice, this despite twenty years of gratifying service to the philanthropic organization which he'd help found. The exchanges had progressed from heated to inflammatory over the topic he'd finally felt forced to introduce, which admittedly was not within the normal jurisdiction of the council. Their sole function was to give comfort and, whenever possible, financial aid to the recently widowed, and the others had argued they'd only been successful because they'd kept this narrow focus.

Schecter had expected the outcry and knew he would personally bear the brunt of it. It had happened before, when he'd asked them to take an active stand against domestic terrorism and other atrocities that had come to his attention over the years.

That they considered him an eccentric was something he'd learned to live with. During the past meeting, however, they'd actually become abusive. He had been accused of being a "paranoid" and "a crazy old alarm-ist."

But it hadn't been the personal attack that left Schecter feeling empty. He'd failed to convince his fellow members that the evidence was now indisputable. He'd shown them the newspapers with their reports of seven dead infants; the last two had been in yesterday's paper.

"Coincidence," most had called it, and those that held some sympathy for his view motioned for him to turn over his "file" to the proper authorities. Of course, there were no "proper authorities" in such cases. There never were, he'd reminded them. He'd seen the fearful denial before, during the war, when he'd discovered that people would close their eyes and convince themselves that a fire could be put out simply by calling it something else.

But a fire was a fire, a murder a murder, and a conspiracy a conspiracy.

Aaron Schecter held one hand on the telephone and squinted at the listings under "State Government" in the directory. A half hour later he was still debating whom to call, wondering how to say it in a way that would get someone to listen when even his own people hadn't; hearing the phrase "crazy old alarmist" echoing around the empty boardroom.

Chapter 17

When the mail came and Joni saw the Metropolitan Hospital letterhead, she immediately thought that Amaloff, after a week's silence, had finally set the inquiry in motion. She was glad she'd fought the urge to phone him, since he'd obviously come through for her.

Then, suddenly she wondered why he hadn't phoned her with the news.

The letter nearly slipped from her hands as she tore it open, expecting to see some documents needing her signature, something of an official nature. Instead, there was a single typewritten page. "My dear Mrs. Lawrence," it began:

> After considering the facts in your case further, I'm sorry to say that I probably won't be able to help you.
> I have made several inquiries to medical authorities, but met with firm

resistance. None of those I contacted
wants to become involved in what they
view as a legal matter. Further, my
colleagues felt there was no real cor-
relation of your claim to the evidence.
This, I suspect, is more a result of
their lack of knowledge about the syndrome itself than a denial of your as-
sertion.

Of course, as a doctor I am inadequate
to advise you on the appropriate legal channels, so I suggest you begin
the process with a lawyer whom you
trust.

I hope you can understand that, within my field of medicine, I have chosen a
direction most others view as eccentric. My approach to preserving life
for the relatively limited time during
which a sickness is possible completely ignores the causes with which researchers are normally preoccupied.
Perhaps, in this context, you can see
why I would be a rather unpromising
sponsor for your investigation.

Naturally, I will remain available
to you to corroborate the findings
which we have developed, and will
help you with any further questions of
fact.

In the meantime, may I suggest again
you get in touch with a good lawyer?
Also, I think a nice, long vacation
would go a long way toward putting you
more at ease.

                *   *   *

There was a postscript:

```
The list we worked from is enclosed,
should you need it to go further.
```

When she finished reading it, the letter fell to the floor.

She was alone. Again.

Book III

Chapter 18

Captain William Thompson hadn't been told about the impatient woman waiting for him in the lobby, and continued his congenial interrogation of the prostitute, the first that had been seen in the well-to-do town of Edgewood in years. When he finally emerged from his office, the attractive woman pressed a kiss to his cheek before being led away by a matron. The scene caused a snicker from the desk sergeant, but neither he nor any of the others said anything directly to the captain.

Thompson walked toward Joni when he recognized the familiar face.

"Mrs. Lawrence, isn't it?" He shook her hand firmly. "A pleasure. What's the matter, you got trouble?"

When she nodded, he led her into his office.

"Remember when you said how hard it was for you to come see me?"

He smiled kindly.

"I guess that's how I feel right now. I just don't have anywhere else to turn."

"What happened?"

She fidgeted nervously, and before long he saw her eyes begin to brim with water. He offered her a handkerchief, but she refused and became annoyed with herself.

"What's happened is I think I'm losing my mind. I thought I was getting over it—my son, Stephen— but . . ." Her voice trailed off, until she came to a decision and tossed back her full, long hair. "Sorry, I swore there'd be no histrionics. I guess you get more than your share of self-pity. Actually, I came here for a specific reason."

Again she went silent.

Thompson sat at the edge of his desk. "If you're having trouble saying it, maybe I can make it easier for you. You came to ask me if I can help you get an autopsy for your son."

She glared at him, astonished.

"How could you possibly know that?"

"You and I have only one piece of common ground, Mrs. Lawrence, so your waiting to speak to me suggests it's got something to do with the reason we met. And that means one of two things: either you believe your son met with foul play or by now your grief has made you irrational. In either case, an autopsy would be the next logical thing you'd want."

It was an incisive piece of reasoning and it reassured her about coming to see him. She nodded her agreement.

"Tell me, though," he continued, "why come to me with this request? Why not start with your lawyer, to find out the procedure?"

She swallowed hard. "The only lawyer we had was my husband's. I never met him, and I don't think he's someone I want to deal with now."

"Because he'd tell your husband?"

"No, I hadn't thought of that, actually. I think Doug's lawyer probably wouldn't help me. He'll be handling the divorce for Doug, and . . ."

"So you came to me? The cop who had to question you?"

"Before you left, the things you said made me believe there was something about you I could trust."

He looked deeply into her eyes. "If that's what your instincts told you, I think you should listen to them."

"But you also made me feel even guiltier than I already did. The way you questioned me about my husband. I can still see you studying the picture of the two of us."

Thompson nodded, as though he finally understood something. Then he looked relieved.

"Well, you may find this a surprise, but when I heard that Mr. Lawrence had left I *was* a little suspicious at first, about him, and what might have happened that made him leave. But as far as your part in it, well, the only feeling I had was sympathy. I felt sorry for you to have to go through the double loss, and I was studying the picture to see what kind of man could have left after you'd gone through so much."

Curiously, she still felt protective about Doug and didn't respond.

"How does your husband feel about it?" the officer asked, "the autopsy, I mean."

"I called him as a courtesy. I was afraid he'd be upset about disturbing the grave, but he didn't care one way or the other, so long as he didn't have to be there. Of course, he thinks I'm off my rocker—and maybe I am."

"Why do you say that?"

She sighed. "Force of habit, and maybe because I'd rather say it before you do. What about it? Do you think I'm crazy?"

"I'd bet against it."

"I'm not so sure you'd win that bet," she said, becoming more relaxed.

"Well, let's assume for the moment you're holding your own. Do you have any new information to share with me?"

She looked uncertain, but said yes.

"Good. Evidence is the best place to start, especially sitting down." He went back to his chair.

Joni studied him from across the desk. His easy manner had helped to calm her, but she still wasn't sure of him. He was a larger man than she remembered, but there was still that easy grace about him, the way he moved, even sat. He was comfortable with himself. Like Doug, he wasn't handsome by modeling standards, but his face held great strength. His angles had been softened by age and his skin creased by dozens of small lines that gave him a weathered texture, even though he wore the pallor of one who worked indoors. His hair showed no signs of age. It was jet black and worn full at the sides. He was clean-shaven and his skin was smooth. He had extremely long fingers and large, hard hands.

Carefully she took him through the first of the reasons that brought her to his office, Dr. Amaloff's surprising findings, which she discussed with the help of the list he'd sent her. She tried to describe the findings in as emotionless terms as possible, and deliberately left out the part about Amaloff's desertion. She could tell he was weighing her presentation as much as what she had to say.

Thompson listened intently and without interrupting. His expression didn't give away what he was thinking, but as soon as she finished he shook his head and his solid features turned unhappy. After he hadn't answered for an uncomfortably long interval, Joni pushed back her chair and stood up to leave.

"Sorry to have taken up your time for nothing," she snapped.

"Sit down," he said firmly. "Please."

"If you don't think it's important enough, I'll find—"

"Mrs. Lawrence, the only thing I find more disturbing than your report is that brave front you've been putting up. If I'd found out what you have, I'd be more shaken up than that. I hope I haven't been one of those who've made you so . . . cautious with your feelings."

His healing words caught her by surprise, and she settled back into the chair. His kindness was armor-piercing.

"You think what I've found out proves something is wrong?"

"I wouldn't say *proves*. I need to know more."

"That's as much as I have, except for . . ." She stopped but had gone further than she'd intended.

"Please go on. Anything else you can tell me now could be critical to the success of your request, and if you're worried about your credibility, don't be. I've heard enough to know you're in control of your faculties. First, you've gone about this too systematically to be crazy. Second, my intuition tells me so."

She hesitated. "You'll think I'm crazy for sure."

"Try me."

A number of disclosures raced through her mind. She started with the episodes at the funeral and the photography studio, hastening to add that she was sure they were only products of her imagination. Then she launched into the story she hadn't thought important enough to reveal at their first meeting in her bedroom.

"The morning before my son died, I thought I saw something on the front lawn, something going toward the house, the nursery, I think."

His face showed irritation. "You tell me this now? Not when I came to question you?"

"I was far away and couldn't be sure I really saw it. I've been accused of overreacting where Stephen was concerned, and I thought it might just be another instance of that."

"What did you see exactly? A man?"

"No . . . more like the shadow of a man. No, just a shadow, actually."

"What did it look like?"

"It's going to sound silly," she paused, "but it was like a tree, tall and . . . spidery. It was only another silhouette until—"

"Yes?"

"—until it moved. But I couldn't see it clearly from where I was."

"Which was?"

"The top of the big hill in the park. I was running. It's about a block away from the house."

"Anything else you can think of about this *shadow?*"

She was having trouble. "As I said, I had the feeling it was sort of sizing up the nursery, as though it was figuring out how to get in."

"You mean walking toward it?"

"No, more like, well, stalking it. I know it sounds silly. That's why I didn't have the courage to bring it up until now, but it was the same day, and now, with everything else that's happened—"

Again, he held off any readable reaction and her impulse was to end the exchange right there, grateful for his continued open-mindedness. Still, it didn't appear he'd be easily alienated.

"There's something else, but I'm almost afraid to say it."

"Go on."

"I had a strange experience yesterday afternoon, in New York City."

"I'm listening."

Despite the skepticism that he now let show, Thompson listened patiently to the story of her vision at the tunnel. After she finished, he was thoughtful, then circled his desk and put a hand on the arm of her chair.

"You're aware that hysteria takes many forms, some of which are very subtle."

"I know what you're implying, but I was completely calm before it happened. It was a response to something I thought I saw."

"But evidently you *were* highly suggestible."

She knew hers was an impossible premise to argue, and she suddenly felt foolish for telling him.

"Let me illustrate what I mean with something that happened to me a few years back, in the winter," he continued, putting his large hands behind his neck. "It was snowing, you know, the kind that freezes on the windshield and won't melt? I was following an old Ford, with the big taillights they had in the sixties. It was a two-lane road, with oncoming traffic and a ditch on either side. All I could see through the ice were the two blurry red spots on the back of the Ford.

"Anyway, the road was slippery, so I was only doing about twenty. Then I saw the lights get bigger and I knew the guy in front had hit the brakes. I did the same, pumping them the way you're supposed to."

He waited for a response, then went on without it.

"Anyway, I turned the wheel very slowly, but it didn't help. My car was in a full skid and there was no way I was gonna stop in time. Well, the crash was what I *expected*—remember that word—the crunch of glass and metal, the jarring impact. The crash knocked my car into the ditch and we both stopped. I was full of apologies, 'cause, legally, it's always the fault of the guy in back. Well, the driver looked at me like I was insane when I asked to see the damage."

Again he waited for her to guess, but she didn't make any connection.

"The fact was, there had been no crash," he announced.

"What do you mean?"

"I never hit him."

"A hallucination?"

"Something like that. I imagined it so hard it became my reality, right down to the tinkle of glass. I *expected* it, so it happened."

The analogy was clear. "I wanted to see my son so badly I *did* see him, is that the point?"

"Sorry, but I thought it might help explain it. In my case, I thought I'd gone off the deep end, but what I went through was a form of hysteria. The police shrink told me that."

"What happened after you found out you hadn't crashed?"

"I was relieved. Also, I felt pretty stupid."

She made a weak try at a smile, but it came out angry.

"Well, I felt more . . . disoriented than stupid."

"Did you get a license plate number? I know it's a lot to ask."

"No. It was a Mercedes—new, I think. Blue or green. That's all."

"Or a Chevy or yellow?"

"I wasn't thinking about the damned car, only what was in it," she answered sharply. "Listen, why don't we just forget this part? Obviously I'm not over it yet, that's all, but I want the autopsy. Maybe I can't prove what I'm feeling, but I know something is wrong, I just know it." She fastened onto his eyes. "A few minutes ago, you were acting like you wanted to help. After what I've told you, do you want me to go somewhere else?"

He studied her for a long time, then cocked his head to one side.

"Listen, I'll level with you. Some of your story strikes me as bizarre, some not. Also, you're still very shaken up over what's happened. But your research with that doctor in New York is very interesting. What did he have to say about your . . . vision at the tunnel?"

She reddened. "Amaloff is a doctor," she said, remembering his letter, "not a detective."

"Then there's that thing about the man on the lawn. We've had similar reports lately; it's possible it's the same man. Probably we'll never know, but all in all it seems that an autopsy is a legit request and one sure way of finding out what you want to." He broke it off abruptly, debating with himself. "There's one last point, too, but I have to admit it's not a very professional one. I think you're a very smart lady."

She wasn't prepared for the frank compliment.

"Are there grounds for an autopsy in this kind of case?"

He smiled briefly. "Well, the truth is, you don't need much in the way of grounds here. An autopsy takes place as soon as anyone believes it's a suspicious death, a medical examiner, for instance, but normally it would happen before the burial, not after."

"You made me go through all this and I didn't have to?"

"I wanted to hear what you had to say."

"When can it be done?"

"I'll find out, but I have to ask you another thing first. Sorry, but do you happen to know whether your son was . . . embalmed?"

She turned away as though she'd been slapped.

"It would make an autopsy less conclusive, is why I'm asking."

For the second time in the visit she was near tears.

"No," she answered weakly, "I don't think so."

"Well, it would be unlikely," Thompson agreed. "In theory, the procedure is supposed to take place, but it's almost never done any more, at least not with infants. Not in ninety-nine percent of the cases, I'd say."

She pushed herself back from the desk and stood again.

"You'll help me get it done?"

"As soon as I check out a few things, yes."

She understood. "You can find Dr. Amaloff at Metropolitan Hospital in New York. He said he would help."

"Nothing personal, I have to verify everything."

"And you'll stay on the case, too?"

"First we have to see if there is a case, Mrs. Lawrence."

"And if there isn't? If we don't find anything, and there was no one on the lawn?"

He put his hand out. "I wouldn't put too much faith in our finding that intruder, or whatever it is that you think you saw. We get these reports all the time. And as far as the rest goes, if nothing develops from the autopsy, you'll just have to get over it the best you can. In time, you'll let it go, you'll have no choice. You don't seem like a quitter to me."

She thought about it. It was a way of describing her no one had ever used before and, despite her current state of confusion, it had the ring of truth.

"Well, not yet, anyway," she answered.

On the way home, she reviewed their meeting and noticed she was getting good at remembering details. After a short time she concluded that Captain Thompson was a lot more cunning than she'd given him credit for. Yes, he'd promised to help with the autopsy, but that was something she really didn't need him for after all, and as far as her story went, he'd shown interest but had never come out and said he believed her. What he'd offered was sympathy when she wanted conviction. By the time she'd turned into the driveway, the hopefulness she'd begun to feel, for the first time since Amaloff, was again in question.

Chapter 19

Monday, August 16

Dr. Robert Herrington sat alone in the back seat of the squad car, looking like a scaled-down version of Orson Welles. His 240 pounds of bulk were draped in a sports jacket that had too many stripes for the paisley on his casual shirt. Thompson was at the wheel, speeding. At the moment, Herrington wondered why he hadn't been satisfied with his thriving private practice and had also opted to become one of the five Medical Examiners for Palisade County.

Now in his third year of part-time public service, Herrington found an increasing part of his time taken up with lecturing, court appearances and, the most disagreeable of all the services required of him, autopsies. The one he was about to perform was as unpleasant as they came. Not only was the subject an infant that had been buried for almost two months, but the mother was in the car with them, in front with the officer.

But there was another reason for Herrington's present discomfort, which upset him even more. The

Lawrence boy's death had originally been part of his own caseload. It had been an obvious case of SIDS, and was confirmed as such by his old friend, Dr. Lazarus Geffs, the baby's pediatrician. The death of this infant had been the third that fell to him in as many months and, like the others, he'd decided there was no need to involve the grieving parents in the ordeal of an autopsy. Geffs had concurred. Also, he'd learned that burial was to take place the next day, and it would have been impossible to free himself from scheduled surgery. So, as he'd done a number of times before, he'd entered "pneumonitis" as the cause of death, the acceptable and common way of precluding an autopsy. Now, of course, the unexpected request cast an unfavorable light on his original evaluation.

Thompson's argument for an autopsy was certainly provocative and, since there had been no embalming, the autopsy would be valid even though the baby had been dead for two months. In any case, once ordered, the procedure had to be carried out, especially since the request had come from the police department itself.

Herrington impatiently shook his head. As in the other deaths, the autopsy would show there was *no* cause; therefore, nothing would be learned.

The grimy police Chevy headed off the Interstate toward Woodlawn Cemetery, a mile away. It was nearly seven-thirty and Herrington's family would be starting the barbecue without him. As usual.

The ride had been an uncomfortable one for each of them, and no one had spoken after the brief introductions. The Lawrence woman hadn't uttered so much as a word or turned her head since the trip started, so Herrington had learned nothing more about her reasons for being there. He decided that she must be a bit peculiar. What in hell could she be thinking? he asked himself. Thompson, too. They couldn't have thought it through. Didn't they understand what the box contained by now? The memory of tonight's visit would stay with the mother for the rest of her life.

Herrington was still shaking his head in disbelief when Thompson guided the car through the pillars that marked the entrance to Woodlawn. In another minute they pulled up and parked near the gravesite. Two workmen were waiting, silhouetted against a spectacular red sky, leaning on their shovels with their backs to the newcomers. When they heard the car, they turned to face the visitors, as though they were expecting death itself.

While Herrington considered helping Joni out, Thompson circled the car and took her arm. Then, looking toward the grave, Joni was suddenly startled by the sight of the gravediggers.

"It's him," she announced to the officer. She pointed at the larger of the two workmen.

"Who?" Thompson said with a start.

"The same one who was there . . . at the burial."

It was true. The gravedigger remembered Joni, too, and seemed uncomfortable with the coincidence.

Herrington turned to her.

"Captain Thompson explained your desire to be here, but I strongly suggest that you stay in the car. There's nothing to see, except the actual transfer, of course, and I don't think—" He broke off a moment. "Well, I've done it many times myself and never really gotten used to it."

For the first time, Joni looked directly at him. "I'm sorry my presence makes you uncomfortable, doctor. I know it seems strange, but I can't really explain it."

"I'm only asking you to consider what you're doing. Are you sure you want to be here? Right here?"

For a long while, Joni didn't appear to breathe.

"No," she said finally, "I'm not sure at all. It's just that he shouldn't . . . be alone for it," she said, indicating the coffin's resting place.

Thompson shuffled his feet. "I've had the same concern you do, Herrington, but Mrs. Lawrence has a clear idea of what she needs to do. I think it best we just get it done as fast as possible."

Herrington shrugged deferentially. He'd done what he could to dissuade her. As he walked away to speak to the workers, he decided he hated his second job very much indeed.

The gravediggers looked nervous, and the bigger of the two stared at Joni for so long she had to look away. Herrington noticed it and gave the order to start. He could only guess what she'd read into the man's gaze. Then the gravediggers exchanged a furtive glance and the first spade touched earth.

The digging progressed slowly at first; the normally blasé workmen seemed reticent about completing their task. Shortly a mount of red clay formed around the edge of the grave, and as it grew Thompson moved closer to Joni. By the time a shovel made a hollow sound that made them all jump, he'd taken her arm in his. His presence seemed to reassure her, and the medical examiner could overhear him asking her again to leave the scene.

"Get it under your shovel," the larger worker announced without warning, "I'll grab it by hand." It had taken only a few minutes, probably because the earth was still easy to dig.

The other gravedigger grunted his approval.

Clumsily, the worker raised one end of the coffin and put rough hands on the tarnished brass handle. As the coffin was hoisted from the ground, Herrington heard a low moan and turned in time to see Joni's legs buckle. Thompson supported her, until she revived.

Seeing her collapse, the gravediggers stopped everything, but neither of them could bring himself to look at
Joni.

Thompson was strong at her side. "There's a limit to
how brave you have to be."

"It's not bravery," she struggled, "I have to be
here."

"Well, at least go back to the car and wait. I'll make
sure they handle things . . . carefully."

Joni looked at the casket and for a few moments
seemed to be communing with it, waiting for something. She closed her eyes, as though listening. Then,
looking disappointed, she agreed to leave. Gently,
Thompson guided her away from the grave and eased
her into the car. When he said he'd be back soon, she
just stared off into the distance. She was in such a
trance when they returned that she reacted with a
terrified start when the door suddenly swung open and
she was staring into the confused features of both
Thompson and the medical examiner. They were standing against a darkening sky, nervous. Her attention was
absolute.

"We removed the cover," Thompson finally said
unevenly. "I wanted to see—"

"And?" she pressed, as though to finally end the
agony.

Thompson looked away and Herrington drew a deep
breath. When the examiner could bring himself to
speak, his eyes were wide with curiosity.

"I don't understand what's going on here," he said.
"It was empty. There was nothing inside."

Chapter 20

The pounding had become deafening. She pressed her hands to her ears, but it came again, one explosion after another, until she felt herself disintegrating into a thousand pieces.

It had started sometime around midnight, first with the fever that soared to over 103, then the chills that followed and, finally, a number of hours later, the noise that came from below in the living room. Something was down there in the dark, in a hurry, stumbling into the furniture. When the loud crash came, Joni went rigid.

Someone is in the house. She woke in a hot flash of terror that made her naked body tremble.

For a moment it was silent while she listened, afraid to move. Suddenly the sound began again. She could hear a scraping noise, too, as though *it* was dragging something, something big. She strained to make it out. No, the sound was part of the person—or thing—that was down there. *A leg? Dragging a leg?*

The clock read 6:30. It should have been light, but

153

wasn't. Nothing seemed real; she felt lost in her own house.

The noise increased until it shook the house with evenly spaced tremors that grew stronger and stronger. It was coming closer.

The loud creak on the staircase came so suddenly that she let out a harsh, sharp, scream. *Do something,* she commanded herself, but when she tried to move she couldn't.

The Presence was well up the stairs when she first heard the disgusting, wheezing sound. It was an eerie kind of breathing, strained and full of congestion. *Wet?* She shuddered, shooting a glance to the door. It was open, but she couldn't bring herself to get up and lock it.

She gulped some air and tried to think. "Who's there? Who is it?" she finally said with manufactured courage.

When there was no answer, her reason worked furiously. It had to be a burglar, no, maybe only a neighbor. Jake Jacobs, needing a fuse. *Please let it be Jake.* She dismissed the thought. He would have called or rung the bell; waited until morning. *Jeremy? Josh?* One by one, she discarded the possibilities, until she came to the only other possible explanation.

"Is that you, Doug?"

There was no answer.

"Doug, for God's sake, say something."

She pressed herself into the bed, the covers drawn up around her throat. *Doug? Back home and trying to scare her? So angry he wanted to punish her in a new way?*

The answer came in a vicious-sounding growl that stopped her heart. It was an animal, a big dog or . . . bigger. Again it began to move up the stairs, steadily coming for her.

Her body was soaking wet, and she was panting for air. She was alone in the house, naked in her bed.

She could sense when it got to the top of the stairs and went still, as though not knowing which way to turn. Maybe she hadn't given herself away. Maybe it wasn't coming for her. She listened, frozen by fear, trying to think of anything she might use as a weapon. The snarling had given way to forced, watery breathing.

Almost too paralyzed to move, she willed herself off the bed. It was already too late for the hallway. She thought of the window. The drop would be over twenty feet, but it was the only way out. *Who was it? What is it?* She would survive the fall, and then run if her legs— *Some local youngsters, playing a joke?*

She got down on the floor and crept to the window. Suddenly her nostrils were assaulted by an odor that disgusted her, a dark and musty smell like the decay of animal flesh. It make her want to vomit. There was no escaping it, no matter which way she turned her head. She held her breath until she was forced to take in air and gagged.

When she finally reached the window, she put both hands on the sill and slowly hoisted herself up. The breathing in the hall had become louder. She told herself it was some kind of hysteria, like Thompson had talked about, but it was too real. Something *was* walking to the bedroom, something hideous.

Shaking uncontrollably, she forced the window, trying not to make any sound. It only went up a few inches before jamming. She tried harder, but it wouldn't budge. *A few more seconds,* she pleaded. *Please!* She started to cry softly. *What is it?* Her palms struck out at the window frame with all the force she had and it went up.

The noise was answered instantly by a howl of

recognition from the hall, and when she spun around to face the door, it was there. In her fright, all she could make out was a cloud of haze, which emanated from a large, pulsating mass. She couldn't force her eyes away as she screamed and screamed again.

In mortal panic, she went back to the window, knowing even as she did so it would get to her first. In desperation, she stood ready to fling herself through the glass. The stench filled her senses and she reeled. She was still screaming when she felt the claws dig into her shoulders, felt herself being pulled back into the room by two burning hooks and lifted off the ground.

Enveloped in the deadly fog, she squirmed uselessly to free herself. She prayed she would pass out. It was a huge, fantastically hideous demon, which reeked of human excrement and decay. Her resistance crumbled and she gave herself up to the rotting monster. At the edge of eternity, Joni was only able to make a pathetic little squeaking sound.

The demon carried her outside and, in the dim light of a clouded moon, she could see they'd entered the woods. The demon moved ahead with her as though she were weightless; a filthy, gurgling sound came from inches away in the fog. The heavy breathing was coating her nakedness with a fine mist of mucus that made her retch. Futilely, she turned her head and looked up until she could make out two empty sockets deep within the haze, the places where there might have been eyes. The creature looked down at her, sightless. Incredibly, despite the fact that the face was otherwise featureless, something about it suggested it was a woman.

Joni could not look away as its grip became icy, unbearably frigid. Wherever it had touched her, she'd gone numb. Again she writhed to escape the monster's grasp, as they left the forest and came to a clearing.

When it finally stopped moving, it held her away from its body, away from the fog, lowering her until she was fitted into a hole beneath the earth. The stench was in there already. The hole had hard sides; it was cold, and the bottom was pitch black. When she reached her hand into the blackness, it came away with splinters and ooze. It let her go. The only light came from above, in the dim night sky. She was barely breathing, her back and legs without feeling where it had touched her.

Bammm! Bammm!

The first explosions almost shattered her eardrums, and a portion of the light overhead was suddenly taken away. The pounding came again, and quickly another shaft of light disappeared. The idea came to her all at once, too obvious to be anything else. She was in her coffin, and the demon was nailing it shut!

With scarcely any light left, Joni pushed off from the bottom of the coffin and slanted her head into the last remaining opening for air, but the moment she did the hateful force from above pushed down on her head with an angry howl. Her neck almost broke under the pressure, and she fell back, pounding her fists on the rock-hard planks above. Her head throbbed merciless-ly. Her lungs sucked in the last of the putrid stench.

Bammm! Bammmmm!

When she felt the transformation start, she froze in disbelief. Her hands had grown smaller, the fingers and palms. Then it was her arms. She felt her legs shrivel-ing, as though she were . . . *shrinking!* She felt for her breasts, but her chest had become flat. Around her, the coffin was becoming larger as her body filled less and less of the space.

Bammm! Bammmmm!

Just before the last shaft of light was taken away, she looked up and saw it outside. The demon was spewing a thick, inky substance, laughing. It held the last plank over the opening. As she watched, the fog lifted around the demon enough for her to see through to where the face had been a vacant plane but now revealed prominent features. It *was* a woman! Joni's mouth opened and she cried out in disbelief, but instead of her own voice, she heard a baby's wailing.

Her mind was almost gone. In the last few seconds before it became impossible to think, she remembered what she'd seen above her and finally understood what was happening.

Inside the coffin, she had become her baby, Stephen.

And the hideous monster she'd seen above her for one terrifying moment was—*herself!*

Bammmmm. Bammmmmm. Bammmmmmmm!

The pain exploded in her temples and she awoke from the worst nightmare of her life with an excruciating migraine.

Chapter 21

"First Captain" Kenneth Scarpone sat behind a large oak desk in the largest office of the Edgewood precinct. "First Captain" was a nickname that had come about to differentiate him from Captain Thompson. Scarpone had started out as a rookie in Edgewood—unlike Thompson.

The working relationship between the two captains had deteriorated since the post of police chief had become vacant and the issue of succession for officers of equal rank left unresolved. While the legal apparatus was being untangled, Scarpone's seniority made him the acting chief, as well as the acknowledged heir to the job, unless some unforeseen calamity spoiled his chances. To Scarpone, Thompson's collusion with the madwoman who was now with them augured just such a disaster.

The unshielded light bulb showed the senior officer to be in his late forties. His balding skull was fringed with jet black hair, which it was rumored he dyed. His face was angular, dark, and, as usual, scowling.

159

"Okay, Thompson, why don't you walk me through it again, just so I'm sure you haven't lost it this time, if you know what I'm saying."

Thompson looked like a general who was stoically biding his time while the war went badly. He knew his boss was getting ready to blow, and if there hadn't been a lady present he would have already.

"The autopsy was perfectly legal and done at Mrs. Lawrence's request. She wanted to know if there was another possible cause of death."

"Which was described as a crib death, according to the people who are *supposed* to make that call." Scarpone turned his dark eyes on Joni.

"Sudden Infant Death syndrome," she corrected. "That's the proper term."

"Whatever," he continued, "but I still don't know what you thought you had to gain by an autopsy. Your doctor said it was a crib—sudden death syndrome thing. The medical examiner, too."

"The examiner officially labeled it a kind of pneumonia," Thompson interjected.

"But only to spare Mrs. Lawrence here the need for an autopsy, the same thing that their family doctor recommended. I checked with the medical examiner, and he admitted it to me, off the record."

"But the grave was empty," Joni said strongly. "I think that proves some—"

"It doesn't *prove* anything, except an isolated case of grave robbing. Even Thompson will tell you that, right Thompson?"

The younger man remained expressionless.

"Maybe," Joni continued, "but when you put it together with what we already found out, something looks wrong."

"And what you had earlier was a long-shot hunch from some smart New York doctor."

"If you mean the research I did, yes. Dr. Amaloff took me through the main causes of the sickness and my son's case didn't match. Dr. Amaloff is a respected expert in the field." But so unrespected at the same time, Joni thought, that he'd been unable to help.

Scarpone sipped cold coffee from a yellow mug, made a face, and took another sip.

"Okay, this doctor tells you he's not a hundred-percent sure. Fine. You're already a little nervous about the whole thing, so you order an autopsy. Fine. It's your right, even though it's a bit late. But then you find out the grave's been tampered with—"

"Not tampered with, dammit, robbed! Someone took my baby!" She knew it sounded as if she believed Stephen had been kidnapped, as if her baby were alive, but somehow it did feel like a kidnapping. "And they did it so fast; he wasn't even allowed to find his peace," she said, her voice breaking.

Scarpone waited for her to calm down.

"And that's just as suspicious as the robbery itself," Thompson added a moment later, "maybe more so. It suggests that whoever was behind it might have been waiting for the body. That leads to the question of how they knew. The newspaper blurb about the Lawrence boy hadn't run yet."

"And how could you possibly know when the body was taken?"

"The gravediggers were there when the medical examiner opened the casket and found it empty. When I asked if they could tell me anything about it they buttoned up like clams. So I leaned on them a little."

"It was the flowers," Joni said.

Scarpone was losing whatever patience he had left.

"Part of a gravedigger's job is to come back the next morning. A fresh grave always settles and needs some minor leveling. When the men came back, they noticed the plants around the grave had been crushed."

"Some of them had been uprooted," Joni added. "I went to look after Officer Thompson told me the grave was empty."

Thompson continued. "They thought it was vandals and were angry because they had to replant the flowers —except now it doesn't look like vandals any more. Evidently the robbers didn't notice the flowers around the grave in the dark, though they'd been careful not to disturb the look of the grave itself."

"Which still doesn't explain why the first thing you do is come charging in here asking for a full investigation," Scarpone said.

The younger captain went somber. "As a matter of fact, it wasn't the first thing I did."

Scarpone glared at him.

"The first thing I did was check out some other graves, on a hunch. The workmen took me to several other places in the cemetery where infant graves had been dug within the past six months, and it was the same."

"The same what?" Scarpone shouted.

"One of them was the same as the Lawrence boy's, empty. And I think there may be a lot more."

Scarpone had a full head of steam up.

"You mean you dug up another grave? Without permission of the relatives? Without a court order?"

"No, two others, actually," he admitted. "One was intact. And it wasn't exactly without official permission. The medical examiner was present, after all, and he agreed to the search."

"Cause you leaned on him, too, right?" Scarpone sprang from his big chair. "You are in big trouble, Thompson," he bellowed. "I guarantee it. You can't go around digging up people's families like that, not in a small town like this one."

"I said the M.E. was there, didn't I?"

"Irrelevant. There was nothing official about it. You didn't have time for court orders, did you, so you went ahead without them. It'll never stand up."

"It doesn't have to now, considering what I found."

Scarpone shook his head. They both knew that once the news got out it wouldn't matter who actually exhumed the graves illegally. As acting chief of police, everything was Scarpone's responsibility.

"Jesus, don't you know what they'll do when they find out?"

"Probably thank us for uncovering the conspiracy," Joni followed.

"What *conspiracy*, for crissake? The work of a deranged deviate? How do *you* know anything about it?" He turned to Thompson. "Or you, either, without finding out more?"

"That's what we came for, an investigation," Joni answered for her partner.

The trap he'd fallen into sent Scarpone into a new rage.

"Well, I'm telling you, Thompson, I'm not gonna let your street tactics stir up a crisis where there isn't any. Here you got to play by the rules, *my* rules. This isn't Newark. We have a blueblood City Council to deal with, if you know what I'm saying."

"That rich people don't give a damn about their children's graves? I don't buy it."

Scarpone was quiet for a moment, thinking.

"Was there any sign of damage, other than the missing bodies? Were the tombstones overturned?"

"It's not the work of vandals," Joni answered. "The coffins were left behind."

"What's that supposed to mean?"

"We don't know for sure," Thompson went on. "If only for convenience, you'd expect the robbers to take them. Whoever did it was either well-prepared for the trip or had something else in mind."

"A motive that didn't require the coffin," Joni continued. "I think the theft of my son's body is part of something bigger."

Scarpone sank back into his chair. He was dazed and fuming mad at the same time. "Jesus Christ, why'd you have to go freelancing at a time like this?"

Joni raised a defiant hand and pointed at Thompson. "Because he has the sense of responsibility he's supposed to have. That's something you seem to be lacking. What are you so afraid of, upsetting a few powerful people? Well, I'm upset, too, and I want the investigation. And I want Captain Thompson to head it until it's solved."

"*You* want? *You?* You think you can order this office around?"

"And if you don't help me, I'll go to anyone I have to in order to get help, the Town Council, the State or County Police. I have a legitimate claim now, and I won't be treated like I'm crazy."

Strangely, her threat had made him suddenly smug.

"Well, I guarantee you won't get far. Look Mrs. Lawrence," he said, mellowing, "I'm willing to use some of my resources to search for the creep who disrupted your son's grave. Personally, it sickens me, but I will not be stampeded into joining your personal crusade. Your grief is obviously the real problem here, and I sympathize with you, but if you try to use this office to cure it, I'm gonna come down hard on you. As far as I'm concerned, you're out of line." He brought his fist down on the table, hard. "Now, you can go to whoever you want to, but I'm telling you now they'll only come back to me for clearances, if you know what I'm saying. So just let me handle it my way."

Before Thompson could answer, Joni's hand shot out in front of him. She stood and leaned toward Scarpone over the desk.

"The goddamn hell I will," she shot back, "because there's still one alternative you can't ignore: the newspapers. Maybe you can get the authorities to stop me, or the town council to think I'm crazy, but you won't have any luck with the press. There's enough of a story here to make them jump for joy, and you know it. So either you give me what I want or I'll take my case to the public." She paused long enough to bring her own fist crashing into the table even harder than his had. "If you know what *I'm* saying."

Scarpone cursed loudly. "You gonna talk some sense into her or what, Thompson?"

He saw an irritating look of calm descend over his subordinate's face.

"I don't see what I can do about it. I'd say Mrs. Lawrence has us over a barrel."

"Oh, shit." He drilled Joni with ice-cold eyes. "Get out of here, lady, get out. Thompson, you get your ass on this full-time until you catch that lousy deviate, you hear?"

"Yessir."

"And you do it fast, or you can find yourself another town."

"Yessir, as fast as possible." He saluted smartly.

Joni fought to conceal a satisfied grin. She thanked Scarpone curtly and pivoted to the door. She'd found his Achilles heel, and it felt wonderful.

Chapter 22

The Visitor felt a trickle of perspiration roll down his back and cursed the uncomfortable wool sweater he'd had to put on. He knew the task at hand was critical—without it, the merchandise would be of little value. The procedure itself was simple. Child's play, the very tall, thin man said to himself, chuckling at the appropriateness of the analogy.

Despite the lateness of the hour, the Visitor felt good. He'd gotten there right on time; not too early for the guard's patrol nor too late for the body.

Because it wasn't his first trip to the Vorhees Funeral Home, he easily traveled through the dark rooms, past the holding areas for the bereaved, past the Twilight Chapel, then down the stairs never used by the families, to an unused storage room.

As soon as he slipped into the storage vault, he heard the sound of music from the other end of the central hall. The radio belonged to the young night watchman, a

*college student named Ron Burns who never ventured
into the depths of the private morgue, where there were
stiffs who could pop up under sheets and scare the crap
out of you. Nor did the young preppie have a weapon;
his sole function was to turn in an alarm if he spotted an
intruder.*

*So the Visitor didn't worry about the guard as he
maneuvered by flashlight in the underground caverns
and eventually found the heavy iron door handle. Then,
carefully, he pushed in the door to the coffin room and
was greeted by a blast of cold air, the reason for his
sweater.*

*The casket containing the baby girl was easy to
identify. It was always the smallest coffin in the
room and seldom was there more than a single small
one.*

*The flashlight darted from one coffin to the next.
Tonight there were only three, including the one small
one. The Visitor closed the door, shutting out the distant music as well as locking in any sound he might
make.*

*He crept forward and caressed the coffin, then he
quickly raised the lid. As expected, the body had been
fully prepared for the upcoming festivities, which would
take place early that afternoon. The Visitor grinned with
satisfaction. He shifted the flashlight to his left hand and
pulled the Instrument out from his shirt pocket, underneath his sweater. Carefully he held it to his ear and
listened for the barely audible hiss. He smiled. The
Instrument would continue to work long after he had
gone.*

*In seconds, the Visitor had placed the Instrument in
the coffin, his hand working its way under the folds of
cloth until it came into contact with the inert flesh where
it was to be left.*

When it was done, he allowed himself to gaze at the little female form, who lay on her back in sublime repose. More relaxed now, the Visitor let one hand stray to the gray cheek and stroked it.

"Hello, Samantha," he said with a sing-song voice. "Remember me?"

Chapter 23

For Joni, the week following her tumultuous meeting with Scarpone was an exercise in slow torture. Now, added to existing doubts about the nature of Stephen's death, she'd had a terrifying glimpse of a child that looked exactly like him, and no matter how hard she tried to erase it, the scene kept playing over and over in her memory. For a time it had made her so confused she couldn't think.

Also, now that she'd finally enlisted a believer in her search, she was paradoxically at the end of any personal effort she could make to take the investigation forward. The task of breaking new ground fell to her police captain partner, who himself was having a difficult time developing leads. Once they'd promised Scarpone not to go public, there was little chance of help from anyone they couldn't contact directly.

Now also there were more frequent visions of Stephen, always at night, in which his eyes would plead with her to help him or blame her for having let him die. Perhaps the most frightening part was the image itself. Since his death, his face had changed, growing larger, and taking on more definition. It was aging, just like he would have.

Then there was the issue of Thompson, and just how much she could really trust him. His quick adoption of her cause was almost too good to be true. She'd always had a problem trusting; it had begun long ago, before Doug. As in her youth, her benefactor's concern had come with a complex set of rules, this time police rules.

The gnawing doubts she harbored about Thompson forced her to re-examine her childhood, and she realized for the first time just how cloistered her life had been. Strangely, the main result of her overprotection was not only naiveté, but a bonding to the source of her innocence, her father. When he died in the fire that night, she was too young to interpret it in any other way but as a betrayal of the ultimate trust.

If the seeds of distrust for men were planted in childhood, however, they were nurtured by the other men she met later on. The first was the one in high school, who introduced her to alcohol and then took advantage of her in a meadow on prom night. It had been a monumentally unimpressive way to lose one's virginity, especially after it had been so well guarded. Then there were those she met after fleeing Florida to U.C.L.A., where she forced herself into a series of affairs with several younger students and a professor. They were a selfish bunch, who used up her scant reserve of trust, and after them the new criteria with men became self-protective. Eventually she opted for seclusion again, and it lasted until two years later, when she dropped out of school, moved to New York and met Sid.

Still aching for a genuine relationship, Joni threw all caution and experience to the wind again, and fell blissfully in love. For one euphoric year, she and Sid made love on the beach of La Semanna in St. Martin, dug clams in Amagansett, partied, worked, and even took an apartment in New York together. And she experienced her first soul-shaking orgasms. But the same day he confirmed in person what she heard from a friend on the coast—that he had a similar arrangement with a woman in L.A.—she took her dishes and said good-bye. It was the last time she ever talked to Sid. It was a matter of trust.

Years passed between Sid and Doug, the next man for whom she'd let down her guard, but evidently she hadn't waited long enough.

Now, however, the trust she needed to cultivate for Bill Thompson was of a different sort and for a different purpose. Though in theory it should have been easier, the old fears still held her back from revealing herself to him.

There were legitimate causes for caution. His quick sponsorship of her cause could be his way of punishing his boss, of exploiting her for his career. Then, too, it was possible he was attracted to her more than to her claim. In one of her more mixed-up moments, she'd even entertained the frightening notion that he was part of the conspiracy against her son. Yet, with all her doubts, in the end she really had no recourse but to put her faith in Bill Thompson. The reason was simple: it was him or no one.

Fortunately, the more time Joni spent with Bill the more she felt comfortable with the complexity she saw. As a cop, he was capable of great breaches of propriety in the pursuit of the truth, yet under his surface deviousness was a surprising amount of integrity for one who'd been around the criminal element so long. He was not a cynic, as many policemen ended up being, and after all the negative things he'd probably seen, he still spoke positively about life in a pure, almost naive way. Finally in understanding his values Joni began to find a basis for trust.

When he arrived at her home late one August afternoon, he appeared more relaxed than usual, a sign that often meant he'd had a success in some aspect of the investigation. But when she opened the door, he remained outside.

"Thought we'd climb out of the fire for an afternoon," he announced. "A little change of pace." His hand came from behind his back, revealing a huge Burger King shopping bag.

It made her grin.

"Anytime I can be a big spender for under three bucks," he said. "Staked out a section of the park, so get a jacket and lock up."

She was warmed by the small adventure he'd planned.

"What kind of wine goes with a Whopper?"

His other hand held a bottle of champagne. "Now, if there are no further questions?"

Their picnic table was an old army blanket. After luncheon on the green, they lay on it in a mellow mood. The afternoon was lush and fragrant. A large weeping willow hung over them, affording a degree of privacy from the playground nearby, and an ephemeral breeze with the sweet aroma of wild rose nudged welcome coolness into their clothing.

During their quiet times, Joni realized how easy they'd become with each other. Yet, it was a curious relationship, with no objective except their common purpose.

At one point, the stillness was broken by two youngsters, who crept up on them and ran off giggling.

"Does it make you anxious when you see other children, I mean in a normal situation like this?"

The question took her by surprise. Up until then, she'd assumed he was protecting her by avoiding the topic, like everyone else.

"I'd like to say no, but I'm afraid I still have some healing to do."

"Are you jealous of other parents? Other mothers?"

"Not that much. I think about the injustice of it, the 'why me' is a big problem." She looked away and became pensive. "Guess it's so hard because after years of not knowing what I wanted, I finally found it, only to lose it so fast again."

"A family?"

"The one thing I can't seem to get or hang onto."

She didn't look at him until he asked, "Can you think of a time when you might want children again?"

At first the question irritated her. The thought hadn't occurred since Doug had mentioned the morning after Stephen's death. No, that wasn't true. It had come after that too, but accompanied by a sense of betrayal that made her repress it. That's what was making her feel uncomfortable now.

He touched her arm tenderly. "Sorry if I opened old wounds. Next time I get too personal, give me a shot."

"Actually, I know it's good for me to talk about it, at least to get back to the possibility, so no, I don't think you got too personal." Before she knew what she was doing, she leaned forward and kissed him nicely on the cheek, but instead of straightening up again, she let him put his lips on hers. Then she pulled away abruptly.

"Hell, I didn't mean to—what a lousy time."

"I understand how you meant it. It's all right, Bill."

"Well, the truth is I feel really lousy about it."

"Don't be silly."

"No, I do—because we have another kind of relationship, Joni, friendly, yes, but still . . . well . . . professional." He was really flustered. "Aw, hell, now I'm even blowing the apology. Listen, it's just that the problem you came to me with is the most important thing, and I don't want to do anything that makes you question my motives. Does that sound dumb to you? Or corny?"

She studied his face. "Uh, huh. Dumb *and* corny, but if you'd said anything else I'd have been disappointed."

He cleared his throat and she realized for the first time he was blushing.

"And speaking of business, there are several pieces of news," he said, regrouping, "even though I'm not sure what to make of them."

"Why didn't you tell me before?"

"'Cause I'm not sure how important they are. Anyway, does the name *Roth Drug* mean anything to you?"

She searched her memory. There was something familiar about it, but nothing she could pin down.

"Just a coincidence, probably. I went through a number of sheets on SIDS parents, like the kind I had to write up after visiting you."

"Yes?"

"Just by chance I came across two fathers who happened to work at the same company, Roth Drug, and both lived within the sample area I set up. Nothing?"

"Sorry."

"Well, it's a long shot. Anyway, something much more interesting came through a connection I have at the County Clerk's office. I spent a few hours going over old records and I'm not sure whether to believe it or not." Thompson paused, considering his words.

"For heaven's sake, what?"

"Well, I started by compiling a list of birth and death certificates for our area, then did some rough indexing with the recorded SIDS cases. I thought it might be interesting to check the number of crib cases from year to year and correlate them to the number of reported grave robbings."

She got the general drift.

"I figured if the number of cases of both had risen or dropped together it might point me somewhere, but no dice. The numbers didn't show anything, and I was about to walk away when something made me go further. So I set up a different table. This time I made Edgewood the center of a circle with a hundred-mile radius. The size was bigger, but completely random."

"So far I'm with you."

"The area ignored city and county lines. Broken up that way, there was nothing to read in the number of robberies, but there was a surprising increase in the number of infant deaths themselves."

"How much?"

"On the order of twenty-five to thirty percent."

"And the normal differences in cases year to year wouldn't account for that?"

"That's a question for your doctor friend in New York, but it seems high to me. Of course, it could have been a fluke year, plus we're dealing in dozens of cases, not thousands like a good sample, so it doesn't take much change to yield a high percentage."

Thinking about infants as though they were columns of numbers was unpleasant, but Joni reluctantly decided she'd have to get used to it.

"I'll ask Amaloff. What else?"

"Something so strange I can't make heads or tails of it. Using the circle, the area with the increase, I looked for other similarities. I was in over my head, I'll admit, and I probably violated some obvious rule of statistics, but anyway, I studied the sex of the babies, towns, ethnic background. There was nothing until, with the death certificates spread out in front of me, I noticed it."

"Go on."

"In an abnormally high number of cases the deaths occurred on a weekday, mostly Monday, Tuesday, and Wednesday. Fewer on Thursday and much fewer on weekends. Suspiciously fewer. I don't think I need to be an expert to know that."

Joni struggled to go somewhere with the information, but couldn't.

"With seven days a week," he continued, "you'd expect out of every seven deaths, roughly two would be on the weekend. Two out of seven, four out of fourteen, etcetera. But in my sample the average was almost a hundred percent less than normal. A very strange difference."

In a flash, the larger implication of deaths grouped around specific days of the week dawned on her and she reached for his arm.

"God, Bill, do you know what you're saying?"

"Yeah, scary."

"It's not grave robbing, any more, it's a plan, a pattern to the *deaths*." She was discovering the connections as she spoke them. "Bill, it's . . . murder. Murders! My God!" She covered her mouth with her hand.

"I can't deny it's a possibility, but as much as I want to get somewhere with this thing, right now I'm praying I didn't know what I was doing in that office. This is one time I'd rather be wrong."

They looked at each other with mutual apprehension. Then, as she moved closer, he opened his arms and held her tightly. This time, for sure, it had nothing to do with romance.

Chapter 24

Tuesday, August, 24
7:00 P.M.

Joni closed her eyes and pressed herself deeply into the cushions of the couch. This time she knew she wouldn't be able to talk herself down. The feeling was building. Everything was coming back at once, the phantom in her dream, the voice at the cemetery, the *thing* that Lottie had feared but had been unable to name. The shadow on the lawn played again in her mind. Somehow they were all part of the same thing, a dark and threatening presence that was close, trying to touch her, force her beyond the brink.

She thought back to the phone call of a few minutes earlier. The moment she'd heard the voice she'd frozen. A woman was crying. She'd obviously been driven to call by her own extreme suffering. Joni tried to talk to her, but the caller hung up. The second time the phone rang, the woman was calmer. She told Joni that she needed to speak to her, that her own infant daughter had also died under upsetting, puzzling circumstances.

Joni quickly dressed and then phoned Bill and left a message that she was tracking down a new lead. The trip to the most elegant section of a neighboring town only took ten minutes of fast driving.

The address turned out to be a Tudor mansion on an impressive estate. A small forest surrounded the house, proving that it had been built in another era. The housekeeper ushered Joni into a formal drawing room and introduced her to her obviously troubled, but poised hostess, Mrs. Post. The first thing Joni noticed about the woman was her age. Obviously, she was well into her forties, maybe older, yet she had spoken of her daughter as though her death had been a recent event.

Mrs. Post calmly explained that she lived alone except for her elderly housekeeper whom, being aged, she now cared for. But her brave front was contradicted by a face full of anguish and too little sleep.

"I'm so grateful you've come," she said after they were seated. "I didn't know where else I could turn."

"How did you get my name?" Joni asked.

The woman produced a box full of newspaper clippings. Several were yellow with age. They were all stories written about crib death victims. Near the top of the loose pile was the story that ran in the local paper about Stephen Lawrence.

"The police don't believe me, either, you know."

"What do you mean?"

"About my baby's murder." Her accusation was delivered as a fact.

"What makes you think it was murder?" Joni asked nervously.

"The child's age. And my intuition."

"But why are you so certain? Even in my case I have no real reason to—"

"—Mrs. Lawrence, my daughter's death was a result of the foulest act." She moved to a nearby drawer and produced a document that had been handled many times.

"Eleven twenty-one," she recited without looking at the certificate. "Cause of death, Sudden Infant Death syndrome. That's what it says, a horrible, filthy lie."

Not long ago Joni had been in the same position as Mrs. Post, but now she found herself just as suspicious of the woman's fears as others had been of hers.

"How do you know?" she asked again. "Your baby was examined by doctors, wasn't he? Didn't they all come to the same conclusion?"

"Of course they did. There was nothing else they could find. They had to say it."

"But you must know—"

"—about the apnea? Of course. I've made myself an expert on crib death, Mrs. Lawrence." She clasped and unclasped her hands repeatedly. "I only had my baby for a few months. When she was six months old she died—like yours. SIDS, they said, like they're saying now."

Mrs. Post urged Joni briskly out of the room, and they went up a winding staircase, the woman leading her by the hand like a child. At the top of the stairs she turned right and entered a relatively small room with fabric walls and an ornately inlaid oak floor. Joni looked around and noticed uncomfortably that the nursery had 1950s furniture; the Swedish modern chairs and the slick plastic crib looked like museum pieces. When she ran her fingers along the top of the crib it was covered with dust.

"This is where it happened, what *they* called an accident of nature," Mrs. Post explained.

"When the baby stopped breathing was anyone else around?"

"I got to my baby's side within seconds. The nurse was already applying respiration."

"Is it possible—"

"Her method was flawless. She was an expert."

"Your baby never started breathing on his own?"

"Young woman," she said with an intensity in her eyes that startled Joni, "my baby was dead *before* the nurse got there."

What she said made no sense. From what Joni had learned, it took several minutes before brain death took place, certainly not the few seconds she claimed.

"Impossible? That's what you're thinking? That's what the doctors said. Of course, there was no way for them to verify the exact time of death, but I could tell they didn't believe me."

"I must admit it doesn't fit with what I've been told."

"That's why I know it wasn't a crib death. Instantaneous death in infants is unheard of. The odds against a baby having a heart attack or brain hemorrhage are prohibitively high."

The woman's story was confused; her logic was off. "Someone inside the house did something to your child, is that what you believe?"

Mrs. Post narrowed her eyes, and when she had made certain no one else was lurking in the hallway, she came back in and nodded her head. "And I know who, too. It was my husband, Mrs. Lawrence. My husband killed my child. He hated it, hated all children, even the one we adopted. He was jealous of them, but no one will believe me."

Now it was obvious what had been making her so uneasy ever since she began to speak to the woman. The child Mrs. Post spoke of had obviously died years ago. Apparently the shock had been too much for her,

and she had concocted the horrible belief that her
husband had been to blame. But for her immense
fortune, Mrs. Post would probably have been institu-
tionalized. Even if there had been any truth to her
claims once, clearly the woman was now stark raving
mad.

There but for the grace of—Joni took a few steps
toward the window and looked down at the serene
setting of the front lawn. The gentle sweep of the
sculptured hedges took on an Alice-In-Wonderland
quality as had the goings on inside the house. She
traced the line of shrubbery to a point where a fountain
was gushing liquid light and saw Bill Thompson on the
run waving frantically in her direction.

After a hasty departure he confirmed what she had
already surmised. Joan Lawrence was only the most
recent of the many SIDS mothers Mrs. Post had
contacted since the death of her own baby in 1961.

3:00 P.M.

*The Visitor carefully closed the distance between himself
and the young woman, cautiously picking his way
through the scores of people who came between them.
She was one of those modern mothers who carried her
baby on her chest, in a harness. Pressed between her
breasts, the baby was sleeping, oblivious to the thousands of other commuters in the human ant colony
known as Grand Central Station.*

*Twenty times fifty thousand equals a million, he
repeated to himself. One hundred times fifty thousand
equals five million. The beauty of the numbers had taken*

on a fascination separate from the plan itself. It was amazing how much the right people would pay for so little, but it had happened often enough to be a fact. The best part was that all the recent money was pure profit. No, that wasn't the best part. The best part was that very soon it would be all his.

At first the Planner had been smarter than he was, clever enough to have bought his services for a pitifully small sum. The insult would be redressed soon, however, and permanently. This time he had taken enough of the Instrument for an extra job, the same way he had once before. He was setting it all up so perfectly. Soon he would have the way to keep doing it; then all he'd need were more babies.

The idea made him tingle, but it was becoming difficult to focus on the mother. He hadn't let her out of his sight since they got off the bus and, now that she'd gone indoors, he wouldn't take his eyes off her until the work was done.

This afternoon, like every Tuesday afternoon, she'd been right on schedule for her weekly trip from Greenwich to the Park Avenue pediatrician. He was the only doctor to whom she trusted her baby and had been her own doctor a generation earlier.

The job had to be done quickly. As she picked her way through the crowd to the end of the Amtrak line, he was right behind her, staring at the canvas straps of the harness, which formed two openings at the bottom. There the baby's wobbly legs protruded and hugged her on both sides. One foot was thrust more forward than the other, shoeless. Just fine.

When he joined the line, his arms were folded across his chest, the right hand with the Instrument under the left forearm. Unnoticed, he repositioned his arms until the Instrument was level with the exposed heel of the

*infant's foot. Then he turned sideways, leaned in toward
the mother and probed the instep.*

*By the time the train was ready for boarding, he had
already ordered a frankfurter and an orange drink at the
coffee counter next to the train for Connecticut. It wasn't
the most private spot for lunch, but it was a good place
to watch the baby die.*

Chapter 25

Bill Thompson had been this scared only once before—
on the day he was shipped overseas to Vietnam. But
what he'd found out at the County Clerk's office in
Hackensack scared him in a very different way.

He'd gone over the numbers a second time, then a
third, before accepting it. He wanted to share his
finding with someone, talk to somebody. Scarpone was
the logical choice, but he couldn't be trusted to be
objective, since Thompson knew he was more concerned with remaining chief of police.

He decided that he needed outside confirmation.
After a frustrating series of phone calls he finally got
Aaron Schecter on the phone. Schecter told him all he
needed to know, in fact told him too much. After the
conversation Thompson was even more concerned.

Then there was the difficult problem of how to break
the news to Joni. And that was what brought him to the
fourth and last flight of stairs leading to the Manhattan
apartment of Douglas Lawrence.

It was interesting to find that Doug had chosen such a lonely part of town in which to begin his separation, but then his leaving home in the first place had been strange. Contrary to the notions he'd had about New York's East Side, Thompson thought Doug's address just off Park Avenue was empty and isolated, even though the whole neighborhood seemed wealthy.

When he saw Doug waiting impatiently in the doorway of his apartment, he began to understand his choice of location. Doug looked like he belonged. He was every part the prosperous East Side stereotype. His face and arms were beautifully tanned, his clothes casual but stylish. Inside the four-room apartment, it was also apparent he'd made a swift adjustment. The space had been heavily decorated with art nouveau, glass, and chrome, and two enormous lambskin rugs stood out in bold relief against a hardwood floor. There were wine glasses near the sofa, two of them, and two brands of cigarettes in the ashtrays.

"If you don't mind, I'd like to get this over with," Doug said as soon as they had settled onto a mocha velvet couch that was too deep for comfort. "I said I'd see you as a courtesy, but I've been through this thing too many times already."

Thompson raised an eyebrow. "Does it upset you to discuss your wife's problems?"

"Of course not, but it is upsetting to know that she still refuses to accept reality. You may not realize it, but our son was so important to her it led to our breakup. Now I see she's even involved the police in it."

"And you think she should drop the whole thing? After what we've been finding out?"

Doug stood up and poured himself a drink. Thompson shook his head when Doug offered him one.

"I'll admit the grave robbing was weird, and I hope you crucify the guy that did it, but it doesn't prove a damn thing." He shot a glance at the officer. "What are you smiling about?"

"Nothing, sorry. You just reminded me of someone else I know who said the same thing."

"Just what *is* it you came to talk about, captain? Why you didn't want to tell me over the phone is beyond me."

"First of all, I came because I wanted to tell you in person that your wife is okay. She's not off her rocker, as you may think. Not completely recovered, maybe, but not out of control."

"Did she tell you to say that?"

"You know her better than that."

Doug was silent for a moment. "Aw, shit. Hey, I'm sorry I didn't ask about her, but it's been rough, you know?"

Thompson looked at the loaded ashtray. "Yeah."

"We're not really in touch for the time being. We've only spoken a few times, before and after the grave thing."

"Well then, you'll be happy to know what I just found out will probably make her give up her theory that the grave robbing was some kind of conspiracy against your son."

Doug shook his head. "Jesus, is she still on that one?"

"Not for long."

"So what have you found out, did you finally locate the body? Was there an autopsy performed that confirmed the cause of death—as *no* cause, I mean?" He was slightly thrown by his own words.

"No, nothing like that."

Doug finished the last of his scotch and poured himself another.

"Listen, I hope you don't mind, but I have plans tonight. A friend is coming over soon, so would you mind just telling me what it is that's going to cure my wife? I presume it's important enough for you to have come here on your free time."

Thompson scrutinized Doug closely, and as he began the story, Doug's expression turned smug, then superior. He sipped his scotch casually and was obviously prepared to dismiss whatever he had to say. Nor did his stony features change at all until, at the end of the story, when Thompson told him what he'd learned earlier that day, Doug's deep East Hampton tan turned white and he spilled the drink on one of his exquisite lambskin rugs.

10:00 P.M.

Thompson hadn't spoken to Joni all day, and when he arrived at her house late he realized that he almost didn't know where to begin.

Joni poured drinks for both of them and curled up at the end of the couch, waiting for him to speak. She could tell that he was elated and eagerly searched his face for clues.

"Remember the large increase in SIDS I found before?" Thompson asked her.

She nodded attentively.

"Well, it was beginning to drive me nuts; it was just too large to ignore."

"Yes, I called Dr. Amaloff at his office in New York this afternoon," she interrupted. "He confirmed it was all out of proportion."

"Good, that's important. Anyway, that left me with the thing about weekdays, and I went with it until finally I asked the right question: not what *happens* on weekends, but what *doesn't* happen. Then I remembered something from when I was a kid. In the old days, in Newark, a buddy of mine was accidentally killed in a fight with another gang. The boy's name was Stewie, Stewie Shapiro, the only outside kid on the block, by which I mean he wasn't either Irish or Italian. When Stewie died, we called a moratorium to pay our respects, cause that's the way it was in those days; a life still meant something.

"Well, at first there was some confusion about the day of the funeral. First we thought it would be on Saturday, then it was changed to Sunday. Because of Stewie, I learned that Jewish people aren't allowed to bury their dead on the Sabbath, the Jewish Sabbath, Saturday. Stewie was Jewish. That's why it was put off a day."

"What's that got to do—"

"The fact that most of our SIDS cases happened midweek might mean someone doesn't want to chance a weekend funeral, don't you see?"

"But who's talking about Jewish babies only? Non-Jewish funerals can happen on any day."

"Now you understand what I mean about an amazing twist."

"You mean it's only got to do with Jewish babies?"

"I couldn't think of any other reason to explain it."

The implications of what he said became suddenly clear. If it were true, it was unlikely that Stephen's death was connected to the plot they were uncovering. She and Doug were Catholic and Protestant, but neither of them practiced religion at all. That made it more likely that Stephen was an authentic SIDS death after all, and very likely that her feeling of dread and all the rest *were* actually a hysterical reaction. It was a startling and confusing piece of news, especially after Amaloff had almost confirmed the unlikelihood that Stephen was an SIDS victim.

Bill held up his hand. "Before you go jumping to any conclusions, hear me out."

"What did you find out about the babies?"

"It was all there on the death certificates, a large proportion of the deaths listed as SIDS *were* Jewish."

"What's going on, Bill? Why would someone only go after Jewish children?"

"I wanted to know, too. Also, I even wondered whether I'd messed up the research, so I contacted a group of people that might be knowledgeable on the subject, a Jewish counseling organization in Trenton. Although they're only set up to help widows, the Chairman of the Council had already spotted the increase in Jewish infant deaths, but he didn't know what to do about it. Of course, the increase was not as great from his perspective, since they look at the whole state and we're concerned with a smaller area, where the difference is magnified. When I told him what I'd learned, he was frantic to help. In fact, too much so. He'd already met with his people. They hadn't believed him, but with my information he wanted to demand an immediate public investigation. So far I've convinced him to hold off on anything official until we have a chance to meet. He agreed to wait until after Labor Day, September the eighth. I told him I was close to solving the case, which I think qualifies as a white lie. If they go public, it'll scare off the people we're after."

Joni felt sick. The idea that there was a conspiracy involving babies was repugnant enough. But against Jewish babies specifically? It was yet another grotesque turn.

"But what about Stephen?"

"It's possible it's all been a big mistake, an incredible set of coincidences," Bill said, somewhat bewildered himself.

"You think you'll find another explanation?"

"Truthfully?"

She nodded.

"I think we're onto something."

She sighed deeply and looked depressed, but a moment later she spoke with assurance.

"Well, I'm with you, Bill, no matter what. Even if it looks like it has nothing to do with me or Stephen any more. I'd be a sorry excuse for a human being if I dropped out just because my stake has changed."

She waited for a response that wasn't forthcoming. He was thinking about something.

"Well, that's why I wanted you to hear the rest," he said suddenly, "because what I have to tell you may mean it's not the end for you after all."

"But it has to be, now with—"

He touched her shoulder gently. "Before I was content to sign you off the case, I did one more bit of checking. Joni, I made paid a visit to your husband tonight."

"Why? What's Doug got to do with it?"

"Just a hunch I had that he should hear what I found out, in case he could add something."

"To the news about the babies?"

"Yes, but there's more to it than that, and it wasn't until I spoke with Doug that I found out. I gotta tell you, I never dreamed what he was going to tell me."

Joni still didn't know what he was getting at.

"Doug was the son of Russian immigrants, as you probably know. His father came over to escape serving in the army, but arrived in America penniless. He and his wife almost starved while he tried to find work, but no matter what he did the doors stayed shut. He couldn't get a job with the big companies and even the unions turned him down."

"This is what Doug told you?"

"Yeah, why?"

"Nothing. I never knew, that's all. He never liked to talk about his father, and I used to think it was strange."

"Well, it gets stranger, believe me. After a while Mr. Lawrence, senior, becomes desperate. At first, he thinks it's because of his skills or lack of them, then because of language problems. Eventually he gets so paranoid he decides to change the one thing he believes will improve his chances. He changed his name."

Joni absorbed the information blankly at first. Then the idea became shockingly clear at the same instant that Bill was saying it.

"Lawrence wasn't Doug's real name, Joni," he said, barely above a whisper, "because it wasn't his father's real name, either. Not even close. It's a lot more Jewish than that."

Chapter 26

Joni and Bill drove to Trenton the next day to meet Aaron Schecter, the director of the Jewish counseling agency. He appeared to be an aged gentleman, good-natured yet intense. Although he looked frail he turned out to be as tough as an old rooster when they asked for more time. The director was adamant that the September 8th deadline be kept. In fact, he said he would feel sorry he had agreed to wait at all, and would feel personally responsible if the delay caused any more deaths. After he had shared Bill's findings with the other council members, they'd dropped their opposition to Schecter's original request. Suddenly there was great pressure to go to the authorities. If he hadn't been so persuasive on the subject of honor, he said, it would already have been done. He promised to wait the thirteen remaining days, but no longer.

Joni and Bill finally realized that they wouldn't be able to convince Schecter, and so Bill told him about their latest discovery—that Doug was actually Jewish. After the account, Schecter let out a heavy sigh.

"That your husband did not choose to return to his faith is not surprising. Since his education was stopped at a young age, he had no doubt lost touch with his Judaism, not to mention the great adjustment the restoration of his name would have entailed as an adult, and in his business. In any case, what's more important is *your* technical status as the wife of a Jew, which is what those behind all this may believe you to be."

"*My* status? How could that be?"

"You don't consider yourself to be Jewish, now that you know?"

"Of course not, why? The law doesn't make me Jewish because my husband turned out to be."

"Quite right. Neither the law of the state nor Jewish law. Quite the contrary. There are only two conditions under which one is considered to be Jewish. The first is if one's mother were Jewish, as your husband's was, or two, if one wishes to go through the education leading to his or her conversion."

"Neither is true in my case."

"Then I must ask how you think your baby was thought to be Jewish and, presumably, taken for that reason?"

Bill cleared his throat. "I think I can answer that, if Mrs. Lawrence doesn't mind."

Joni nodded her permission. Bill had gone over it with her that morning.

"When Mrs. Lawrence's husband discovered his background, it must have come as a shock. Whether he felt angry at his father or ashamed of his Jewishness, he kept it a secret for a long time, but eventually he must have had a change of heart. Maybe it was his way of resolving years of guilt, I don't know, but anyway, when the baby was born the hospital records depart-

ment requested information on the infant and Mr.
Lawrence handled it while his wife was still in recovery.
The records were sent to the county seat in Hackensack. It turns out the data on these documents is more
complete than on the simple birth certificate they send
to you later. For example, there's a space on them for
religion, and in the Lawrences' case it's given as Jewish.
That's how he was able to set right something that had
been wrong for many years and, by accident, he also
created the mechanism by which our ghouls must have
judged his baby's religion."

Schecter was rubbing his head. "He must have been
terribly confused about his father's earlier choice. He
could only let go of his past up to a point." He closed
his eyes for a few seconds, then spoke. "Now, if you
don't mind, I'd like to ask you a question that's been
tormenting me ever since you discovered these . . .
crimes."

"Of course."

"In my lifetime I have had the misfortune to witness
every type of anti-Semitism, sometimes personally, as
in Germany. I have seen the haters of this world go
after the Jews through their religion, attack them
through discrimination in business, in unions, in clubs
—even at the highest levels of government. I thought
I'd seen it all, but I admit that what you've uncovered is
a new one for me."

"Yes," Bill said. "I can see how terrible this must be
for you." He looked at Joni. "For all of us."

"Aside from that, none of this seems to make any
sense, unless we're dealing with absolute insanity. All
the risks these people are taking, whoever they are.
The expense and organization it must require. What
motive could they possibly have to murder Jewish
infants and take their bodies? Why? I don't understand
it."

There was timeless sorrow in the old man's eyes, a sense of desolation even in the way he stood.

Bill waited respectfully, then offered a suggestion.

"I guess we have to allow for the most likely thing, the one that's always possible."

"Nazis?" Schecter barked.

"Or one of those neo groups, like in Germany and the Middle East."

"Or in America," Schecter added. "Do you think we're dealing with a plot to attack the Jewish people as a whole? Say, to kill off its population at its roots, its children?"

Joni shook her head reflexively, but neither she nor Bill had an answer.

"Is it possible the bodies are being sold? That it's for the money?"

"Who would buy them?" Joni asked weakly.

"Perhaps one of them is a doctor, or was. Maybe barred from practicing. It's a terrible thought, but perhaps he or they could be selling off pieces of bodies, or using them for experimentation. It must be difficult for someone to get hold of infant cadavers for research purposes, especially if the research isn't normal."

Joni felt her stomach contract. The idea that someone might have taken Stephen's beautiful blue eyes and used them in some such horrible way revolted her.

"If we're talking about research," Thompson said, cutting the direction of her thoughts, "there's another possibility. What about a religious group, fanatics of some kind who want the bodies? Cult worshippers who might use them for sacraments."

Joni hesitated, then spoke as though she was embarrassed.

"Some of the feelings I've had make me think we could be dealing with some evil force, something satanic. I know it sounds extreme, but—"

Schecter's face told her he wasn't prepared to deal with the idea on any level, perhaps because the concept of evil was more related to Christianity and its early obsession with the devil. Bill was trying to be sympathetic, but Joni remembered the trouble he'd had believing in her earlier premonitions. He had thought she was hysterical. In truth, she was uncertain herself about everything. In the beginning, she'd put all of her faith in feelings, but now she was increasingly unable to trust them.

"Let's try to be logical about this. What would anyone want from a baby? Parts of the body? Organs?" Schecter speculated. "When an infant is born with a defective organ, can the parents go somewhere for another one? An organ bank? They must be harder to obtain than for adults. That might have given rise to a black market." He looked at Joni and stopped. "I'm sorry. This must be hard for you, too."

"I'd hate to think there are minds out there sick enough," she answered.

"Evidently they're sick enough to *take* the babies," Thompson added.

It was becoming apparent that an endless amount of speculation was possible, but it wasn't leading anywhere.

"In any event, the question remains as to why Jewish babies and, as far as we know, exclusively Jewish babies." Schecter rose, indicating an end to the interview. "And it's because of our inability to answer that question that I must insist on the original deadline."

"I understand," Thompson said.

"After that time, we'll be forced to call in—how do you say it—bigger guns?"

Bill signaled his agreement.

"I must tell you, though, my instincts at eighty tell me to fight back, not wait."

"If it's any consolation," Thompson said, "in this case you *are* fighting by waiting. If I'm wrong, or not clever enough, I'll be right next to you, with the biggest club I can find."

"And me," Joni said.

Schecter bowed. "Shalom."

"L'chayim."

"And just where did you pick that up, captain? Or have you changed your name, too?"

"No. It's something I learned from an old friend I used to know in Newark. It was a long time ago."

Chapter 27

Monday, August 30
Midnight

"This time," the Planner muttered to the helpless, semi-conscious animal as it was lifted to the table. The animal looked afraid.

This time, like the others, it had been easy to get a dog for the experiment. Nearly every community had a pound, and they never refused someone one of their wretched charges. The virtually inexhaustible supply of research specimens was just another indication to the Planner of the righteousness of the work.

There were other signs: the way the agents had appeared precisely when needed; the way the Jews had unwittingly provided the sacrament, without which the first part of the plan could not have succeeded. And the infant affliction itself. It had provided the perfect camouflage.

Examining the makeshift laboratory, the Planner noted the clutter that had accumulated over time, most of it in recent months. It had been necessary to assemble *more and more equipment as the success of the experiment became more pressing.*

It was never a pleasant thing to kill the dogs, even though most of them would have met the same end in the pounds. This one had looked especially healthy and grateful for the last-minute reprieve. A golden retriever, about eight years old.

Once the dog was strapped securely to the table, the Planner put aside a nagging affection for the animal and went to the refrigerator. Inside, the half-filled vial of sea-green liquid was removed and shaken carefully until its tiny particles were in an equal suspension. Great care was necessary at this step. There was very little left.

Even in its imperfect state, the drug had taken years of research to create. The project had been suspended before the chemical was perfected, but the experiment continued without the rest of the team.

The retriever began to whimper from the tight restraints placed on its four legs. It wasn't used to lying on its back for so long and like those that had come before it, the animal soon realized it wasn't a game. It was also unaccustomed to the small patch of white where its hair had been surgically shaved. Two large black eyes watched anxiously as the Planner held a small bottle, from which the foul-smelling liquid was drawn off. A receptacle was brought past the dog's head to the shaved part and the exposed skin rubbed with something cold that burned the eyes.

"This time," the Planner repeated, readying the Instrument. Once the drug was perfected, the sacred retribution would be carried out.

Slowly the Planner touched the Instrument to the dog's skin and remembered they were running out of Jews.

*   *   *

Bill Thompson tossed in his bed, unable to sleep. For days he'd known what he had to do but hadn't been able to take the first step. The plan was dangerous and required clearances he wouldn't be able to get.

He reached for the lamp on the night table and clicked it on with a grunt. The pack of Marlboros was on the other side of the clock radio. Below the radio, in the top drawer of the night table, he found the picture he'd brought with him from Newark when he joined the Edgewood Police Department six years earlier. It showed a sixteen-year-old, street-hardened punk, gesturing obscenely at the camera. The punk was wearing a leather motorcycle jacket over a T-shirt and had a cruel, wiseguy leer Thompson had always hated. A cigarette dangled from his lips—Lucky Strike, as he remembered—and the kid looked like a potential killer. Thompson had kept the picture as a reminder. It was a picture of himself.

The plan he wanted to set up needed to be accomplished quickly and it would demand a great deal from at least three other police officers under Scarpone's command. Bill knew which men he wanted, but still he'd be in trouble if one of them decided he didn't want to go along with it. The scheme was highly irregular, to say the least, and they'd be risking their badges as much as he was. But he didn't have a choice—they'd have to start staking out all the local cemeteries and find a judge who would let them dig up the graves. Without telling anyone.

Thompson was still up when the Sony read three-ten. Right after that, he looked at the picture in the drawer again, shook his head, and made up his mind. Right after that, he went to sleep thinking, *with or without the judge*.

Chapter 28

The next week flew by. The cemeteries were being staked out, but the grave robbers did not show up. Joni and Bill were both silently depressed. By then, with only six days left in which to solve the crimes, they began to discuss it constantly. Not surprisingly, the frustration took its toll on their relationship. For the first time, Bill lost patience with some of her ideas, and seemed to be brooding himself.

Bill spent his time thinking of every possible bizarre explanation for the crimes. He even read through the Old Testament, in the hope it would yield a fresh religious angle he might have overlooked. One of the parables suggested that the plot could be a terrible sort of revenge, a retribution that had waited two thousand years.

"The idea goes back to Egypt in the time of the pharaohs," Bill had explained. "As the Bible story goes, the pharaoh wouldn't let Moses and the Jews leave Egypt and Moses called down seven plagues on the Egyptians. One of the plagues was the killing of the first-born male of each Egyptian household. That's what struck me the instant I read it. What if someone is re-enacting the plague, taking the first-born of the Jews?''

It was an incredible thought, but there was nothing in the evidence they had so far to negate it. Both of the empty graves they'd originally uncovered had once contained first-born males of Jewish families, plus Stephen's case, assuming the grave robbers took him to be Jewish.

Schecter had been calling them repeatedly throughout the period, at first to check Thompson's progress, but then, five days before his deadline, to announce that one of his fellow council members might be about to leak the news of the conspiracy over his objections. Then, with only three days left, he called again, pleading to be released from his promise, but Bill wouldn't agree. The conversations with Schecter were pressure they didn't need, not that they could blame him. If he'd known the truth about their progress, not even his promise would have prevented him from turning in the alarm.

Increasingly throughout the last week, Joni grew so terrified, she needed sleeping pills every night. Now the dreamlike visitations from Stephen were happening at any time of the day or night, and after each one she was left with the same feeling: wherever Stephen's spirit was, it was in pain. It was as though he were dying all over again, or would always be dying. Bill could do nothing for her except listen, but she was beyond being calmed by his words. Joni could feel a climax was building, both in real life as well as in her dreamlike connection with Stephen. Each day the feeling that something terrible was going to happen grew stronger. Her headaches refused to go away overnight.

* * *

The summer night was unusually moist, the air thick and charged with tension. The temperature was holding near eighty-five as it approached midnight, cooler only by contrast to the searing heat of the afternoon.

When the thunderclap jolted the house, Joni was alone. Again there had been an unsettling phone call, which had come just before the storm broke, another disturbing burden to bear at the worst possible time. It was Doug.

In the course of their separation, they had spoken only a few times, and never had he brought up the subject of reconciliation. Tonight there was enough sibilance in his speech to suggest he'd been drinking. Joni had let him explain away his secrecy about being Jewish, and as soon as he did he began to proclaim his love for her and a desire for them to reunite. Her heart had gone out to him, but only out of compassion for someone who was suffering. As much as she tried, the feeling wasn't there.

During the call she found it difficult to listen to Doug without thinking of Bill, and the more he pressed, the more loyalty she felt toward the new man in her life. It wasn't that she and Bill had anything approaching a romantic attachment yet, but there was clearly something unspoken between them, as though something were waiting.

While she and Doug talked, the full fury of the storm broke directly over the house and, a few seconds later, the light flickered, then failed. Doug was pleading with her for an answer he wouldn't have wanted to hear when the phone went dead in her hands.

The storm was still raging when she crawled into bed, seeking escape in sleep. In the dark, cut off from the world, she knew she could panic if she let herself, so she forced her mind away from all dangerous areas of thought. Later, when sleep still hadn't come, she groped her way downstairs and finished a second glass of wine by candlelight. It was past two in the morning when she finally slept, and still the lights hadn't come on.

. At first she thought it was the yelp of a neighborhood dog scared of the lightning, and then she felt the anxiety taking over her body. *Oh God, not again,* she prayed in the dark. This time she knew it wasn't a dream.

In an instant, her slip was wet with perspiration and the insides of her arms and thighs were tingling. The headache struck a few seconds later, after a crack of thunder rattled the windows. Drawing a thin cover around her, she closed her eyes, waiting for it to go away, trying not to hear the insistent whine which had already changed into a more maddening sound. A baby was crying.

She knew it was Stephen, and he was nearby. In another upstairs room. *The nursery?* There was no doubt. The thought froze her in bed, and she weakly said his name out loud. Her entreaty was answered by an echoing chant, which she heard with frightening clarity.

Mamaaaa!

When the cry stopped, another sound continued, a thumping; a *heartbeat!*

She felt for the radio and held it to her ear, but it wasn't on. A burst of lightning lit the room for a fraction of a second, followed by the sound of wood shattering somewhere in the neighborhood.

It was a while before she slowly drew back the covers. His call came again, over the sound of her

thundering heart. She forced her legs to move and
stepped out of the bedroom and into the hall.

"Mammaaaa!"

The thunder struck again ahead of a gale that seemed
to be blowing inside the house as well as outside. Her
thin nightgown wasn't warm enough to keep her body
from shaking. She felt for the nursery door and found it
closed, as it had been ever since Doug destroyed the
room. Heedless of her insane thoughts, she reached for
the doorknob, turned it until it clicked, and pressed.
The wooden plank glided effortlessly forward, but she
stayed outside. There was suddenly a clatter inside and
she lost her breath. It was the rain hitting the window.

Someone . . . something is trying to drive me crazy.
Please let me be dreaming again.

There was only blackness, not even the light from a
street lamp to help show where the crib once stood,
near the back of the room. She felt lonely for Lottie's
reassuring company, even Doug's. Stephen's presence
was there; she could feel it all around her. Needing her.
Coming for her!

Or was that what someone wanted her to feel?

Mercifully, the crying stopped as soon as she entered
the room and she stood in the dark silence, breathing
with effort. Then, before she knew what was happening, her head jerked around in response to a new
sound. It started as another cry from Stephen, but now
it had been joined by a second and a third voice. The
chorus contained an unearthly suffering, as though
their souls were . . . *burning in hell.*

The imagery wasn't hers; it had been put in her
mind.

Now the unholy incantation was coming from downstairs. Nearly mad with fear, she shouted for them to
stop, then she angrily called out again, demanding

those who were making the noise to show themselves. The answer came in a huge chorus of voices, and she raced to the steps that led downstairs to where they were coming from.

"Who are you?" she cried. "Why are you doing this?"

Her hand clung to a banister thick with humidity as she crept tentatively down the steps. They were coming from everywhere, the den, the kitchen, the living room. There was another ear-shattering clap of thunder, followed by:

Maaaamaaaaaaaaaaaa!

She was moving quickly again when she hit the landing and felt her way into the pitch-black living room. Once she was there, the voices again stopped abruptly and started in another room.

"Stop it, for God's sake. Stop it!"

She made her way to the desk, knocking over a freestanding lamp and a planter before she found the phone. Without light, her finger counted to the nine position, then the one, then one again.

Her last and longest scream, before she fled the house, was because of what she heard in the receiver an instant after she remembered it had gone dead: a single, strident baby, older than Stephen had been, but with his voice.

Help me, mama. Heeeelp meee!

She could feel the corner of her mind go numb. She dropped the phone and turned toward where the door should have been. The entire house vibrated with the cries of the damned. The din rose to a deafening level as she stumbled ahead and felt the door, then worked the latch until she was stabbing blindly into the storm on the front lawn. She was oblivious to the dark, to the torrent that soaked her instantly. Unaware of the direction she took, she fled into the garden and fell into dense bushes that scratched her arms until they bled. Pushing herself to her feet, she eventually found the street and continued to race away from the house of madness, crazy and blind, until finally there were two small spots of light that drew closer and became the glistening car of Captain William Thompson.

Chapter 29

It felt like mid-afternoon, not morning. When her name was called for the third time, the voice broke into her sound sleep.

"Hey, you okay?"

Bill was standing over her with a cup of coffee in his hand. He looked worried.

"I thought . . . they were over. The nightmares, or whatever they are," she said softly. "God, Bill, when will they stop?" She shivered under the covers.

"You ever walk in your sleep before?"

She tried to remember, but only got as far as the voices from the night before.

"Is that what I was doing? No . . . never."

"Do you remember being out on the street?"

"The street?" She didn't know what he meant. She rubbed her eyes. That was it, her mind, her memory, they were finally going.

Bill reached down and turned the cover back, revealing her left arm. It was covered with scratches.

"I did that . . . and I don't remember?"

"Last night you said something about Stephen calling you. You were running to get away from it."

More of it came back. "It wasn't a dream, but it wasn't real, either. Stephen needed me, he was crying for me from all over the house. I felt him there, I swear I did."

Bill nodded tenderly. "Of course it was a dream. Here, take a sip." He gave her a steaming cup.

As she drank, she noticed the bed was soaked. Bill told her she'd been in the rain and insisted on going to bed without changing.

"Why were you there last night? How could you have known?"

"I didn't. It was partly because I thought the black-out might spook you," he turned shy, "and possibly because I felt like seeing you."

She smiled limply. "Just *possibly?*"

Joni fell silent for a while, thinking about what had happened during the night. Then she turned to him again.

"A long time ago, in your office, I asked you if you thought I was crazy. I think right now I need very much to hear that you still think I'm not."

"Okay, ask me."

. "Do you think I'm crazy?"

"Nope. I think I am."

"What are you talking about?"

"Crazy for leaving you alone in this depressing house all these nights."

She studied his face for a long time, that warm, strong face that she could now read so well. Then she knew she was ready, and they kissed with a yearning they'd both held in check for so long. Later they held each other without moving, and when they finally separated, Bill pushed her away and held her at arm's length.

His face was full of information, and she sat up in the bed.

"I should have known. You found out something!"

He nodded. "It's just happened again."

"Another Jewish baby?"

"More than that. The surveillance I set up at the cemeteries has turned up something. As of this week, the guys had already located a lot more graves, and all this time I've been trying the legal channels. It's gone so slowly because of the secrecy we needed, but this morning we finally found a judge who was willing to sign the court orders without telling the parents."

"What made him go along with you?"

"Remember Stewie Shapiro, my friend from Newark? Judge Knowles remembers him, too. His brother used to be a member of the gang that accidentally killed him. When I reminded him, we had the basis of an understanding about the leniency of the law."

"Still pretty gutsy of him, considering."

"Anyway, the graves were located by then, so once the court orders were signed, the digging started. Scarpone still doesn't know."

"And what did they find?"

"Of the twenty-one infants buried in the last year and a half, a number of Jewish ones were no longer in their graves. Only the Jewish ones."

"How many?" she asked, quickly propping herself up on the bed.

There was no way to cushion the blow.

"Sixteen," he said mournfully. "Nine boys, seven girls."

Book IV

Chapter 30

It was pouring when Joni woke up. Her first thought was that in two more days it would be all over, one way or the other. And there was nothing she could do that would make a difference.

Joni spent much of the morning surveying the household, something she hadn't done in earnest since the day everything changed. What she found was random disorder and chaos, and so she began to take stock of all that needed to be done.

A little after three in the afternoon, she was startled by a loud crash in the entrance foyer. The door burst open and Bill charged into her home without knocking. Without any greeting, he launched into a new disclosure and she had to ask him to start over again.

"Okay," he said breathlessly, "first, remember Roth Drug, the company I asked you about?"

She did.

"Two more people connected to them had SIDS deaths in the family, though not the immediate family."

"It can't be a coincidence now."

"I guessed it was some kind of vendetta, but I don't see how the other ones had anything to do with it. The occupations of the fathers are too diverse, their ages, everything. So far there's nothing that connects all of them except the religion."

She shrugged.

"But here it is, what we've been waiting for the most. Two cases of SIDS have just been reported within a twelve-hour period, both Jewish."

Joni sat up on the sofa. It was the break they both needed and feared at the same time.

"The names are Levinson and Gordon, and both are within our control area. Schecter called me at headquarters."

"How did he find out before you did?"

"He's set up his own relay system throughout the state, specially selected friends and colleagues call in when they hear about the death of a Jewish baby. Well, he got his first two calls today. He was nearly off the wall, and I can't guarantee he'll stick to his Wednesday deadline any more."

"Are the board members likely to break the silence?"

"They don't know about the two new cases. He's deciding whether to tell them."

"So what do we do now, assuming Schecter can hold out till Wednesday?"

"I'm not sure, but if what the grave diggers told us was true, the robbers will probably go after the bodies quickly. At least, we have to assume that's true and sit there until they show up. Or until Schecter cracks. But at least if he sticks to Wednesday, we have a chance."

"When are the burials?"

"Well, faithful to Jewish law, they're both scheduled

to be buried tomorrow, so our problem is which to cover. Two different cemeteries, plus either of the infants might be a victim, or both. If it's both, of course, it doesn't matter."

"Maybe Scarpone would help us cover one?"

"Already checked. I haven't been keeping him too up-to-date on the case for obvious reasons, but it's gotten so big I had to tell him we suspected there would soon be two more robberies. When he asked how I knew, I lied and told him it was a phone tip. Now he's nervous enough to do something just so he won't look bad, in case something happens. He said he'd back me up on whichever cemetery I decided to cover, but he won't send anyone else to the other one because he doesn't want word to get out unless he's there to verify it. He's coming himself."

She shook her head in contempt.

"How can we take a chance on leaving one unguarded?"

"I think I figured that out. Just listen to this. The father of one of the babies, Gordon, claims to have found a footprint in the garden he raked only an hour earlier. A cop on the scene thinks it was Mr. Gordon's own print, since it's roughly the same size foot. Mr. Gordon is considering an autopsy. Meanwhile, his wife is crazy with grief and her doctor is recommending against it for her sake. As of now, I have to lean to the one with the suspicious father, but I'll keep working on it until tomorrow night. I have to go to the right one or I might blow it."

"*We've* got to go to the right one," she corrected, "and by the way, try to find out the ages of both babies. I have an idea."

He just looked at her. "All right, but don't think I didn't hear you say *we*. I hope you're not—"

"Anything else I can do?" she asked quickly, cutting him off deliberately.

"Yeah. Fix me a drink, something strong enough to make me sleep so long I can do without it tomorrow night."

"Enough for *us* to do without it tomorrow," she added, and scooted to the liquor cabinet.

Chapter 31

Both burials were earlier that afternoon in distant cemeteries, the one for the Gordon baby was the furthest away in a town near the New York State line. Bill watched the Gordon burial from a distance, and saw no one who looked suspicious. He took note of the exact location of the grave. By the time he reported back to Joni, however, their decision was much easier.

"The footprint was too shallow for identification," he said. He'd found that out late in the day at the precinct. "And Mr. Gordon has been persuaded to cool his suspicions. Just like in your case, the medical examiner has put down 'pneumonitis,' and there won't be any autopsy."

"What about the ages of the babies?" Joni asked impatiently.

"Got that too. Levinson's baby was just four months and the Gordon's turned out to be a little over seven. Why did you want to know?"

Joni lit up at the news.

"Because that just told us which cemetery to go to. Don't you see! SIDS is common under six months and rare over six. The Gordon baby is questionable as a SIDS case, but Levinson's is normal. That's what made it so hard for me to tell about Stephen, he was right at the six-month cutoff."

"I never knew that, all this time."

"I wouldn't have either, if I hadn't been *hysterical* enough to do the research with Amaloff."

"Well, that just about clinches it, but I wasn't going to take chances, anyway. I've asked one of the guys at the precinct to stake out the other cemetery, and I won't call him off, but I do feel better about where we're going."

There was little else to do then but wait for sunset, since night was the undoubted time the ghouls would show up, if they were going to. Sunset came very fast.

8:30 P.M.

By the time the cemetery was visible in the distance, the sun had already set and a mist blanketed the lowest portions of the ground. Close up, the burial ground was shrouded in gloom and appeared old and not well cared for. It was on a hill on the outskirts of a working-class area.

Bill slowed the car to a crawl and asked Joni to watch for Perry Street, but the signs, where there were signs, were difficult to read. Finally she shouted the name and he quickly pulled off the road.

"Damn! Scarpone was supposed to meet us here," Bill said, thumping the steering wheel. He squinted, trying to penetrate through the fog, but visibility was poor.

"I wonder what Schecter is thinking and doing right about now," Joni said.

There was almost no daylight left when a horn sounded one short blast right behind them. It had come so close without being heard that it startled them, and they spun around to see a white car with Captain Scarpone at the wheel.

"Jesus, why didn't he bring a marching band?" Bill snapped. "He gets here a half hour late and the first thing he does is blow our cover."

"At least he came."

Bill rolled down the window to motion and the senior captain left his car, sauntered over to theirs, and got in.

"So this is where it all ends, eh, Thompson?"

Bill checked himself, with difficulty.

"Maybe, but we've got this one chance. My guess is the body buried here today is going to be stolen like the others. I'm betting it'll happen sometime before dawn."

"Sounds like a long shot."

"We know the robberies can take place within a few hours of burial, at least that's how it happened in Mrs. Lawrence's case. There was no way of telling with the others, except that common sense says it would be pretty quick. They probably want the bodies intact."

"What makes you sure there's more than one?"

"It just feels like too big an operation for one person."

Scarpone looked at her, then him. "I think it's pretty farfetched, but I suppose you figure any time after dark?"

"They'd have to be stupid to do it in daylight, even here, and they're not stupid."

"Terrific," Scarpone moaned. "So we just sit around all night in the middle of nowhere, waiting to bust these ghouls of yours, is that it?"

Bill swung an arm over the back of the seat, his dark eyes flashing. "Look, why don't we put this personal war of ours aside for a while and work together? We might get lucky and break this thing."

"I'm here, aren't I?"

Joni kept herself from joining in. She felt uncomfortable being trapped in their ongoing dispute, just as she had been the first time, in Scarpone's office.

"Why this cemetery?"

"The parents wanted an exclusively Jewish cemetery, and this is the only one in the area."

"Jewish? What's Jewish got to do with it? What the hell are you talking about now?"

Bill caught her out of the corner of his eyes. "I haven't told him about that part yet," he muttered.

"What part?"

"Turns out that almost all the robbed graves we found in our area were Jewish babies. For whatever sick reason, someone only wants the bodies of Jewish babies—and is probably turning them into bodies to get them."

"You mean they're being murdered? Are you crazy!"

For the first time, as all the evidence was laid out, Scarpone became truly shaken. He gave up on a cigar stub that wouldn't light and cursed. "I don't believe it. Sixteen more Jewish kids? What about Mrs. Lawrence here? She started this whole thing, didn't she?"

"She isn't Jewish, if that's what you're driving at, but they probably thought her baby was." He looked at Joni. The next piece of unlikely information was about to be released.

"I recently found out my husband *was* Jewish. His father changed his name years ago. My husband knew it all along, and never told me, but he did put it down on the birth certificate as Jewish."

"You know," Scarpone was shaking his head back and forth, "the more I hear about this, the loonier I think you both are. I'll tell you one thing, if you keep going with this Jewish angle and you're wrong, the citizens of our town are going to riot." He turned to gaze out the window. "And they'll hang me right along with you, goddamit!"

When he finished, Scarpone peered out the window at the dreary landscape, then turned back, his mood more cooperative.

"All right, level with me. How much of this is legit? What's the chance you're really onto something here?"

"Pretty good. There's a Jewish aid group in Trenton that keeps records on all families in New Jersey, and when I called them they confirmed an increase in Jewish infant deaths in the state. They were going to put in the alarm themselves, until I convinced them to hold off. Tomorrow is their deadline."

"Why didn't you tell me this before?"

"You would have told me I was crazy . . . like you just did before."

"Christ!"

"Anyway, all this time we've been waiting, and now two more Jewish babies have died. I managed to get some coverage on the other one, and we're here."

"And what if they turn out to be false alarms?"

"We lose a night's sleep, but at least we tried."

Scarpone took a deep drag on his unlit cigar butt. "Well, since you're determined to carry this out, there's something else you might as well know. Even before Mrs. Lawrence came into it, there were a few other grave robbings like the one you stumbled onto."

"A *few* others?"

"They came in on a memo from State, but the locations were out of this jurisdiction. There'd been

about a half-dozen across the area and up into Connecticut. Now that you mention it, I recall some of the
names were Jewish-sounding."

Bill was irate. "You waited all this time to tell us?
When you could have saved us weeks?"

"Use your head, Thompson. There was no way to
connect it till you just gave me the Jewish angle." He
waited and continued, more reserved. "While we're at
it, there was another one in Paramus, about a week
ago. You didn't hear or read about it, because the
parents asked to keep it quiet. They'd suffered enough
and didn't want it to go any further."

"Jesus, suppose that was one of them? What was the
name?"

"Corwin, Joel, and the reason the department found
out was because it rained the night of the burial and the
next morning a lot of dirt washed away. They had to do
the whole thing over again, and when they lifted the
coffin it seemed too light."

Bill yanked at the door handle with a burst of energy.
"We'd better get going, it's already dark. You coming?"

"Assuming somebody shows, you gonna try to take
them?"

"Not unless I have to. I'll try to tail them, to see what
they do with the body. It should lead us to anybody else
who's connected."

Scarpone hesitated and turned to the landscape
again.

"For starters, I think I can do more back at headquarters. Between now and tomorrow we are going to
have a bitch of a story to tell, and someone has to
develop a plan to deal with the media and town council.
That's my job." He turned to Joni, as if she would be
easier to convince. "Besides, there's more chance three
of us will be spotted. In fact, if you take my advice,

Mrs. Lawrence should return with me until I can get more men."

"I'll go along with that."

"Thanks, but no," Joni said definitely. "We've come this far together. Why can't you call for the others?"

"They'd have to be brought," Bill answered in his superior's defense. "Too hard to find their way in the dark, plus they'd risk being seen. And for all we know, the police radio is being monitored."

"Two by two?" Scarpone suggested.

"That ought to do it. Assuming it comes off, you'll have to pick us up visually on the way out. That might be a problem."

Scarpone acknowledged and left the car with a grunt.

When he was out of earshot, Joni's temper burst loose. "I still think he's trying to save his career more than catch anybody."

"Heck of a guy, huh?"

He started the engine and pulled the car into the center of the road. Reversing, he backed it to the curb, then pushed his foot down hard, and the vehicle climbed the obstacle and fit itself into a narrow opening in the tight pattern of trees.

When they were out and climbing toward the ghostly outlines that marked the edge of the cemetery, Bill was scowling.

"I think maybe Scarpone's just plain scared of cemeteries at night."

Joni pressed herself closer to him in the hushed darkness. "Why should he be different?"

Joni felt very vulnerable as she left the relative security of the car and set out for the gravesite. The cemetery seemed like a maze. Instead of getting too close to the Gordon grave, Bill suggested they find a hiding place that offered a good view, preferably on high ground.

Cautiously, they skirted the oldest part of the cemetery, littered by tombstones that had not received care for years. Many of the monuments were canted to one side, as though a force from beneath were pulling them down. Erosion had smoothed the hard edges, until differences between them were all but obliterated. One monument towered above the rest in the old Jewish cemetery. Atop its twin spires were a Star of David *and* a crucifix, clearly an exception to the rule of exclusivity.

The wind had picked up and was driving the mist deep into their clothing. Too late, Bill noticed Joni was not well-clad for the dank night and that she had begun shivering. He remembered a raincoat he kept in the car, and offered to go back for it, but she convinced him not to because of the lateness. She raised the collar of her poplin jacket around her neck and urged him to continue. It was one of several decisions she would regret before the night was over.

A while later, they found a location that offered the needed cover and visibility and they made their way tediously to the highest point on the forty-or-so-acre tract. After making sure they were the first to arrive, they cleared a space under a massive, half-dead elm.

Huddled there, receiving some protection from the elements, the wait began. It was just after nine-thirty.

During the hours that followed, both of them became

chilled to the bone. The mist turned into a soft rain, and though the thick leaves offered some shelter, the night was so uncomfortable they were forced to get up and move around from time to time.

Joni and Bill tried to ignore the sounds issuing from nearby thickets. They were made by things of unimaginable shape and intent. One night creature in particular rustled about for almost an hour, and once it seemed to be moving directly for them. At that moment, Joni clutched Bill for all the daddy he had in him.

Shut off from the sights and sounds of the familiar world, Joni felt the desolation down to her bones. It was easy for her to imagine how their ancestors must have felt when they peered into the blackness and wondered what it was all about, the mystery even greater than her personal one, which connected all of humanity through all of time.

It was impossible, too, not to think about Stephen. During the tedious waiting, she tried to remember how he looked in his happy moments, when he'd gaze up at her from his crib and break into a cherubic smile. How often she'd seen him that way when they were alone in the nursery and the world outside was a million miles away. But now, each time the picture came into focus his expression always turned frightened, and she had to force the image from her mind. Wherever his spirit was, she thought, it couldn't be any lonelier than she was.

She'd been rubbing her arms during the reverie, and when she was back in the present she recognized the sensation. It was an aching for him, the need she felt to hold Stephen and be complete. The thought made her colder still, and she moved even closer to Bill. Later a tune began to play over and over in her mind. She'd only heard it once or twice, but never forgot it. *Don't know how I came here, don't know where I'm bound;*

lost among a million stars, no hope of being found. It seemed to sum up her feelings about everything. *Lost* was the word that said it. Everyone was lost, with no one to find them.

"I can't help thinking that Stephen is with me, somehow, somewhere," she said to Bill. They were sitting close together on the ground. "In a way, I don't think I've ever really lost touch with him; it's as though he's still part of my consciousness, still part of the universe. In a way that death hasn't ended."

Her words touched him, and he enclosed her in his arms. She wept. Her spirit ached for her lost son and for a world full of lost children everywhere. As they held each other, she knew she had never felt closer to another person nor as removed from all humanity, and for a while she could feel his breath coming in short bursts, too.

Chapter 32

The hours passed at a crawl, and by early morning it began to look as though their last hope had fled. A light rain had stopped, and the ground fog gradually lifted to reveal a partly cloudy sky boasting a yellow half-moon. The clearing was accompanied by a warm breeze that worked on their soggy clothing. Now, except for the wooded area directly behind them, there was no part of the landscape which they couldn't observe from their position.

But there was nothing to be seen.

Joni had dozed at least once that she could remember, and Bill had just closed his eyes in an unspoken changing of the guard. Leaving him to his rest, she stood quietly, bracing herself against the tree. It felt good to be upright, and she arched her back until her cramped muscles felt looser. The smell of soil and decay were strong.

When she heard the noise, she didn't have time to

229

alert him. Standing there immobile in the silence, she could clearly identify something creeping toward them in the black woods. It sounded large, bigger than a dog. The steps were slow and human as the approaching creature crashed through old leaves and branches. The footfalls came closer, until moments later the intruder wasn't any more than a few yards away.

Slowly getting to her feet, Joni was barely able to make out a shape. It was a man, very tall but not impressively big. Holding her breath, she edged closer to Bill. He was still sleeping, but now the stranger was too close for her to risk a noisy awakening.

The man in the woods had not chosen the nearby path, but had taken another route through the trees. They were lucky he had; they were sprawled across the only path.

When the intruder came to a stop, he was so near it was almost certain he'd stumble over them. Slowly Joni lowered herself to the ground, hardly daring to breathe. The intruder took one more step and was so close she could have reached out and grasped him by the ankles. Then, at the last possible moment, he struck out in a new direction and went past. Only the darkness had masked their presence. But she'd seen the ghoulish face. It had been devoid of emotion. In his wake, a cold burst of air made her cringe and she saw that a large rifle was slung over his shoulder. He looked like a hunter, and maybe he was.

When the sounds of his movement receded into the distance, she felt safer and turned to Bill. Surprisingly, he was already kneeling, his pistol trained in the direction of the figure who had come and gone.

"One of *them?*"

"Not one of ours." He got to his feet, leaving the gun unholstered. "Stay here," he whispered.

She looked at her surroundings and tried to imagine remaining. "Wrong!" she said clearly.

Unable to convince her, Bill ordered her to keep low, and took the lead. Painstakingly, they moved into the woods. If he were one of them, he would lead them where they wanted to go.

As though it were a scene from a 1930s horror movie, they darted from one tombstone to another, the only available cover. After a short distance, one of the old mausoleums that dotted the decaying landscape loomed ahead.

"In there?" Joni whispered. Her imagination supplied frightening visions of the inside of the crypt.

"It's possible."

She cringed. "I don't know how much more of this I can take."

He brushed back her hair. His hands were rough and covered with bits of soil and leaves. "If you want to stay you can, but this time I think you're safer with me."

She looked at the decrepit building again. Everything about it said death. First it had housed the dead, then had itself begun to die. Eventually it would collapse of its own weight, to become part of the ground, another broken, decomposing skeleton.

With effort, she followed him to the crumbling entrance and, after listening carefully, he stepped through the opening. A moment later she followed.

The interior of the mausoleum was in better condition than the outside. A light was coming from somewhere, and they could see that a second story had been dug beneath the first. Between the two levels, steps had been laid in the mortar and a staircase built into the wall itself. Then there were some rustling noises below and a light suddenly flickered.

"Someone's down there," she said.

He signaled her to be silent and crept toward the top of the stairs, but when she started to follow, something reached for her thigh and wouldn't let go. With a gasp, she managed to tear loose and almost fell. Like two statues, they listened. The noises below came again. Bill asked in a whisper what had happened.

"My dress got caught on the stone." The coarse cement on the wall had snagged it and rubbed against her skin. It stung. "Forget it, I'm okay."

He slowly inched down the stairs. About two-thirds of the way, he leaned forward and glimpsed the bottom floor, and saw him. Bill's finger tightened on the trigger of his drawn revolver.

It was a man. At first glance, it was like staring into the face of a cadaverous Viking god. He was huge, one of the largest men Bill had ever seen. His eyes were alive and fixed in deep, wrinkled sockets. In the uneven light it was hard to make out his manner of dress, which had been darkened by neglect. A bulky coat bled into loose-fitting trousers and they were joined together by a rope belt. Massive hands protruded from sleeves which ended in ragged fringe.

The beard deified the image. It was biblical. The man looked more like a prophet than the old hobo who looked up and beamed with friendliness.

A quick scan of the basement showed there was no one else around.

When Joni came all the way down, the apparition took away her breath, but Bill's hand calmed her.

The hobo was crouching, brewing coffee on a can of blue-flaming Sterno. Without showing evident concern over his uninvited guests, he went back to his chore and became oblivious to them.

Cautiously, the two of them crept down the stone stairs and became part of the underground vault. On the far wall, behind the hobo, were sleeping quarters, two hooks in the mortar and a filthy, ripped hammock which hung too closely to the wall. Joni found herself wondering whether he simply endured the cold bed partner or needed a wall for his sense of well-being. Near the hammock, a torn calendar with a naked woman read 1962. It was cold and humid, and the place reeked of old coffee grounds.

"Does he live here in the winter?" she asked, as much to relieve the tension as anything.

"Probably has a mausoleum in Florida," Bill whispered back.

Holding out the saucepan, the old bum picked up a broken piece of crockery, dipped it in a pail of water for cleaning and abruptly turned and offered it to Joni.

"You want some?" Bill asked.

"Maybe we shouldn't hurt his feelings."

"At this temperature, how could he have any?"

Reluctantly, they both took a cup of the steaming brown soup. Whether it was the long damp night or their chilling thoughts that needed warming, the coffee tasted decent.

After they were seated on milk cartons, Bill turned to their host. "We're looking for someone, a man you might have seen around here."

There was no response, just that same smile that never left his lips. It was a far cry from the face that almost stumbled on them by the tree.

"Do you know who he is? The one who comes in from the woods?"

For a few seconds the hobo's face became serious, then, abruptly, it went moronic.

"Rock-a-bye baby, rock-a-bye baby."

The moment he began chanting, Joni felt for Bill's arm. "You think he's one of them? A lookout?"

The hobo heard her and became angry, but instead of moving toward them he reached for his head as though in pain. When he parted a clump of matted hair, a long bloody scab appeared and Bill leaned in to examine it. Quickly the hobo drew back, and when he quieted he went back to his coffee and began humming some tune that sounded like a lullaby.

"You think he fell?" she asked.

"No. I've seen a lot of wounds like that one. Made by bullets."

"Shot?"

"Looks like it, and I'd say it was recent." Bill's eyes were working. "If it was within the past day or so, it's a good bet it was done around here. Maybe he was attacked or surprised by someone—the man in the woods."

The incantation stopped and, before they knew what was happening, the hobo covered the Sterno can with his ape's hand. In a second, they were thrown into darkness and when Joni reached for Bill she could feel his hand going for the pistol. Then there were footsteps on the stairs behind them, and they were alone except for an echoing voice.

"*. . . down will come Adam, cradle and all . . .*"

There were a few more steps, then hideous laughter. He was at the top of the stairs.

"Adam? Adam Gordon?" Bill whispered.

"How would he know?"

"Maybe they've been here before and he saw what they did."

They groped their way to the stairs and climbed up in time to learn there was a front door and that it was slowly being pushed shut. The rasping sound of cement on cement echoed in the cold chamber.

"He's sealing us in," Joni rasped. The thought of

never getting out of the place was terrifying. Her words continued to ricochet off the walls, decaying somewhere in the level below.

When they were in total darkness, they made their way slowly to the entrance and pressed against the weight of the stone, but it did not yield even to their combined effort.

"He must have amazing strength," Bill said.

"What'll we do?"

"Maybe there's another way out."

"Is there enough air in here?"

"Yeah, I think so."

"What if there isn't?"

He didn't answer.

They both fell silent for a few minutes, until a scraping noise came from the other side of the room. Suddenly a match flared and touched a candle. The chamber brightened, and they heard the mindless laughter of a presence that had been with them all the while.

The hobo was at the back wall, and his fingers were probing a portion of the crumbling material, which fell away like sand. He worked steadily, ignoring them, and when he'd finished he picked up the candle and blew it out.

"I should have jumped him when I had the chance."

"Not if you ever want to get that door open again."

There was a new sound, less intense. After it ended, a rectangular shaft of dim light entered the room, partially silhouetting the hobo. He had removed a section of wall, evidently not for the first time, and was excitedly motioning for them to join him at the newly formed window. Cautiously, they approached. It was just wide enough for two people to look through, three if one stood behind the others.

It was like peering out of one's own grave. The view offered a panorama of the cemetery and, as with their earlier hiding place, they were on high ground.

The hobo made the discovery first.

To the right of center, less than twenty-five yards away, they could see two figures against the blue and black sky. The closer one was working. A short time later, a third appeared from out of the woods. He could have been the tall and spidery man Joni had seen before.

"What now?" she whispered.

"Wait to see if any more show up, then go in for a closer look. But the first time I can park you in a safe place, you stay put, understand?"

She agreed, knowing that this time she'd obey the order.

One of the people on the horizon became more animated. He had started to dig, and in a while he became slightly lower on the horizon.

Pointing to the doorway, Bill addressed the grizzly man. "We want to go out. Do you understand?"

Either he didn't get it or didn't want to.

Bill tried again, this time pointing to himself, then Joni. He pantomimed their leaving and the way they would watch the graverobbers. As he finally made their purpose clear, the hobo quickly became fearful and cowered against the wall.

"Okay, then, just her and me." He was trying to calm him. "You stay here."

Joni repeated Bill's instruction, and her voice seemed to have a soothing effect. With more coaxing, the hobo finally went to the door and, with further urging, they got him to pry it open. His strength was tremendous, and the slab gave way.

Finally the opening was wide enough to slip through,

but once they did, the hobo stayed inside. Joni turned back to see him cringing against the same wall as before.

"Maybe if we knew what he does, we'd stay in there, too," she said.

3:05 A.M.

The Planner arrived at the grave alone and in the customary dark clothing. The knowledge that others had been there earlier was reassuring. By now, one of them would have already inspected the area on foot before bringing the van to the fresh gravesite. Even though there was almost no chance anyone would be in the cemetery during the early morning hours, it was the most basic precaution.

Within minutes, the familiar gaunt agent arrived and wordlessly set about his manual chores. The Planner checked the site again to make certain there had been no error and entered the van. Now the contents could be readied.

The vehicle had been turned into a mobile laboratory. The Planner turned on the ultraviolet lamps, creating a sterile environment. Then the container itself was prepped, washed down with alcohol, and sealed against any last-minute contamination. This took less than ten minutes, and with nothing left to do until the exhumation was complete the Planner's mind wandered. Of all the cases, this one had been the most rewarding. It was the one during which the drug had been perfected, and at that moment complete retribution had become possible. Now no one would be spared the wrath of a fitting vengeance, not Jew or Christian.

Staring out into the bleak but familiar landscape, the

*Planner thought about the beginning. The number se-
lected for punishment had grown as swiftly as they were
identified. The first targets had been the most obvious
ones, those who had actually exposed themselves as
being guilty. And, then there had been the unique one,
the one who had performed the greatest evil. She and her
small being had been the most satisfying, even though
the waiting had almost driven the Planner insane.*

*A look of completion came over the Planner's face,
and it did not disappear until there was a shout from one
of the men. The digging was almost at an end.*

The terrain was becoming familiar, and the sky had
cleared. Moonlight now lit the way, but the quiet was
working against them. Any sound would surely carry
into the countryside. Bill and Joni stayed close to the
ground, putting a fresh coat of dew on their clothing
and using the shadows of larger monuments until they
were close enough to hear the muffled exchanges.
Then, looking for cover, Bill spotted a pile of loose
rubble between two adjacent gravestones and they
squeezed down behind it.

Not far from the ghoul who was working, they saw
the van, as one of the men got out and came to the
grave to inspect it. All three were dressed in dark
overalls and caps that fitted tightly. It was easy to see
they were highly organized.

They worked silently as the mound of dirt grew. The
tall man stood guard, continuously scanning the area.
In the absence of other sounds, the digging noises
became exaggerated. The *chcccks* of blade into soil
were regular and ominous, and the laborer's efforts
were rewarded a short time later when his shovel struck
a hard object and he yelled to the others.

When he did, Bill turned to the area that led back to
their car.

"What are you looking that way for?"

"Our escape route. They won't stick around once they get the body, and we have to be ready to move ahead of them."

When the last of the digging was over, the man in the pit threw away his shovel and called for assistance. The one from the van took a last look around and came to the open grave, shouting directions. Doing so, he began to put on gloves, the way a surgeon would, holding his hands skyward.

"For handling the remains?" Joni asked, feeling disgusted.

"Looks like it."

Painstakingly, the other two ghouls raised their load out of the earth. When they had it clear of the ground, they moved quickly to their left and the leader reached for the casket to brush off the remaining soil. Then he unfastened the latch that sealed the box and raised the cover.

For a time, they stood solemnly over the exposed corpse, as quiet as their unseen observers. It was as though, for both sides, even the simplest movement would cause some unknown calamity. Although the two groups had come to the cemetery with opposite purposes, at that instant Joni sensed they might both be sharing a similar emotion.

Breaking the spell, the leader kneeled to touch the contents and said something to his accomplice, who handed him an attaché case. The business case was laid beside the coffin and opened, and the subordinate again backed away to become a nervous sentinel.

What happened next was a complete mystery. The leader worked inside the smaller box for several minutes and, although they could not see what he was doing, it seemed to require great care. No one spoke. When he was satisfied, one of the other men left the area and, a short time later, the van drove up to the grave.

Cautiously, the leader reached into the open casket and lifted up the body. His care could best be described as parental. He stood with the corpse and pivoted stiffly until facing the van, where the driver was busy inside.

As if in protest, one of the cadaver's arms came away from the body and spilled loosely to one side. The helper reached for it, but was warned off quickly, and the leader maneuvered the body into the smaller box. When the body was inside, he closed the lid on the container and took off his gloves.

The remaining tasks were performed without direction. The gravedigger planted the empty coffin back into the hole and filled the opening. The last step was to lay out the pieces of sod that had been saved in strips. It made Joni think of the flowers that had been trampled around Stephen's grave.

Unfortunately for them, only one worker took care of this chore, allowing the second guard to concentrate on his watch, because while he was straining for a better look, Bill leaned heavily into a pile of rubble. Suddenly a section broke away with a loud crash. The noise immediately alerted the sentry, who yelled a warning and sprawled into a prone position. Instantly, he produced a handgun and sighted it at the source of the disturbance. As though it had been rehearsed, the other worker hurried to the van, where the leader was already preparing to shut the sliding door.

"Damn it to hell! If he decides to check us out, I'm gonna have to shoot him," Bill whispered, "and that'll blow our chance of finding their hideout." He had his pistol trained on the skulking figure, who was moving directly at them.

Bill's hand went to her mouth as she was about to

answer. The guard was almost close enough to hear the exchange. He had pinpointed the sound and locked in as though he had radar. Within seconds he'd be upon them.

Steadying his weapon on the tombstone, Bill waited for the last possible moment. He was stoic, calculating. Then, before the gunman could move closer, there was a sudden disturbance from their left. Suddenly a huge creature was charging at the guard from out of the darkness. The beast was on the guard before he could turn and aim, and the ghoul fired a wild shot as he was knocked onto his back. The attacker let out a victorious howl that pierced the night, but instead of using his advantage to finish the man, he continued on into the heart of the cemetery, picking his way expertly through the labyrinth of markers.

"The hobo!" Joni exclaimed. "It must be him."

The gunman picked up his weapon, stood and pointed at the quickly receding figure. "Get that old bastard," he yelled, taking chase. "Over there." He never looked back toward his original destination.

As the guard ran off, Bill grabbed Joni and began a retreat to the car. Moving low, they ran for about a minute before she pulled up short to look back and caught a last glimpse of their benefactor. He was running wildly, his long hair dancing in the moonlight, striking out in the night like the free forest creature he was. He raced into the darkness, laughing like an insane man.

As they continued on, the ravings became muffled. Then a shot rang out and another from a different direction. There were three more shots in quick succession, and the laughter ended.

"He did it for us," she insisted, as soon as they arrived back at the car, out of breath. "I know he did."

"Don't be so sure. He was weird enough to do it on a whim, or for revenge against the one who shot him. The guy with the gun recognized him, right?"

"Then why did he keep going?"

Bill had no answer.

"And why did he keep shouting after he had gotten away?"

"Would it make you feel better to know he sacrificed himself for us?"

When she thought about it, Bill was right. It was less painful to believe the hobo was simply insane, but before she could dwell on it any more they heard the van coming.

Chapter 33

There was only one grave robber in the front seat, and he drove by slowly, with the headlights out. After he passed, Bill waited a long time before turning on the ignition, so long, Joni thought, that they'd lost their chance to follow in the dark.

As they waited under the trees, a second car emerged from the same direction, appearing out of the night as if by magic. When it went by, the driver had his arm out the window, and in his hand was the familiar pistol. Luckily, the sound of his engine masked the sound of theirs.

"Is that why you held off?" she asked as soon as she could feel her heart beating again.

"I'd have done the same thing in their place. I only hope if Scarpone's backup is around they don't mistake their second car for us."

"Got a feeling you won't have to worry about it," she added sarcastically.

She could feel Bill's urgency, but he waited a short while longer anyway. Finally they left the camouflage

without putting on the headlights. Once on the road
they soon caught a glimpse of the van, far ahead. They
remained well behind them as the narrow country road
meandered through the forest, cutting off visual contact
at times, but the van was traveling under thirty and it
was never more than a few seconds before it came into
sight again. More disturbing was the continuing absence of the men Scarpone had promised.

There were several possible explanations for the
missing police backup, the first being that they *were*
behind them and adept at concealment—not very likely. Or they could have been sent but become lost in the
unfamiliar surroundings, still stuck out at the cemetery.
The most obvious reason was Scarpone had never sent
them in the first place, but it was hard to accept that in a
life or death situation they'd been abandoned because
of politics. Then there was the notion that if anyone
could so such a thing, it would be Scarpone.

When the van reached Interstate 80, it took the local
lane instead of the express, which would have meant a
trip all the way to the George Washington Bridge and
New York City. It was a good guess that their destination was somewhere nearby.

The lighting on the Interstate was notoriously poor,
but in this instance it worked for them by allowing them
to stay fairly close. They'd driven almost ten miles
when all at once the gang's car swerved to the right lane
for a turnoff. Wherever they were being taken, it
wouldn't be long before they found out.

Joni looked at the two-way radio.

"Forget it," Bill said, guessing her thought.

"What about sending out a message on a CB chan-
nel? Get someone to relay a call for help." She waved
off his answer. "Yeah, I know, they could be monitoring. So we go after them ourselves? The two of us?

Never mind if there's a dozen more waiting when we get there?"

"Yeah, go be a cop in a quiet suburban town."

The car left the highway at a sign marked Valley Road. Just before they turned, they slowed to allow a longer interval between the vehicles. If the gang believed they were being followed, Bill explained, this would be the logical time to check. At this hour in the morning, with virtually no traffic, anyone who took the same turn would be suspect.

Once off the main road, the streets were deserted and they cautiously reduced their speed. Before long, they found themselves on a brighter, narrower local road and the van, together with its rear guard, had completely vanished.

Bill quickly pulled off the street.

"Either they took off faster than we thought, or they're hiding out somewhere around here."

"Suppose they did see us?"

"Don't get paranoid. We'll just wait a few seconds."

"I wouldn't put it past them." She looked ahead to where the road curved to the right. The thick trees hung over the emptiness like stage curtains.

After an interminable wait Bill announced, "We gotta do something."

"I say go."

He turned it over in his mind again, his knee bouncing nervously.

"No, I think we sit it out. If they're not hiding, we've already lost them, but they would've had to go like hell, and that's a risk I don't think they'd take. There aren't many cops around, but still . . ."

Joni had become aware of conflicting tides within herself. One was the hope that the ghouls were far away and would never be seen or heard again, but another feeling was calling for revenge and a more just finality to their search.

Uncertain, they waited. In these few moments of relative calm, she looked at their surroundings and saw the neat little houses of the community. They appeared to have grown there, something organic that was planted and took shape from seed. She was touched by the innocence of the people living within the sleepy dwellings, maybe because she knew more about their vulnerability than they did.

Finally, their caution was rewarded by a flash of light about a block down the road. A solitary car separated itself from the shadows and backed onto the street.

"Guess who?" Bill said triumphantly.

The car kept moving until it turned and faced them, and the driver turned on his bright lights. A few seconds later, another beam, from a spotlight, lit up the pavement, working its way forward. Joni was unprepared when Bill pushed her down roughly to the level of the dashboard, but after the spotlight played on their windshield it continued on until they were again in shadow. Then she understood.

Once the trailing car turned off its lights, it took off with a screech of tires, and Bill put their car in gear and moved forward. The area was familiar. They were on a road that extended north through a number of small towns that eventually led to Edgewood. They next slowed down in a small village that was quiet even during the day. It only had two or three gas stations, some stores and a bank. It did have one other attraction of note, Joni remembered.

"The King Arthur Theater?"

Bill stopped directly in front of the landmark. If that was their hideout, he hadn't expected it either.

"So this explains it," he said.

"Explains what?"

"This place was shut down for a year or so. It was about to be torn down when a group of investors stepped in and saved it. Everyone thought they planned to build an indoor sports club, tennis or something, but it was rumored they had trouble raising the money."

"Ever find out who was behind it?"

"Uh, uh. Nobody ever cared to, until now." He studied the building. "Not bad. So big it's inconspicuous."

"Maybe it's one of the houses behind it."

"I'll bet on the theater. It's safer than a house, away from neighbors who might hear something in the middle of the night and call the police."

For a while he listened intently.

"Ready to go to the movies?"

After they left the car, they followed the dark alley that led to the back of the theater. The large building didn't have a parking lot, and there was no van in sight, but when they got to the back entrance, they were in time to see a door being pulled shut from within.

Again Joni suggested calling for help, but Bill quickly dismissed it. Surprise was their only weapon, an advantage that would be reduced by time and the number of people.

The ease of entry on the first floor was offset by the risk of a guard, so Bill went looking for another way in. As they crept along the edge of the old building, Joni felt eyes watching, other unseen ghouls lurking in the alleys and behind every car. There was no hint of dawn yet. It was a night that gave the feeling morning would never come, that the dark—and those things that inhabited it—had permanently triumphed over light.

The dim streetlamps spread a cheerless pallor over the cracked masonry of the building's facade. The walls glowed a dingy, pale yellow, and at several places a carpet of sick-looking ivy clung like a tenacious parasite. The rear wall was a windowless plane, broken only by vents for air conditioning. The building next to the theater rose three stories higher and was studded with windows that looked down onto its roof.

"Business offices," Bill explained. "Loan companies, a real estate agency, some doctors."

"How do you know that?"

"Typical profile." He pointed to the entrance. "That's how we get into the theater."

"The door?"

"It's called breaking and entering. Stay here until you see me wave, then run like hell. I still think I'm crazy letting you come along."

"Only if you had a choice would you be crazy," she answered, although privately she found herself agreeing with him.

He crossed the space between the two buildings with surprising speed and, after he fumbled with the lock for a few seconds, the door opened. Disappearing inside, he quickly showed himself again and then motioned Joni forward. Though her legs were rubbery, she managed to duplicate the route he'd taken, and together they slipped into a musty entrance that led directly to a steep stairwell. It felt like the mausoleum.

The stairs provided no hiding places. There were no landings and only one office per floor, but the design gave reasonable assurance that no one would be able to surprise them.

At the third-story level, Bill paused and tried a door marked "Robert Norsworthy, D.D.S." It was locked, though the doorknob jiggled loosely. Taking out a tool that looked like a Swiss army knife, Bill selected a blade and probed the cylinder while Joni stood alert for any change in the shadows.

"Well, it worked before," he said after he met with failure. "Out of the way." He put his back against the inner wall of the staircase and his hands on the interior railing, but as soon as he lifted his foot and aimed it at the lock, she stopped him.

"You'll make too much noise. Give me your wallet."

"My what?"

She fished out one of his credit cards. "Try this."

It worked.

"That's what I like about you," he said, "you watch a lot of prime time."

Dr. Norsworthy's office was out of the Smithsonian, right down to the drilling apparatus, which looked absolutely medieval. The only window was located next to the patient's chair, and Bill went to it right away. One story below them was the roof of the King Arthur.

"That's where we're going."

"Big drop," she said, squeezing by him for a view.

"Me first, then we play catch."

The window gave under pressure. There were no locks on it, since it was inaccessible from the outside. Climbing out feet first, Bill hung from the ledge, let go, and fell to the roof without injury. He held out his arms, and Joni made the same leap in an act of blind faith. His hands broke her fall, his large, wonderful hands, as her sneakers landed with a jolt on the sticky tar roof.

The top of the theater was a flat expanse, broken only by a substantial skylight that rose above them. They approached on tiptoe to the edge of the glass and carefully looked in. But it was hopeless trying to make out anything. The glass was frosted to begin with, and years of accumulated dirt had made it completely opaque.

While deciding what to do, they heard a crash below, followed by an angry, high-pitched voice that chilled Joni to the core. Also, they could hear the faint sound of heavy objects being moved around.

Joni went behind the skylight, in hope of a clearer view, and found a door built into the glass. It was held shut by a hinge, but it was so eroded that Bill pried it off easily. After that they were looking down at an old wooden stairway, lighted by a single flickering bulb.

The steps didn't creak, but they moved carefully just the same. Downstairs, more than one person was shouting loudly. Judging from the volume, the grave robbers were still a distance away.

At the first landing, an old door fell back with a groan and they both froze to see if the noise had betrayed them.

"What do you see?"

Incredibly, the gang was gathered together on stage. The full curtain was in place, cutting them off from the rest of the theater. Evidently, there was no night watchman, at least not any more.

"There's some kind of catwalk over the stage. Pretty high."

"Will it support us?"

"Probably, there's a ton of crap on it already."

She poked her head over his shoulder. It was a narrow platform built close to the ceiling, with just enough room to stand. She drew a deep breath. "You still have your gun?"

He patted his shoulder, but she took no comfort from it.

Bill took the lead, moving a step at a time. When they were fully onto the scaffold, he signaled her to stop. So far it was holding their combined weight, but all at once, to her horror, she realized the entire span was swaying slightly. She saw the explanation overhead: the scafford was suspended by heavy ropes from the ceiling, not from below.

Cautiously, they went as far as they could until the path was blocked by an assortment of theatrical equipment, lights, sandbags and loose wood. Above to their left, metal boxes had been screwed to the wall next to the scaffold. Most of them were open, leaving banks of switches exposed, probably for lights around the cavernous theater. For the first time, Joni looked down and realized she was thirty or forty feet off the ground, and in light bright enough to be seen if they hung over the edge.

There were three of them, the same ones they'd seen at the cemetery, and it was evident they'd used the theater before. The stage had been converted into a medical room of some kind.

But the biggest shock of all was that one member of the crew was a woman. From above it was impossible to see her face, which was covered by a surgical mask. There was something else familiar about her, but Joni couldn't figure it out. She was off to one side, removing apparatus from a case, and was not involved in the dispute the others were having. Now and then she turned to check the progress of the two men, then returned to her work. One of the helpers was almost finished assembling a table made of wood crates with planks laid between, while the other stood ready with an armful of sheets. The woman was wearing a make-shift surgical gown, but underneath were the overalls they'd seen at the cemetery.

Bill studied the scene below. The stage was lighted by two large klieg units, directed at the center of the table from opposite sides. While they watched, both men disappeared off the platform and returned carrying the container they'd seen at the cemetery.

The woman nodded. It looked like she was the one in command, but whether she had planned the whole thing or was only carrying it out for someone else was impossible to know.

Their moves were precise and well-practiced. On the

woman's order, the men lifted the box, eased it onto the table, and opened it. The leader inspected the contents and was satisfied, and the shorter, more subservient helper reached inside, lifted the body clear, and put it on its back. When it was in position, he covered it with a sheet up to its neck. The spectacle was grizzly, and Joni struggled to remain detached. When she felt the pressure increase on her hand, she turned and realized Bill had been holding it all along. The scene unfolding below was having its effect on him, too.

But she quickly forgot about Bill, and even where she was. The woman was reaching for the body.

Chapter 34

Once more the Planner looked down at the inert form that lay on the makeshift table. A boy again, she noted with neither approval nor disdain. Most often they'd been male, even though sex had nothing to do with their selection.

It was a time for great care, for guarding against any unexpected danger. The betrayal by the more powerful agent had become known. He had been observed taking more of the Instrument than instructed and could no longer be trusted with the work. He would have to be dealt with.

The first of the precision Instruments fit neatly between two practiced fingers, and the Planner turned her head away so as not to confront the sightless eyes. The action was a foolish remnant of conscience, and she was always irritated with herself for the feeling.

That thought occupied her mind until the tall agent urged her to proceed. This body had arrived later than expected, held up for a trivial reason at the cemetery. And there was yet another body waiting.

With one hand the Planner reached for the cold flesh and pried the infant's head away from the table by the back of its neck. The still-weighty substance of the skull yielded to the pressure, and she brought the avenging Instrument closer, thinking: Blood for blood.

As the body was readied, it seemed obvious that the ghouls' purpose was dismemberment, but after a few more minutes passed, no butchering instruments were in evidence.

With a great deal of ceremony, the gangleader produced a large syringe and studiously inserted the long needle into a vial she held upside down against the light. Before long, a greenish liquid began to fill the chamber.

"I've seen this at the police lab," Bill whispered. "It's dye, to identify the organs."

Joni didn't pursue it any further. Her stomach was turning over.

Painstakingly, the woman finished transferring the liquid. When she had gotten all but a small amount from the bottle, she wrapped the original container carefully in a towel and gave her attention to the syringe. As she watched, Joni thought of the injections Stephen had been given in his short life, the inoculations that she, as his mother, had been grateful for. It made her wonder if the woman had ever been a mother.

The inanimate body lay on its back, its arms placed palms up at its sides. One man stood on each side of the table, watching as the Planner approached with the hypodermic held high. As the leader bent over the corpse, Joni let out a soft moan and Bill jerked around to caution her. The migraine had started again.

The infant was naked, and the woman leaned over it and pressed her face close to his. With her free hand spanning the rib cage, her fingers carefully traced the bone structure up the side of the chest toward the throat. Evidently, to command a better access point, she edged around the table until her body blocked their view of the upper torso. Soon after, she swung her other arm around, aimed the needle at some hidden point and lowered it.

Her head remained in place for almost a minute and, when she completed the operation, she held the syringe behind her so it could be taken away. Throughout the procedure, the more sinister guard paced around the stage watchfully.

With one hand now visible on the chest, the woman shifted her attention higher and took another small instrument, in order to examine something around the mouth.

Joni shifted position for a better view. Her head was pounding and she felt woozy. The feeling of dread had returned and she wanted to be off the high platform, away from whatever was about to happen. Then, when she looked at the tall guard, she remembered the man on the lawn, the stranger she'd seen while running.

The woman signaled her satisfaction and took a step away from the operating table and become rooted to the stage. Now even the sentinel shifted his attention to the table.

Joni looked down and saw it for a fraction of a second: the changing light on the sheet, the slight rearrangements where the body was still covered. *But no one was touching the table!*

The disturbance sounded like a generator, the whirring of a small motor, possibly an unseen piece of equipment the ghouls had brought. The guard did not look back to investigate. A moment later, a shock of recognition shot through Joni's body as the strange sound changed. Now it was becoming human, high-pitched and mournful, and it came with the tingling feeling that a new presence was near. Then, all of a sudden, the source of the sound became apparent. No other explanation was possible. The sheet moved again, by itself. The uncovered arm stiffened, then released. The motion was followed by another. The fingers on the same side started to quiver.

"Sweet Mother of God," Bill uttered at the exact moment she knew it, too. "He's alive! Dead and buried, and now he's alive!"

Chapter 35

Dawn

Their disbelief hung weightless in the air, awaiting direction. The steady, rising wail became the full-bodied voice of a newly born male infant, crying out in a reassertion of life. The resurrected infant moved his other arm, and then both his legs thrashed violently under the white sheet. His face, which only a moment before had been blue and lifeless, was quickly infused with color as his active breathing hastened the return of a normal supply of oxygen.

The realization of what was happening registered with absolute alarm and denial. In confusion, Joni lost all sense of caution and suddenly came to her feet, but she was near the side of the platform and the catwalk began to rock.

Bill put his arm out for her to hang onto, but his own movement increased the swaying motion.

Joni knew she was about to spill off the platform into the emptiness below, a plunge toward the impossible truth on the stage that was half-real, half-hallucination. Before he could get to her, she flung a hand out toward the wall for support. Her fingers clawed at the brick surface, but the low railing had already cut into her belly, doubling her over for a fall. Just before her feet came off the platform, Bill lunged for her and caught her around the waist. His other hand went up to her open mouth. Her eyes were wild, and he was afraid she was going to scream.

Still groping for a place to hold on to, Joni's hand found its way into one of the metal boxes on the wall and accidentally knocked a switch inside to another position. Instantly there was a new sound to deal with, the *whrrr* of an electric motor.

The moment she regained her footing, she looked at Bill and saw that his panic was no longer because of her. She turned to face the source of the noise and was stunned to see the entire front of the stage in motion. Those below had also turned to watch the billowing velvet curtains separate at the middle and begin a slow sweep to the sides. The giant picture screen was lifting off the ground on its way to the ceiling. The baby began to scream at the new disturbance, its voice a discordant counterpoint to the motor. As the curtain drew apart, the operating room was fully exposed to a thousand empty seats.

The guard was the first to look for the cause of the commotion. He scanned the stage in both directions, then raised his eyes to the swaying catwalk, where a man and woman were visible on one side of the scaffold. He pointed to them and, shouting an alarm, drew his gun.

Escape seemed impossible. While the guards raced off to mount the stairways leading to each end of the platform, she and Bill quickly tried to crawl to the narrow doorway they'd come through. About halfway there, Bill felt inside his jacket for his pistol but the holster was empty. Reversing himself, he wasted precious time getting back to where they'd been lying. Joni spotted the gun near one edge of the platform, but before Bill could get to it there was heavy breathing at her end of the walkway.

"You move and I'll kill the woman," the gunman yelled.

He was training a gun at Joni from only a few feet away.

"You got it," Bill answered immediately, bringing his hands over his head.

At the other end of the boards, the smaller guard also had him in his sights.

No resistance was possible. The gunman gestured to them, and moments later they were led down the back stairway to the stage, where they were forced to sit back to back with both weapons trained on them. It seemed like the continuation of a terrible nightmare. In her state of confusion, Joni drifted to a place in her mind where reality and unreality were the same.

The more pressing business of the resurrected baby prevented the woman from attending to them personally. After Joni and Bill were rounded up, she performed a series of operations and ended by strapping a resuscitator cap over the baby's mouth. The crying was replaced by the hissing of oxygen. During her work, she never turned to acknowledge her captives. The more studious man had again taken up his role as medical assistant and was checking vital signs. Twice he reported his readings, which were received with satisfaction. The baby was covered to the neck and had become still.

Throughout the process, Joni and Bill were given a complete view of the proceedings; the lack of secrecy indicated the gang must have plans for them.

The large woman wiped her forehead clear of perspiration and, with a last check on the baby, seemed to relax. With her back still turned, she then removed the surgical mask.

The picture that had formed in Joni's mind was of someone older, but actually she was in her late thirties or early forties. She looked masculine and tough; a few seconds later, when she turned to face them, Joni saw the evangelical eyes.

"It's her!" Joni gasped.

There was no equal surprise on the part of the bigger woman. Her jaw was smugly set.

Bill was dumbfounded as the two women glared at each other.

"The one from the parents' group," Joni cried out. "Mrs. Lange! How could it be you—"

"Because of all people I have the most right," the menacing figure boomed. She moved threateningly close to Joni before stopping, but it was enough to concern Bill, who quickly tried to divert her.

"Don't fool with her, you can see she's crazy." He turned his attention back to Lange. "Is this what you did to all of them? This living hell?"

Suddenly the meaning of his question rocked Joni. In her panic she had somehow not made the connection, the incredible end result of what she had witnessed.

"Is this what you did to *my* baby?" she screamed. "Did you take Stephen Lawrence, too?"

Joni started to come to her feet, but the closer guard pressed the weapon into her shoulder. Lange was angered, but held herself in check.

"Tell me. For God's sake, tell me!" The thoughts were racing through her mind. *Was he one, too? What had they done with him? Could he come through it and still be normal? Alive? Oh God, please!*

The eyes were cold, her features stone. "Your baby did not revive, Mrs. Lawrence. It was simply not strong enough; in the genes, no doubt, and beyond our control."

"You . . . low . . . filthy . . . animal . . ." Joni was screaming, still trying to deny what she'd just heard.

"It was a weak child and would have died later anyway."

Joni felt as though she had been kicked in the stomach. Her mind was a notch away from snapping. Stephen *had* been one of them, but he hadn't been resurrected, he'd been murdered.

Unmoved by her suffering, Lange turned to the smaller man. "Put the baby in the carrying unit and watch you don't foul the oxygen line."

The man reached for the quiet infant, something insubordinate in his manner.

Lange eased onto the edge of the table and folded her arms, but she did not address the only question that really mattered.

"I don't understand how you were able to learn so much. For your sake, I wish you hadn't."

"I'm not the only cop who knows about you," Bill snapped, the guard glaring at him as though he wanted to be provoked. "This doesn't change anything. You'll be taken out anyway."

"What kind of people are you, killing babies, taking them away in the middle of the night," Joni raged. "How could you even think of such a thing?"

As the woman approached her, the guard automatically pushed his weapon closer to Bill's head.

"It was you who could have caused a death here tonight, not me," she charged. "Your stupid interference was the only risk."

"Murderer!" Joni screamed.

"Stupid woman. Didn't you see what happened here? No one was murdered, never. This has nothing to do with murder."

"Then what is it?" Bill yelled. "You killed the Lawrence boy, didn't you?"

The Planner turned away.

"What kind of terrorists are you?" Bill repeated. "Or are you just another bunch of crooks with some sick, disgusting angle?"

The accusation seemed to throw her, as though she hadn't expected him to say it.

"That baby was dead until I brought it back," she said, facing him again. "Doesn't that mean anything to you—what I did?"

"He's ready," interrupted the man charged with taking the baby away. He'd put it inside a makeshift case that looked like a large pet carrier.

"Take it to the van and stay with it."

"And make sure no on sees you," the rougher guard ordered.

The subservient man lifted the case with a grunt and trudged off the stage with the case, leaving the building by an exit off the side aisle. Lange followed his movements, grimacing once when he bumped his load against the wall. Then she faced Bill again.

"Even you must respect what we've been able to do," she said defiantly.

"I don't respect insanity, I feel sorry for it and those it touches."

"Shaddup, you," the guard said. "What're you bothering for," he said to the woman.

"Who's giving the orders around here?" Bill demanded.

"What you have seen is only part of it," Lange continued, obviously uncomfortable with being suddenly on the defensive. "What I have done is nothing less than one of the great achievements of science."

"Being so cruel . . . so inhuman?" Joni blurted out. Her hatred was making her reckless, but she didn't care any more.

"Stop it, I won't hear it," Lange said. "Don't you see as a woman I could never—"

"As a woman? A woman? I don't recognize you as a woman, not even as a human being."

"More like an out-of-date Hitler," Bill joined in.

The woman seemed suddenly confused by his attack, then understood. "Oh, yes . . . because they are all Jewish."

"And because whether you are one or not, you're as bad as the Nazis."

The guard had his fill of the exchange and, without warning, struck at Bill's head with the barrel of his gun. The impact knocked him to the floor, a section of his hair suddenly becoming a wet red, but he took the blow without making a sound. When Joni tried to go to his aid, the guard pushed her away roughly, daring her to disobey.

"I don't expect you to understand," Lange raged. "You see it from your own limited world of criminals and the law that governs average people."

"Who buys them?" Bill asked, propping himself up on an elbow. "You must be selling them, but to who? The Germans? The Klan?"

Trembling, she turned away.

"How many have you murdered? Where are the ones that survived?"

In the midst of the horror, Joni sensed a purpose to Bill's continuing antagonism. He seemed to be deliberately provoking his captors.

"*We* don't murder any of them," the guard answered,

"the ones that don't make it are put away by your side."

"Autopsies?"

"Stupid laws, foolish parents who would not accept the obvious," Lange answered.

Joni felt revolted. She could visualize the police surgeons and wondered if some lab technician, working alone in the morgue, had discovered the terrible truth and tried to conceal it, or whether the gang could make the babies appear dead inside, too.

"Those deaths are your responsibility," Bill accused.

The guard edged closer. "Not the babies, but you two will be."

The question came again, even before thoughts about her own welfare. "How did you let my baby die?"

The two women's eyes locked, until the older one turned away from the intense hatred.

"It is a . . . complex question . . . of justice. In any event, I had nothing against your *baby.*" She was shot a disapproving look from the gunman and went no further."

"You're lying," Bill said.

"Enough of this. You're my prisoners." She glared at Joni. "Since you will not let go of the past, the truth is your son was a victim not of me but of you. It was *your* actions that led to his demise, your cheap treachery and lust for money."

The unbelievable charge brought on a new wave of confusion. She didn't know what her demented accuser was talking about.

"You made a mistake. Don't you know that, you made a mistake!"

"There has been *no* confusion."

"You're completely insane," Bill shouted back. "A menace. You're not fit to live in the world with normal people."

Joni had reached her limit and pushed herself forward. She began to crawl toward the woman, clawing the air, her nails razors wanting to rend. Lange shrank back in fear, until Bill restrained Joni just before the guard reached for her.

"I am not what you are thinking, not a murderer. It has nothing to do with that." She moved to the front of the stage, to stay a safe distance away.

"Yeah?" Bill shouted. "And what about us?"

She looked confused again and didn't answer.

Restrained by Bill, Joni gave up her attack on Lange and fell back in fear of what was about to happen to them.

"It's time," the guard said.

"No. You've told us this much, why not tell us how ingenious you really are?" Bill said. "What *are* you doing with the babies, training them for a future Third Reich?"

The guard edged closer.

"Preying on the weak—like some diseased parasite?"

The guard closed the gap with a last step. Bill had left himself unprotected.

"And you, you low-life bastard, they find you in some sewer with all the other rats?"

The crazed gunman raised his weapon.

"Stop!" the leader shouted, moving past them to restrain the guard. She was inches from the edge of the stage. "Not now! We have to think!"

"That's it, slime. Why not use the gun? Go ahead and wake the neighborhood, S.S. scum."

The woman's warning was not enough. Outraged,

the gunman brought his arm down to smash his prisoner, but the moment his momentum committed him forward, Bill shot his feet straight out and they landed squarely on his foe's ankles. The move was so quick the spindly man never saw it. His legs buckled and he fell forward. Bill's knees were already compressed into his chest, and in a flash he thrust them out again at the guard's midsection. On impact, the body reversed direction. The gun came out of his hand as he catapulted backward, out of control.

"Run, Joni. Get out of here," Bill commanded, pushing on her and getting to his feet. He lunged for his staggering enemy, but the man got his bearings in time and intercepted him with a powerful second effort. The two men struggled. Before long, Bill's fist drove into the guard's cheek and the heel of his shoe caught him at the base of the spine on the way down. There was a snap, and the guard went lifeless.

Out of the corner of her eyes, Joni spotted Lange moving toward the weapon, which lay invitingly on the stage floor. Without time to think, she came to her knees, Bill's order to retreat still ringing in her ears. Crouching, she put her head down instinctively and, an instant later, she flung herself forward, aiming at the center of the large body with a howl that rose involuntarily from her throat. Intent on overcoming Bill, the bigger woman heard Joni's cry a second too late, and Joni's head struck her unprotected belly with crushing impact. The collision forced the air from her lungs and folded her in two. She bellowed loudly as her body jerked backward toward the seats below, the retrieved gun now a useless weight in her hand. For a few excruciating seconds, her body hung precariously over the edge of the stage and her arms flailed wildly in an effort to give her balance. Then it was no use, and with a shriek she toppled over onto the seats of the first section. The base of her broad shoulders made contact first, striking the hard metal top of one of the seats. She screamed in agony, as though her back might have been broken. Afterward, she lay there paralyzed, a throbbing ball of pain.

Trembling, but still unable to take her eyes off the woman, Joni could feel Bill next to her and slumped against him, sobbing. They stood back to back, both breathless. Her heart was racing furiously.

The voice that echoed across the silent stage repeated itself.

"Don't move. Stay right there." It was the servile guard, returned from wherever he had taken the baby. His pistol was pointed at them, and it was shaking severely. His course of action was now uncertain with no one to give the orders.

He came closer. Nervously, he nodded his head in the direction of the crumpled body on the stage, which was spurting blood from several places on the face and from the mouth. He looked to the Planner, where she was crashed between the seats. She was trying to move, making low, guttural sounds.

"It's over," Bill said softly, before the guard could collect himself. He detached himself from Joni and started toward him. "There's nothing you can do, it's over."

He continued to speak, taking slow, cautious steps.

"Don't move any closer." The man put the gun between both hands and steadied himself.

"All you can do is become a murderer. Is that what you want?"

Joni watched, unable to move. With the loss of Bill's support, it was even hard to stand. It still wasn't ending.

"I'll shoot," the gunman said as though he meant it.

He was frightened, and there was an audible click in the trigger mechanism as he cocked the weapon.

"No you won't," Bill said, unreasonably confident. "No you won't."

The indecisive man neither moved forward nor back as Bill put out an easy hand and took the gun away.

Chapter 36

Minutes after Joni found the phone, four squad cars came screaming up to the front of the King Arthur Theater, their flashing lights making the deserted building come alive again. Before any police could enter, two more radio cars arrived from the south and, by the time Scarpone and the ambulances pulled up, the street was exploding with a clamor of light and sound that awakened the sleeping town.

The dirty glass doors of the King Arthur shattered like crystal under the nightsticks, and all at once police were pouring down all three aisles of the auditorium. By the time Scarpone made his way to the stage, it was apparent from his pained expression that the calamity he feared had come to pass. It was big, it was ugly, and Thompson, not he, had cracked it.

Later, the medical teams made their way out of the theater with a live infant, a corpse, and two prisoners. Lange had been given an injection and placed on a stretcher, unconscious. Before the ambulance left, Bill conferred with Peter Midas, the paramedic attached to the ambulance in which Lange had been placed, and when he was done he related their conversation to Joni. According to the medic, Lange had only an even chance to recover. The fall had severely damaged her spine and, even if she hung onto life, she was likely to be paralyzed.

After he found out the importance of the information his patient possessed, Midas allowed Bill and Joni to ride in the back of the ambulance with her. If she died before regaining consciousness, so did all hope of unraveling the details of the conspiracy. The only other surviving gang member was claiming ignorance about what happened to the resurrected babies. His involvement always ended at the theater, he insisted, where he was used only for medical assistance.

The inside of the well-equipped vehicle was a scaled-down version of an intensive-care room. The patient's heartbeat was being recorded on an EKG unit complete with its own console, and her temperature read 97.4 on a small electronic screen. Two intravenous tubes, suspended over one side of the stretcher, snaked their way into the back of the patient's hand and forearm, their red and clear liquids slowly leaking into her veins.

Finally Joni broke open the silence that had lasted since the ambulance began moving.

"What you did back there was very brave. I thought I'd cave in just watching you."

"No big deal."

"He could have killed you."

"Nah, guys like that aren't the kind."

Seeing Bill so close to death made her realize how much he meant to her, but she was confused by something he'd said.

"You told him he'd become a murderer if he shot you. Wasn't he one already?"

"Not until we can prove someone actually died at their hands. Don't forget, all of them, not just Stephen, were already dead in the eyes of the law. And the graves are empty."

There was a rasping sound from the stretcher. The patient was waking, but she was racked by pain. Her ability to move her limbs was limited, and when she realized it she became frightened. A line of ruptured blood vessels traveled across her forehead, and the bridge of her nose was covered by a clump of bandages. She did not look like a survivor. She went through a few stages of awareness before she heard Midas addressing her.

The medic looked on attentively when Lange finally opened her eyes and looked around the ambulance. Haggard and drugged, she struggled to blink away the haze. For a moment, she seemed to recognize where she was, but then retreated back into her thoughts and must have found the memory of her fall. Her ruminating was suddenly climaxed by trembling and a burst of hysterical screaming. The bout left her panting.

"Alive?" she asked bleakly a few moments later.

The paramedic adjusted a blanket around her throat.

"Don't try to move You're on the way to the hospital."

"I . . . will live?"

Joni rubbed the gooseflesh on her arms. She wanted to turn away, but couldn't.

"We have a surgeon waiting for you. Whatever you need will be done." The young doctor was pleased with his answer, and his mouth formed a tight little smile of accomplishment.

Lange blinked repeatedly, shaking from cold chills

rippling through her. Eventually, she rolled her head and her gaze swept over Bill, not registering at first. When she came to Joni, the strained angles of her face hardened even more.

"You!" she snarled. "Are you satisfied now?" Again she grimaced at a sharp pain somewhere within.

Bill studied her without sympathy. He looked eager to begin asking questions.

Lange turned to examine the man attending her. "Not a real doctor," she moaned. "Get me a real doctor!"

"If you don't mind, officer," the medic said to Bill, "I'll need a few minutes before you start."

Grudgingly, Bill agreed.

Midas leaned over his patient. "Are you well enough to tell me what you're feeling?"

"What . . . is my condition?" she demanded with surprising vehemence.

"Your body has been dealt a grave insult. Your vital signs are stable for the time being, but there's no way to know how your body will respond to surgery. The situation is serious, but not hopeless."

She digested the information like rancid food. "I can't move my legs."

"Your spine has been injured in the fall. For now you are partially unintegrated below the waist. The feeling may or may not return. Also, there is damage to your kidney, but until we run tests we don't know how extensive. There's been some internal bleeding as well." He looked down sternly. "I'm sorry to be so direct, but I think you have the right to know."

"I might . . . die?" she uttered, with a sense of fascination that for the moment overcame her fear. Again she was ripped by pain, and she bit into her lip, the veins along her neck popping in bold relief.

Midas looked past her. "With the right care and

some luck . . ." he said, letting the rest of the thought drop.

Bill had inched toward the stretcher. "Can I talk to her now?"

The medic scrutinized him suspiciously.

"It may save lives, I've already told you why."

The young man turned to his patient. "From what I've heard, I can't refuse him, but he's promised to make it brief."

When the woman didn't respond, Midas moved away to allow passage for the officer, but Lange became furious and rolled her head away from them.

"I'm not . . . well enough for questions. How can you allow—"

"I'll be right here if I'm needed."

She cut off her attention to him and Bill moved closer, leaning in until he was no more than a few inches from her, but his voice was soothing, if possible, sympathetic.

"Whatever you've been through, you must realize you put others through something terrible, too. Maybe you just got caught up in something we don't understand, a need that took you over for a time. But you've been given a chance—right now—to undo some of the damage. Tell me what it was about, for your sake. For the sake of those you injured. It can't do anybody any good to keep it a secret now."

She closed her eyes and heaved a great sigh, her chest deflating under the blanket. "You tried to kill me; now you want me . . . to help."

"Were you alone, or were there others?"

There was no reply.

"Who's behind it? Where are the other babies you brought back?"

"It is . . . not important."

"You must know the suffering you've caused," Joni

tried. "What kind of crusade can be built on the bodies of babies?"

She saw Bill quickly wave her off. For whatever reason, at that moment he didn't want her help.

Lange continued glaring at Joni even after she stopped talking. "I don't owe *you* anything."

"Your family," Bill started again. "Is there someone you'd like to call? To see?"

A flicker of emotion passed over her, but it was gone instantly. Her mood was changing, and she was drifting, perhaps finding relief in a new thought or old memory that took her away from the ambulance. It was probably the painkiller, but someone seeing her for the first time would have described her expression as *silly*. Joni remembered that look on a child she once met. He had been retarded.

Brain damage?

"Who were the two men with you?"

When she returned to the present, she was more vicious. "You will never find out anything. There was no crime . . . I know. Leave me alone."

The finality of her pronouncement echoed in the small chamber like a death decree. It took a while for Bill to come to a decision but when he did he shook his head angrily, then leaned so close their faces were almost touching. "I won't leave you alone, not if it kills you," he shouted.

Bill jumped up and stood over her, between the red and clear tubes that led into her arms. He made one more entreaty, which was rejected. "Then go straight to hell!" he exploded.

His hand went to the red bottle, which was about two-thirds full. When he located the glass regulator, he took it a half-turn to the closed position.

"Hey, hold on there," Midas shouted.

It was too late. At the bottom of the plasma bottle, a

tiny bubble that was forming on the glass shrank until it disappeared.

"Stop him. Don't let him do it," Lange yelled.

Joni almost protested but held off, thinking that Bill was bluffing.

"Leave that . . . alone."

"One less of your kind," Bill said, closing the valve the rest of the way. In a few seconds, the liquid stopped dripping and the tube began to drain.

"You won't do it . . . it would be murder."

"What you've done is worse." He touched the valve on the clear bottle and turned it part of the way.

The medic jumped to his feet. "All right, that's enough. You can't—"

"You forget what she's done, what she can tell us."

"She's too weak. It could give her a heart attack."

"Then we'll have to try and prevent that, won't we?" He turned toward the EKG.

Watching him with concern, Joni began saying things to herself she didn't want to think about, that he was losing it.

"Before I leave you alone, I'll see you dead!" Bill shouted.

"Stop it," the medic burst in.

"She doesn't leave me any choice. I want what she knows—before it's too late."

Midas came forward, testing, but Bill's hand was in front of him.

"Back off, fella. I'm running this from here on in," Bill said.

The younger man scrutinized the officer, the holster, and was quiet.

Lange's eyes were wide and ferocious as he turned on her. "You're wasting your time," she shouted.

"We'll see how strong you are."

Listening to him, Joni knew that despite his sudden

violence, she wouldn't try to stop him. Though she hated to admit it, inside she wanted vengeance almost as much as an explanation. Silently she vowed to support him in whatever he was planning. The space was a tomb. The ambulance and all in it were in the grip of a calculated hatred.

With one quick thrust of his hand, Bill yanked both the wires off their terminals. Inside the EKG unit, a shrill monotone alarm sounded in response to the insult. In a second, the black screen showed a bright dot that traveled from left to right and started over again. When it went flat, Lange gasped, clutching her throat.

"How many of you are there? Why did you do it? Where are the babies?"

Midas wanted to move again, but froze with a threatening look from Thompson. Now even Joni couldn't hide her alarm.

"Maybe you shouldn't go so far," she said softly. "She doesn't look like she can take it."

"And that'll be enough out of you, too," he snapped.

It was a Bill Thompson she had never seen. Suddenly, there was a distance between them she didn't understand. Even the Lange woman seemed to sense it, and it terrified her more. She began to yell for help.

"Scream all you want. Nobody gets in here until I say so. Tell me what I want to know."

When there was still no response, he reached up and turned off the flow of glucose. Then he sat down to wait.

It took five minutes, then a rattling sound came from the head of the stretcher.

"It's so cold. Please . . ."

He didn't look at her.

"It's enough, no more. You will kill me."

"You'll talk?"

"Hurry," she said, looking at the I.V.'s. "Turn them on."

He said nothing and didn't move.

A dull smile came to her lips. "With all you found out . . . you never guessed the obvious."

"Which is?"

"There are no others. It was in your mind, always . . . in your mind."

"Just you? No one higher up?"

She shook her head.

"What about the gunmen? Where did they come from?"

"They were needed to do work I couldn't. Foolish, mercenary men."

"What work?"

"Getting to the babies . . . in their homes, anywhere they were."

"How many babies did you take?" Joni burst in.

Lange shifted toward the new speaker, but when she saw Joni a sneer spread across her face.

"Answer that," Bill ordered.

"Will you turn them on?"

"How many babies?"

"Twenty-four," she howled.

"Were there going to be more?"

"Yes . . . those . . . all those who deserved it. Many."

Bill shot a quick glance to Joni, then went back to Lange.

"Why? Why did they deserve it?"

Her expression was changing. Her eyes softened and held a hint that her battle was ending.

"You will understand. You will . . . not be so sure," she said evenly. Then she was suddenly venomous again. "They killed my baby . . . tortured him and killed him."

"Who did?"

"The doctors, the ones who made the drug . . . all of them." Her eyes went to the useless bottles hanging overhead, then closed. She looked as though she might be dying.

Bill rose abruptly. "All right, we'll try it your way, but I want it all or they go off again." He moved around the cot and reached for the plasma valve. Her eyes widened, but he didn't turn it on until she nodded. The red fluid began to drip.

"I was pregnant . . . needed medication, for depression. Hormonal. The doctor prescribed a new tranquilizer, still being tested. When my baby was born . . ." she trailed off, pressing her lips together until they were white. "I trusted him, but it was the drug. A freak of nature! My baby was a *monster!*" she cried.

"Your baby died from the drug?"

"I prayed for it . . . for three years. He deserted me, and I was alone with him."

"Who, your husband?"

"He nearly went insane . . . the pitiful little boy." She focused on Bill and seemed to be accusing him. "There was nothing I could do. Finally he couldn't stand it any more and left me. They had to pay."

Joni and the medical man exchanged glances.

"Revenge on the doctor? All those children to avenge a single doctor?"

"All those days, I tried for justice, with all the authorities, but they told me I was irrational—crazy from the grief. They refused to listen, but I was right. Someone had to pay—all of them!"

The similarity between herself and the woman wasn't lost on Joni nor was the irony. The hatred the woman had harbored for so long, that drove her to take the

babies, had actually been born out of the love she'd had
for her own baby.

"All of the people who made the drug?" Bill asked.

"All of them. The chemist who discovered it, the
ones who manufactured it."

Bill's face was alert. "People connected to the company that made it?" He shot a look at Joni. "Roth
Drug?"

At the mention of the name, Lange became resolute
and looked to her left. "The other one. Glucose."

"At the end."

She turned her head further away from him.

"Okay," he snarled. He reached for the red bottle
again, as if to turn it back off.

"I'll tell you," she said quickly. "Don't!"

"Who did the babies belong to?"

"All those who profited from what they did to my
baby. Salesmen, the pharmacist who sold it . . . the
writers who advertised it . . . the lawyers who hid the
truth."

"But they couldn't all have had babies for you to
take."

Her head turned slowly in their direction. Her eyes
held no emotion. "Somewhere in their families . . . in
every family . . . there is a baby."

There was a long silence in the ambulance. The
revelation was chilling.

"So they weren't all local people?"

"Most, the company was here." She shuddered.
"Why is it so cold?"

"For God's sake, turn the bottles on," Midas
broke in.

Joni edged closer to Bill and whispered. "Don't you
think she's too badly hurt for—"

"Do you want to find out the rest?" he said sharply.

"Yes, but—"

He cut her off again to address Lange.

"How were you able to fake their deaths and then bring them back?"

"I was a chemist once . . . worked with others on a serum to . . . prolong life at low temperature."

Bill cocked his head. "Like in a morgue, or a funeral home?"

She closed her eyes.

"So you duplicated the drug and used it on the babies?"

"Perfected it."

"And injected it into the babies to make it look like sudden infant death?"

"It produced a coma . . . no traces."

"Then you brought them back—"

"A stimulant, strong . . . injected into the heart."

"The drug you used to inject them, did it have a limitation?" Joni demanded, risking Bill's anger.

Lange was beyond resistance. She nodded. When she did, Bill looked surprised and let her continue.

"It only worked for a short time, is that right?"

This time she refused to acknowledge Joni's question.

Bill bolted toward the bottles again. "I've had it with your games, lady. You're out of time." He reached for the tubes.

"No, Bill!" Joni cried.

It was too late. Bill grabbed both tubes and ripped them out of their bottles. With no place else to go, the liquids squirted out of them and splattered the bedsheets and pillow. A few drops fell on Lange's forehead.

"Nooo!"

"Go on, Joni," Bill ordered.

She was horrified by what he'd done, but continued falteringly.

"So you had to get the infants back before it wore off, isn't that what happened?"

"They would have died if we didn't get to them—suffocated when normal respiration returned . . . when the oxygen was exhausted."

"What oxygen?"

"Small capsule that leaked oxygen . . . the babies hardly breathed . . . didn't need much. One of the men put it in the coffin the night before burial."

Joni remembered the hissing sound she had heard at the chapel the morning Stephen was buried.

"And all of this, it's all why they had to be Jewish babies, isn't it, Mrs. Lange?" she asked.

Bill, was astonished. "Jesus, that's why—"

"Yes," Lange cried.

"Because Jewish babies have to be buried right away," Joni said, "and you were sure you could get them back in time. And you also knew that babies are almost never embalmed any more, so there was no risk anyone else would tamper with the bodies."

"That's why you didn't inject them before a week-end," Bill went on, "because their burial might have been held up for the Jewish Sabbath."

Lange closed her eyes, signaling agreement with the battery of guesses. Midas looked hopelessly lost as Bill backed away from the woman.

"You only went after Jewish babies right from the start, but all of your enemies couldn't have been Jewish?"

"Enough . . . enough to start with. The doctors, the *professionals*," she sneered, "the ones who owned the company . . . until I could purify the drug . . . make it last longer."

"For the Christian babies you wanted," Bill guessed without needing confirmation.

The ambulance was moving, but more slowly. Midas

remained silent. Everyone looked cold and seemed to be shivering. The Lange woman was deathly pale, and Joni wondered how long she would last.

"The plasma. Give me the plasma!"

"What did you do with the babies?" Bill roared. "The ones you revived?"

"Placed them with other parents . . . adopted by those who deserved them more."

"You gave them away or sold them?"

"I needed the money for expenses . . . research. One of the helpers demanded more and more for himself, threatened me."

"How much did you charge?"

She hesitated. "Fifty thousand . . . each."

"You needed all that money for expenses?"

"He threatened me," Lange repeated.

Joni did the math quickly. The total was astounding, over a million dollars, but was it the money or the hate that had driven her in the end?

Bill stood. "And where are they all now? Tell me or—"

"A list, I have a list," she blurted out, and began to sob.

The last question sprang from her lips before she even knew it. She was only a few inches away from Lange.

"Why did you take *my* baby? Don't you know what a terrible mistake you made? We had nothing to do with the drug company. He wasn't even Jewish!"

There was enough strength left in the woman for a last torrent of hate.

"You . . . were the face in my dreams . . . always that face. The model."

Joni looked at Bill, but he was just as lost as she was.

"Your ad in the medical magazines!" she said.

The words instantly stirred old thoughts, back to

when Joni had just started working as a model, before
the first cosmetic jobs came.

"You more than any of them," Lange shrieked,
trying to get up from the bed. "It was you who brought
the drug to the doctors, you more than the rest. Your
face!"

In the picture forming in Joni's mind she was wearing
a white lace peasant blouse and was barefoot. They had
put her in a meadow of wildflowers, to show her
contentment. The copy had claimed that until the day
before she'd suffered from a pre-natal problem—
possibly it had been depression.

"You did the ad for the drug," the woman shouted.
"It was because of you the doctors gave it to me. I
wanted your baby to die. He was never meant to be
brought back, the only exception. so you could suffer
the way I did." The fury over, she collapsed into the
blood-spattered pillow.

Bill looked at Joni for some kind of confirmation, but
she was staring off into space. They'd shot the ad in a
single afternoon in Central Park. It was the first time
anyone used her face to sell something, and they'd put
their product in her hand. What she held up to the
camera and, eventually, the medical community, was a
small package of tablets. On the side of the package
was a list of contents, including several drugs she'd
never heard of.

In an instant it had all become clear, and for the first
time since Stephen died, she felt true pity for his
murderer.

But it was all coming so fast. There was no way to
imagine what it must have been like for the pitiful
woman, slowly going insane with hatred and helplessness, day after day for years; so crazed she had prayed
for her own baby's death. Perhaps it was a suffering
even greater than her own and, in a bizarre way, the

unwitting part she'd played by doing the ad *did* give her a share of the responsibility. She'd never asked about the product she agreed to sell.

Joni stood and walked to the head of the stretcher bed. Like the figure in it, she felt cold, bereft. When she came to her knees, both faced each other with probing intensity, a clearly different feeling from that which had existed only minutes before the last disclosures. It was as if the air had been vacuumed of hate for both sides.

They continued to stare at each other, without looking away, searching for the knowledge they now had in common. After a while, the ambulance lurched to a stop. Both front doors slammed and there were footsteps at the side. When Bill unlocked the back doors, he and the young paramedic were met by a single intern.

Joni closed further on the stretcher.

"With all you've done to me and to others like me," she whispered, "I think I can understand. I feel sorry . . . so sorry for both of us."

Lange's eyes traveled the features of the face she'd hated enough to take everything from, and she seemed to undergo a profound change. Her rock-hard features softened and she was somehow diminished in size. By the time more gowned men from emergency entered the ambulance and started for her, she held up a feeble hand to stop them and turned to Joni, her eyes glistening the way they had when she lectured to the SIDS mothers. She said something that Joni couldn't hear, and she moved in so close that for an instant they accidentally touched. Then, in a voice barely above a whisper, Lange said it again.

"One of the men . . . the greedy one. I found out later, through my contacts."

"Found out what?"

"He took him without telling me . . . for the money. We didn't think he was Jewish, didn't care, but you buried him so quickly. There was time . . . unexpected."

She heaved a great, purging sigh.

"The greedy one . . . he wanted the money."

The miraculous idea registered on Joni with the image of a single human face, Stephen's, and when she was able to speak she was suddenly screaming.

"What did you find out? What are you saying?"

"A . . . writer, I think. Book about Jupiter, yes, Jupiter. He's the one he sold him to. Stole some of the drug . . . visited your son's grave . . . in time . . . sold him to the writer."

Lange was becoming incoherent. Her voice was weak and trembling with emotion as she turned to look directly into Joni's eyes.

"Before . . . I lied to you . . . forgive me. He's alive, your baby is still alive!"

Chapter 37

The phone call to Doug had been a requisite kindness, which she managed to keep brief. She knew if she took any time with him she risked an emotional outpouring, and that would have only convinced him she was having another neurotic episode about Stephen.

Fighting back a confusion of feelings, Joni quickly detailed to him what happened at the theater, ending with the bombshell that Stephen might even be alive. At first Doug listened without responding. She sensed he wanted to believe her, but after a long silence he began talking about doctors and a program he'd heard of that dealt with stress sickness. The story she'd told was so strange that this time she couldn't blame him for not believing her. Obviously it was going to take Stephen himself to convince him she hadn't lost her mind completely.

The call ended with an agreement to meet as soon as she had the final information, but when she hung up she knew that no matter what she found, nothing could ever bring her and Doug close enough again. Even the return of their son.

It was unusually crisp for early September. Along the expressway that ran from Manhattan to Eastern Long Island the end-of-summer foliage became more and more dense as the car speeded toward the East Hampton writing quarters of Harold Beresford, author of *Jupiter Diary,* one of the most successful science fiction novels in years, and the possible new father of Stephen Lawrence. Bill had gotten Beresford's home address from his publisher after an early-morning call to his home.

As they drove, it was ironic to realize that at this very moment Schecter would be talking to the press. The story of the gang would greet them in the papers on their return to New York.

Only now, did Bill have the time to tell Joni how he'd manipulated Lange.

She started to tell him how cruel he'd been to the dying woman when he told her to listen to his story.

"When I talked with the medic at the theater," he explained, "I found out Lange wasn't in any real danger, only a lot of pain. The damage to her spine would heal with rest and the internal bleeding—well, maybe some small blood vessels like you'd get from any bad spill."

"But she was paralyzed," Joni said. "She couldn't move."

Bill's look was almost prideful. "Might have had something to do with being strapped in so tightly under the blankets."

Joni was getting the idea. "And her face? The bloody bandages?"

"Real enough, but I can't say the same for Midas's

performance. Before we got into the ambulance, I convinced him to go along with a little act. Figured if we could get her to believe she was dying, we'd have a better chance of getting information out of her."

"Especially if she thought you were going to kill her in the process." Joni was still unnerved by the memory.

"There was never any danger of that."

"What about the intravenous units you shut off?"

"She got all she needed at the theater. Morphine to kill the pain and blankets for possible shock. The I.V. bottles were only props needed to make it convincing. They weren't even connected to her wrists under the bandages. The tubes drained into other bottles, hidden under the stretcher."

"What about the cold? She kept feeling cold and you couldn't have faked that."

"Didn't you feel chilly yourself? Truthfully?"

"Well, yes, but I thought it was . . . emotional, from what was going on."

"And helped along by the air conditioning. We controlled it with the help of the driver in the front seat. He was instructed to keep turning it colder as we questioned her."

"Jesus, Bill."

He shook his head. "It was a real case of poetic justice, if you think about it."

"In what way?"

"Well, we ended up doing to her exactly what she'd done to the babies. Like the victims, she was the victim of an elaborate death hoax."

"And so was I. How come you never let me in on it?"

He turned to her and shook his head with a soft smile. "Are you crazy? One look at that honest face of yours and she'd have seen through it in a second.

Besides, you did pretty good without knowing, the way you got connected the Jewish angle for us."

Joni blushed. He was probably right. She never could play poker.

As they got closer to the end of the expressway, Joni felt less and less like talking and Bill instinctively remained silent. The thoughts about Stephen and Lange came one upon the other until she was tangled in a web of fears and facts that raced in and out of her mind without letup. There was no way to be certain whether Lange had told the truth near the end. She was still delirious from the morphine and might have been adding one last torment before what she thought was the end of her life.

The migraine had begun to pound in her head when she realized there was a possibility Lange had lied, and now it was nearly blinding.

Bill kept it at sixty-five or better until they left the Montauk Highway and joined the only main road that serviced all the resort towns up and down the coastline. After Labor Day weekend, it was relatively easy to get to East Hampton. Gone were the thousands of nonresidents who choked all roads to the area during the steamy summer months.

The trip took a little over two hours and, as they neared Beresford Manor, Joni felt her nerves stretched to the breaking point. It was clear that in a matter of minutes she'd either be at the end of an unbelievable journey or at one of many new torturous beginnings. Just before they left, Bill had called the residence and spoken with a visiting brother, who said the family was on an outing and would return shortly. Unhappily, the man evaded all direct questions. He was very protective of his successful relative and advised Bill to put his questions to the writer himself, once he showed his

credentials. There were people, he said, who might
want to take advantage of his brother through his
family.

Finally the plush estate came into view. The residence was tucked away on a private lane, a starkly
modern home made of glass and steel and set off in the
center of a large parcel of open land which fled to lower
ground and the ocean on one side. There in the
distance, Joni could see the rough morning surf that
surged angrily into the face of a number of tall sand
dunes, which guarded the rear of the premises.

They approached the house from a driveway that
circled right and carried them to the front door. There
was no one to be seen, no guard to intercept a visitor. A
single car was parked in front of the stately entrance, a
late-model Mercedes that gave Joni a start.

They paused at the door, shoulder to shoulder.
Then, with a tender glance, Bill let go of her hand and
she rang the bell.

The wait was endless. A strong wind that blew in off
the ocean seemed to be pushing them back from the
house, warning them. All memory was compressed into
the vision of a single face, another entity that was once
a life within her and might now be part of her again.

Footsteps inside gave way to the creaking of a thick
oak door that slowly drew back, and a slight man with
long, curly graying hair and a loose-fitting sweater was
looking at them suspiciously. Behind him a woman
clenched her wrists nervously and appeared to be more
of a mourner than mistress of the house.

"Mr. Beresford? Harold Beresford?"

"Yes. What is it?" He held the door only half open,
its edge cutting into his side.

Bill flashed his identification. "I'm the one who
called. This is Mrs. Lawrence. We're here to see the
child."

He checked the badge and nodded with resignation. "My brother told me. Are you sure you have the right place?"

"If you don't mind," Bill gestured to the inside of the residence.

The man gave way and ushered them through a paneled library into a sitting area.

"Funny," he said. "This all seems so surreal." He looked toward his wife. "Frankly, I hope you don't find what you're looking for. There's a chance you won't, you know. We went through several . . . channels before we were successful. Maybe not yours."

His wife was closely scrutinizing Joni.

Looking for a resemblance, Joni wondered.

For a few seconds, they examined each other with unbearable tension, until Mrs. Beresford came over to Joni.

"My name is Helen. I know what you must be going through. I hope it will end for you . . . one way or the other." There was a sense of great resignation in her manner.

"Could we see the child?" Joni finally found the courage to say, with no attempt to conceal the terror behind her question.

The husband examined her. Obviously she represented a threat to his family. When he was done, he turned to meet the worried glance of his wife.

"Leslie is out back at the dunes, with my brother."

"Leslie?" Joni froze at the sound of the alien name.

"Yes, our son," he said, at first uncertain about the surprise she showed.

In her anxiousness, it hadn't occurred to her that the name could have been changed or that the one they had chosen could have belonged to either a boy or a girl. Somehow she'd expected him to say *Stephen*.

There was no awareness of the rest of the house, only

the many steps it took to leave it. When interior dimness gave way to light, they were shown through a door and the ocean was straight ahead, beyond the dunes. The writer and his wife did not follow.

A man and a baby were playing in the valley between two dunes. Walking was difficult in the deep sand, but Joni did not stop to remove her shoes. She was throwing herself forward against the maddening doubt that made her want to turn back. Bill's arm pressed strongly around her waist, but allowed her to proceed at her own pace. Once she stopped completely and only moved forward again through an extreme effort of will.

She was still too far to see clearly. The brother was sitting facing the child, trying to help him stand, but when he spotted Joni and Bill he ceased his activity and leaned forward to say something to the boy. The youngster was full of energy and tried to continue the game they'd been playing. The man grasped him under the arms and turned him in a half-circle until he was almost facing her.

A few dozen yards away, she stopped again and Bill loosened his grip on her.

"No matter what," he said, "I'm here for you." Tentatively, he let go.

"No matter what," she echoed. She smiled faintly, but a second later her face was gaunt. She turned to face the ocean, her skin insensitive to the harsh gale that drove bits of sand near her eyes. A first step was followed by another, and she continued on alone. Somewhere along the way, the migraine had suddenly gone away.

The little boy's head was only partially visible. He had turned away, so all she could see was a small portion of his face ringed by long curls of silver-blond hair. He was bigger than she remembered, more grown up, and then she realized that if it were Stephen, he would be.

As she approached, the child pulled himself loose from his older playmate and tilted his head with a clever, amused expression, but almost immediately he fell forward, burying his face into thick folds of sweater.

His face was still there when she reached the two of them and went to her knees to gently pry him away. Before he turned, one searching eye peered out from between the layers of wool and studied the profile of the woman who was crying his other name.

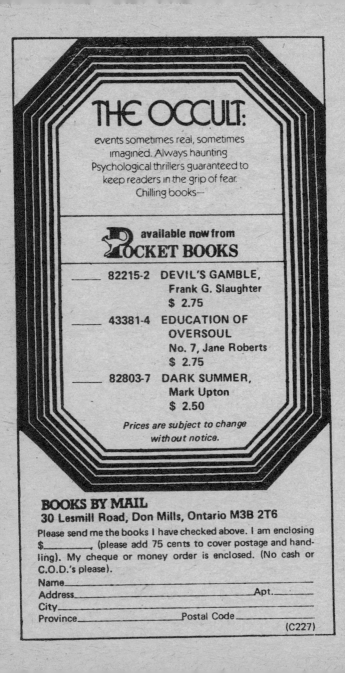